aloha lagoon

www.alohalagoonmysteries.com

D1736321

ALOHA LAGOON MYSTERIES

Ukulele Murder
Murder on the Aloha Express
Deadly Wipeout
Deadly Bubbles in the Wine
Mele Kalikimaka Murder
Death of the Big Kahuna
Ukulele Deadly
One Hawaiian Wedding and a Funeral

BOOKS BY CATHERINE BRUNS

Aloha Lagoon Mysteries:
Death of the Big Kahuna

Cookies & Chance Mysteries:
Tastes Like Murder
Baked to Death
A Spot of Murder
(short story in the Killer Beach Reads collection)
Burned to a Crisp
Frosted With Revenge

Cindy York Mysteries:
Killer Transaction
Priced to Kill

DEATH OF THE BIG KAHUNA

an Aloha Lagoon mystery

Catherine Bruns

Best wishes!

Catherine Bruns

ACKNOWLEDGEMENTS

There are always people who assist me with my writing process and play such pivotal roles while asking for nothing in return. It is an honor and a privilege for me to know them. Thank you to Retired Troy Police Captain Terrance Buchanan for his willingness to always answer my questions, no matter how numerous they might be. Judy Melinek, M.D., Forensic Pathologist, provided much needed assistance in the medical field. Beta readers Kathy Kennedy and Krista Gardner are true gems with their honesty, and I adore you both! Special kudos to reader Constance Atwater who also lent her knowledge about the State of Hawaii, as it's been a while since I last visited the island. Any Reger and Sharon Hmielenski provided some of the original recipes in the back of the book, for which I am deeply grateful. Thank you to my family, especially my husband Frank for always believing in me and to publisher Gemma Halliday for the opportunity to be a part of the Aloha Lagoon series.

CHAPTER ONE

———

When I was a little girl, playing waitress was one of my favorite pretend games. Together with my friends who lived next door at the time, we'd rush around and serve imaginary people at my mother's dining room table. In nice weather, we would use the back deck of my house. The state of Vermont has beautiful foliage during the autumn season, and we enjoyed gathering the multicolored leaves, pretending they were different types of entrees. The customers never complained about how long the food took to arrive, nothing was undercooked, and we always received hefty tips. And I *never* spilled food or broke glassware.

Yeah, only in a perfect world…

"Carrie Jorgenson?" A deep male, accented voice boomed in my ear.

I jerked myself out of my thoughts. A tall, powerful-looking Polynesian man was standing to my left, glancing down at me with a somewhat impatient look upon his face.

With trepidation, I rose from my chair. "Yes, I'm Carrie."

The man looked me over without comment and extended his hand. "Hale Akamu. I'm the owner of the Loco Moco Café." He gestured for me to sit down again.

"It's very nice to meet you. This is such a wonderful location for a restaurant." The café was close to the beach and situated smack in the middle of the highly popular Aloha Lagoon Resort in Kauai.

It was a perfect day weather-wise, something I had learned not to take for granted growing up in snow-ridden and rural Vermont. The sky was a cloudless blue like the ocean, waves were gentle, and the temperature warm without nagging humidity. Hale and I were the only ones inside the building, besides a server and two customers at the counter.

He ignored my comment, perhaps thinking I was sucking up—which, of course, I was. Desperation can do strange things to an unemployed person.

Hale eyed me sharply. "References?"

I swallowed hard and produced a manila folder from my shoulder bag. "Yes, they're from back home on the mainland. I just moved here a few weeks ago."

He gave a curt nod and glanced at the page while I took a moment to study him. He was very good looking, similar to Tom Selleck from his *Magnum, P.I.* days, with thick, dark hair and eyes black as coffee without a hint of cream. I knew he was in his early forties because I'd checked him out on Google the night before. In addition to the restaurant, he owned a mammoth-sized shopping mall on the island of Oahu. Hale had inherited a vast amount of wealth from his parents when they'd died in a car accident about twenty years ago. It sounded like a horrible tragedy for a child to endure—anyone actually—and for a moment I pitied the man. Unfortunately, there was something about him that immediately registered high on my radar in terms of dislike.

Even during our brief exchange, he managed to puff his chest out in an exaggerated manner while looking down his nose at me. He clearly thought I was beneath him. As if this wasn't enough to repulse me, I saw his eyes focus on my chest for the briefest of seconds. When he raised them again and found me staring back at him, his mouth twitched into a small grin.

Yeah, not in a million years, buddy.

Hale tapped his pen on the tabletop with an authoritative air. "I don't see any serving experience here."

Darn. Kim was right. I had called my best friend from back home last night, and she had advised me to lie about my experience. "Make up some hole-in-the-wall restaurant," she'd advised. "He'll never check."

But I couldn't do it, especially now, not with those calculating eyes pinned on me. "I-I did work in customer service."

Hale pointed at the sheet of paper. "Walmart. You worked for a *Walmart*. It's not the same thing."

This was not turning out the way I had hoped. It was my third interview in as many days, and I was slowly running out of options. Brad, my boyfriend, worked as a surfing instructor at the resort and had told me that the Loco Moco was hiring.

I decided to level with the man. "Please, I really need the job. I'm willing to do almost anything."

He narrowed his eyes, and a sly smile formed at the corners of his mouth. "Oh really?"

Ugh. Bad choice of words, and this guy had *letch* written all over him. I heard myself babbling. "Um, I meant wash dishes or sweep the floor."

His eyes swept over me, and my discomfort grew. "Well, that's a shame."

Yikes. Yes, Hale was a pig. I was almost certain of it.

"Excuse me, Hale."

Hale glanced up. "Yeah, what is it?"

A man about my age glanced from me to Hale and seemed embarrassed. "You asked me to let you know when Carmen got back from lunch."

Hale scowled and rose to his feet. "I'll be back in a minute, Miss Jorgenson. Don't go anywhere."

As he spoke the words, I noticed how quickly the color rose in his neck and cheeks. Whoever this Carmen was, I sensed she might be in for a bit of a tongue-lashing. Hale swaggered behind the front counter on his long, powerful legs, head held high and erect. His dark eyes circled the restaurant while he walked, as if afraid he might miss something, and the well-defined nose stuck out so far I feared he might suck up all the air in the place. He disappeared through the double swinging doors with portholes, which I assumed led to the kitchen.

I let out a long, steady breath and tried to calm myself. I seemed destined to strike out again. Maybe panhandling on the beach was in my future.

I looked up to see the other man watching me with unabashed interest. Well, he wasn't just any man. This guy was as hot as the inside of a volcano.

He flashed me a perfect, gleaming white smile. "Interview?"

I nodded. "I don't think my chances are good."

"Ah, I wouldn't say that. We've all been working overtime because the place has been so busy. And Hale does *not* like to pay overtime." He extended a hand. "I'm Keanu Church."

"Carrie. Nice to meet you." His hand was smooth and cool to the touch.

"Likewise." Keanu had dark wavy hair, a natural tanned look to his skin, and crystal blue eyes the same color as the ocean. Although he was slim, powerful muscles bulged underneath the short-sleeved white T-shirt that said *Loco Moco Café* on it. The jeans he wore fit him perfectly everywhere, and I do mean everywhere. He was tall, but anyone was tall when compared to my five-foot-four-inch stature.

Before we could exchange any more pleasantries, the sound of a woman shrieking met our ears. I glanced around. There was now one lone customer at the counter, reading the newspaper, and he seemed disinterested.

"I don't care what he did," Hale yelled. "The customer is *always* right. And since you have no idea how to treat the public, you're fired."

"You're not firing me because of that idiot, and you know it."

Hale's voice was similar to a low, angry growl. "Get your stuff and leave."

The woman's tone was menacing. "I would advise against firing me, Hale. For your own sake."

"It's Mr. Akamu to you now. And your empty threats don't bother me. You're no longer an employee here. Pick up your things and get out."

I expected more sobbing, but instead the woman's tone was venomous. "You'll be sorry for everything you did to me. I'll *make* you sorry."

Hale laughed. "Threatening me, huh? Yeah, like that's the first time I've heard that line before. Get your pathetic self out of here."

Keanu's expression was grim while his eyes remained focused on the swinging doors.

Less than a minute later, a woman who looked to be in her midthirties pushed through them, a purse in one hand and a tote bag in another. She turned and lifted her middle finger in salute toward the kitchen. "You haven't heard the last from me, you freaking tyrant."

Only she didn't say freaking.

As I watched the woman depart amidst a sea of sobs, my insides filled with dread. I turned to Keanu. "Why did he fire her?"

Keanu sighed. "A patron left her a nickel tip, and she made a snide comment to them. Hale overheard and went nuts. It's nothing new. Believe me. He fires someone at least once a month. It's like he needs to make a quota or something."

A giant knot formed in the pit of my stomach. *Do I really want to work here? Uh, no.* But then again, what other choice did I have? All of my life I'd wanted to escape from my hometown and had dreamed of living on a tropical island. When my boyfriend had landed a position as a surfing instructor, I'd asked if I could tag along. Although his reaction had been less than favorable, he'd agreed.

Brad and I had been dating for close to a year, but instead of becoming closer over time, it seemed as if we were growing apart. He'd come out a few months ago to get settled and had recently started to ask around about a job for me. Another surfer had told him there might be an opening at the café.

Keanu broke into my thoughts. "It sounds like your chance for a job might have improved."

Before he could say anything further, Hale pushed through the swinging doors and strode back over to us. He had papers in one hand and a giant coffee mug that read *Hale Rules* in the other. He placed the papers in front of me.

"Carrie, is there any chance you could start work right now?" Hale pointed outside to where the tables were starting to fill. "Our dinner rush will be starting soon, and as you might have overheard, we're suddenly shorthanded."

I wasn't a superstitious person. Plus, I needed the job. Yet I had a bad feeling about coming to work at a place where the owner was obviously disliked. Plus, what if he came on to me? I didn't need that hassle. Maybe I could accept the position for now but still look around for something better.

Hale waved an impatient hand in front of my face.

"*Hello?* Are you still with us, Miss Jorgenson?"

I gulped and forced the words out before I had a chance to change my mind. "Ah, yes, I can start right away."

He nodded and pointed at Keanu. "Good. Take her into the kitchen and show her around until Vivian frees up. Then she can shadow her around for the rest of the day—get drinks and stuff for the customers. A little later on you can show her how to run the register."

Keanu nodded. "Sure thing."

Hale pointed at the papers on the table. "Fill out your W-4 and I-9 and give these to Keanu before you leave."

"Of course. Thank you very much."

He looked down at me, but it felt more like a leer and practically made my skin crawl. When he reached for my hand again this time, I flinched. It was moist and clammy and sent a shudder of repulsion through me. *Ick.* I hastily pulled away.

"I look forward to having you here."

Before I could muster a reply, he was over at the register, laughing with a customer who had come inside to pay his bill. Hale slapped him on the back and rang the man's credit card through the machine, between taking sips of coffee from his egotistical mug. He then turned and disappeared into the kitchen again. I turned to Keanu, who gave a slight shrug.

"I guess congratulations are in order. Come with me. I'll show you where you can put your purse and find you an apron. I'll get a name tag made up for you too."

I followed him through the swinging doors into the shining kitchen, still shocked that I actually had a job. I couldn't wait to tell Brad.

"You're an import, aren't you?"

It took me a moment to realize that Keanu was talking to me. "Yes, I've lived in Vermont my whole life."

Keanu grinned, and for the first time, I noticed the adorable dimple on the left side of his mouth. "Did you get tired of all that white stuff?"

I laughed. "Something like that. Plus, I've always wanted to live in a tropical paradise."

He ran a hand through his dark hair, and I found myself wondering if it was as soft as it looked. "Tropical, yes.

Paradise—eh, not so much. So tell me, what's snow like? I've never seen it."

"Shut up."

He smiled. "I'm dead serious. I've always wanted to ride a snowmobile. Maybe I'll go check out Vermont sometime."

From his physique, he seemed better suited to a pair of swim trunks and a surfboard than a ski parka. "You were born here?"

Keanu shook his head. "I was born on the mainland, but my parents moved here when I was a baby. The island's all I've ever known. Don't get me wrong—I love it here, but I really want to see other places. Experience other seasons. You know, watch the leaves change and maybe shovel a driveway or two."

I raised an eyebrow at him in disbelief. "Believe me— you're not missing much. So, did your parents name you after the actor?"

"*Keanu* means 'cool breeze' in Hawaiian. My mother tried to convince me she came up with the name because of the long walks she loves to take at night, but I wasn't fooled. *Bill and Ted's Excellent Adventure* is one of her favorite movies, and it happened to premiere the same year I was born. Coincidence?" He grinned. "Nah, I don't think so."

I glanced around at the gleaming, stainless steel kitchen. A short, balding man in a white chef's hat was stirring something on the enormous ten-burner stove. There was a walk-in freezer, two dishwashers, two three-bowl sinks, and endless counter space. The one nearest to the chef held a whole pineapple, red peppers, and spices. My stomach rumbled as the smell of whatever he was stirring hit my nose. I hadn't eaten yet today— primarily because of nerves—but now I was starved.

Keanu brought me to a smaller room that branched off from the kitchen and pointed at an open, empty locker. On the opposite side was a flight of stairs that I assumed led to an office overhead.

"You can put your purse in here," Keanu said. "We don't have locks for them. Your welcome to bring one in, but no will bother your stuff. Only the employees are allowed back here." He reached over it into a cubbyhole above the locker and produced a white apron that said *Loco Moco Café* on it. "Put this on." Then he glanced at my hair. "Hmm."

"What's wrong?"

"I'm not sure if Hale will insist that you wear a hairnet or not."

I made a face. "But I'm not cooking, only serving. Plus my hair's in a braid." It fell way below my shoulders. I'd been growing it for what seemed like forever.

He nodded. "You've got a point. Still, the man rules with an iron fist around here."

"Yeah, that's pretty obvious."

"It's a shame to cover up something so beautiful." Keanu's tone was so low that I barely made out the words. "I hear Viv out in the kitchen. Come on. I'll introduce you."

I followed him out the door. Did he mean I was beautiful? *Oh, get a grip, girl.* "Are you a server here?"

Keanu shook his head. "I'm the assistant manager, so I run things when Hale isn't around. I keep the books for Hale but also help out with serving when needed. Hale lets me make my own schedule, but I usually put in ten-hour days. I'm studying to be a CPA."

"Wow, when do you find the time?" I asked.

He shrugged. "I'm here so much these days it's getting tough, but I manage."

The portly male chef was standing in the doorway of the walk-in-freezer, chatting on the phone with someone. A pretty woman who appeared to be about my age was writing something down on an order pad. As we approached her, she looked up and flashed me a genuine, warm smile.

"Viv, this is Carrie Jorgenson," Keanu said. "She's starting work tonight. Hale wants to know if you can show her around."

"No problem." Vivian extended her hand forward. She was pretty, with delicate features and short, blonde hair worn in a pixie cut. Slim and about my height, she moved around the kitchen in a graceful manner that reminded me of a bird.

"Nice meeting you," Vivian said. "Mainland, right?"

I laughed. "Is it that obvious?"

She smiled. "I've lived in this state my entire life. I'm pretty good at picking out the imports, such as you. Mainlanders aren't as relaxed and always seem to be in such a hurry."

Speaking of which, the sound of someone running down the stairs could be heard. Hale's face appeared before our eyes as he leaned over the railing and pointed at Keanu. His dark eyes raged with an internal fire. "I want to see you in my office. *Now.*"

"Okay." Keanu winked at me. "Nice meeting you. Catch you later."

"You too," I managed to say while Hale glanced over at me. His gaze met mine and then raked slowly over me. Instinctively, the hairs rose on the back of my neck. Why did it seem like this guy was undressing me in his mind? *Pervert.*

I watched Keanu casually start up the stairs, and then he disappeared from sight as the wall separated him from my view. "Is he in trouble?"

"Nah." Vivian shook her head. "Hale always acts like that. It makes him feel more important." She studied me closely. "Cute, isn't he?"

I grinned. "Are you talking about Keanu or Mr. Akamu?"

She laughed. "You know darn well who I'm talking about. Not the big kahuna, that's for sure. He's a jerk. As soon as I can catch a break, I'm out of this place." She looked at my hair. "Oh, I see we're going to have a problem."

I sighed. "Yeah, I know. Hairnet."

She fiddled with the lone braid that fell past my shoulders. "You're gorgeous. I'd kill for those big dark eyes of yours."

I'd actually been thinking that I preferred her amber-colored ones to my own. They were striking in her oval face and framed with long, thick lashes. "Thank you."

"So what do you think of your—ah—new boss? Barrel of laughs, isn't he?"

That was definitely one way I *wouldn't* describe him. Since I was new, I didn't think it would be a good thing to start bashing Hale right away, so I struggled for something positive to say about the man. "He's good-looking but not exactly my type."

Vivian frowned. "He started right in with you, didn't he? Seriously, the man is about as disgusting as he can get. I mean, he sits in that office upstairs all day, staring outside at the customers and counting his money. You can always see his face pressed up against the window. His parents left him a gorgeous mansion that overlooks the ocean too. He pretends like he works, but Keanu does most of the daily operation items. Despite all the cash he's got, do you think he'd give me a raise so I don't have to eat ramen noodles three times a week? Fat chance."

"That's awful," I said.

Her eyes looked weepy as she nodded. "He hates me."

Vivian seemed too pretty and sweet for anyone to hate. "Why?"

She pressed her thin lips together in a stubborn manner. "Because I wouldn't go out with him. He humiliates me every chance he gets."

A sick feeling of dread swept over me. "Well, I have a boyfriend, so I doubt he'll ask me."

"That makes no difference to Hale," Vivian said. "He'd have to have morals first. And don't suggest I file a sexual harassment claim either. I need this job. I think of him as gum on the bottom of my shoe. Useless and disgusting."

"Ah, you must be talking about our fearless leader."

I jumped, startled at the deep voice. The chef was standing there, watching us with a bemused look upon his face. He held a pineapple in one hand and a chef's knife in the other, the phone now sticking out of his breast pocket.

He appeared to be in his late forties or early fifties with a balding head, eyes as black as coal, and a slim moustache on his upper protruding lip. Short and stocky, his stomach protruded underneath his white double-breasted chef's jacket like a small basketball. There was a huge gap between his top front teeth when he smiled, and I found the effect strangely endearing.

Vivian gestured at the man. "This is Poncho, our cook. Poncho, this is Carrie. It's her first day here."

Poncho placed the pineapple on the counter and shook his finger at Vivian. "It's *head chef*, Viv, remember."

"Yeah right, whatever."

As I extended my hand, Poncho grabbed it and bowed his head in a dramatic fashion.

Vivian groaned. "Cut it out, Poncho. Give the girl a

break. She's already had to deal with Hale, and she hasn't even been here for a full hour yet."

"Delighted to make your acquaintance," Poncho said. His dark eyes regarded me with interest for a moment. Then he turned and thrust his knife into the pineapple. Afterward, he pressed his fingers to his lips with a satisfied sigh. "Ah, do I know how to pick 'em or what? Look how juicy this one is!"

I took a step backward and bumped into Vivian behind me. She patted my arm reassuringly. "You don't have to worry about him. He's a bit strange but overall, harmless."

"We are all a bit like that here." Poncho glanced over at Vivian. "You heard about Carmen?"

"Yeah. It wouldn't surprise me if I'm next on the chopping block." Vivian's voice quivered slightly as she glanced toward the stairs.

"Girls, you *have* to try some." Poncho handed us each a piece of the fruit. "It's to *die* for."

We both sampled the pineapple. It was my first time trying the tropical fruit since I had arrived on the island, and my mouth practically burst from the flavor. I savored it for as long as I could, rolling the sweet, juicy taste around on my tongue. In no way did it even come close to the canned variety I'd always eaten back home. "Wow, this is delicious."

Poncho giggled like a schoolgirl as he plunged the knife into the pineapple again. He continued chopping away to his own beat, as if playing the drums. It was obvious he was enjoying himself. "I've thought about doing this to a certain person. Bet you can't guess who?"

"There's a reason this place is called Loco Moco," Vivian whispered in my ear. "You have to be *loco* to work here."

I was already starting to figure that out.

CHAPTER TWO

———

"Hey, babe, you home?"

"In the bathroom. You can come on in." I was sitting on the side of the tub in our apartment, soaking my feet, which were screaming in agony. I hadn't realized how physically demanding this job could be. After about eight hours of carrying trays and rushing back and forth from the café to the patio, I was beyond exhausted. And the best part? I got to do it all over again tomorrow. I prayed I'd get used to the workload eventually.

Brad stood in the doorway, a six-pack of beer in hand. He was your typical-looking beach bum with an Adonis-like body to die for. His dirty blond hair had turned lighter in the brilliant Hawaiian sun, and his hazel eyes held a hint of green to them that sparkled like emeralds when he smiled down at me with those pearly white teeth of his.

Brad worked out almost every day at the resort's gym, and it showed. His abs, along with the rest of him, were definitely drool worthy. I was ashamed to admit his looks were the first thing that had attracted me to him. He had casually mentioned the other day there had been a recent increase in women signing up for surfing lessons at the resort. It didn't take a genius to figure out why.

He leaned down to kiss me. "I saw your text. Congrats on the job. That's awesome."

"Thanks." I turned on the hot water again.

"The Loco Moco has excellent food. Do you get to eat for free?" He turned and walked back out the door, into the kitchen presumably.

Jeez, he was unbelievable sometimes. "No idea. I didn't exactly feel comfortable asking about free food on my first day of work." Heck, I was grateful to have a job for now. "Are you home for the night?" I asked, suddenly hopeful. "I could make us something to eat, and then we could talk and watch television."

"Nope," he called out in a cheery voice. "One of the guys is having a party. I might be pretty late. Why are you soaking your feet?"

"No reason," I snapped back in irritation. "I only spent eight hours running back and forth on them."

He peered in the doorway again, piece of pizza in hand. "Bummer."

I pulled up the stopper to let the water out of the tub. "I was really hoping you'd stay home for once. You're always working or out with your friends. We never spend time together anymore."

Brad blew out a long breath. "Give me a break, okay? You're already acting like we're married or something. You're the one that wanted to come here. I didn't ask you to."

His words cut like a knife. Okay, he was right about that. Besides wanting to escape my miserable situation back home, this had been a last-ditch effort on my part to save our relationship. Now I was starting to wonder if it was actually worth saving.

My throat tightened with tears that I fought to hold back. "Gee, thanks for that."

"Look, I'm sorry." He leaned down and kissed the top of my head. "I got stuck teaching a bunch of bratty little kids to surf today because their regular instructor was out sick. One even got gum in my hair. Man, talk about annoying. Kids are such a drag, you know?"

It was nice to know that Brad would make a wonderful father someday. "Don't worry about it. Go with your friends. I'll be fine." I was getting used to spending nights alone anyway.

Brad handed me a towel so I could dry my feet then pulled me up gently and put his muscular arms around me. His cool hands moved seductively underneath my shirt. "I have some free time before I'm supposed to meet them."

Usually I succumbed to Brad's romantic advances, but tonight I couldn't bring myself to. His words had hurt too much.

"I think I'm coming down with something," I lied. "I wouldn't want to make you sick."

Brad released his hold and eyed me sharply for a minute. "Yeah. I get it. Well, don't wait up." With that he turned and left the room.

When the front door slammed a minute later, I allowed myself a good, healthy cry.

*　*　*

By early evening the next day I hadn't dropped anything yet—always a good sign. Only about four hours left to go. As I returned from delivering beers and Mai Tais to a couple on Loco Moco Café's wide outdoor patio, I paused for a moment to savor my surroundings. The deep blue sky was tinted with a hint of orange as the sun got ready to disappear behind the clouds.

The island was gorgeous with its lush green surroundings and palm trees swaying lightly in the warm breeze. The pleasant scent of hibiscus filled my nostrils as the waves lapped gently up to the shore and beckoned me. Although not a fan of deep water, the effect left me feeling serene and very peaceful.

The café was only a small part of the very elegant resort, situated in the town of Aloha Lagoon, on the island of Kauai. I hadn't been inside the actual resort part yet, but Brad had mentioned the rooms were gorgeous.

The Loco Moco was not your average café either. The inside of the building was pristine, from its gray tiled flooring to granite countertops, oak tables, and chairs, and long counter with individual padded seats that ran in front of the coffeepot machine and the register. The outdoor venue consisted of wicker tables and chairs, with padded seats for comfort, all covered by large, raised bamboo umbrellas that shielded patrons from the rain.

I found myself thinking of Vermont again but not in a homesick sort of way. When I'd left, there'd been three feet of snow on the ground. It had been no problem for me to say good-bye to the only home I'd ever known. In truth, all I wanted was to forget the first twenty-four years of my life and forge ahead with a new one. There was something better waiting for me here. I knew it. Yes, this was going to work out fine.

I looked up to see Hale's face pressed against the upstairs open window of the café. Even at this distance I could hear him shout, "Get back to work!"

Okay, so things weren't perfect, but I'd get there eventually. At least I had a paying job. I scurried back inside the café where an elderly woman was sitting at the counter. I smiled and gave her a menu. "Welcome to Loco Moco Café. Do you need a few minutes?"

She frowned, the lines around her eyes deepening further. "I've already had a few minutes. You people sure are slow around here."

My cheeks burned. "I'm sorry. What can I get you?"

"Just coffee, honey."

I grabbed the pot off the double-burner machine behind me and reached into the doorless, oak cupboard above it for a cup and saucer. After I'd filled it and had returned the pot to the burner, someone touched me lightly on the arm. I shrieked, and the coffee and cup both went flying, the later crashing to the floor.

I turned around. Keanu was standing there, one side of his white T-shirt stained with coffee and the rest dripping down his arm, which was also turning red above his elbow.

My hands flew to my mouth in horror. "Oh my God. You scared me."

"Obviously," he said and reached for a dishtowel to dry his arm off.

"Coffee," the customer grunted again.

Flustered, I reached for another cup, ignoring the mess I had to step over. After I had served the woman her beverage, I raced through the swinging kitchen doors. Keanu was already in the back room. He had removed his shirt and was reaching for another one out of a locker.

I stopped dead in my tracks and stared at the magnificent sight before me. Keanu's chest was sculpted and smooth, with abs that looked like they'd been carved from stone. He turned around and pinned me with that bright blue gaze of his.

"Something wrong?" he asked.

I shook my head. "Um, I wanted to make sure your

chest—er—I mean, that your arm was okay. It looks like a nasty burn."

Head smack. I couldn't believe I'd said that. Seriously, what was wrong with me? I had a boyfriend and didn't ogle other guys. That wasn't my nature. I remembered something Kim had said to me once, "Looking isn't cheating." Maybe so, but it still wasn't my speed. I turned away from him, thoroughly embarrassed.

Keanu didn't respond as he thrust his arms into another white T-shirt and threw the stained one in a nearby hamper.

"I'm really sorry," I mumbled. "I can't believe I was such a klutz."

Keanu studied me for a long moment then smiled. "That's okay. It only stings a little. Besides, I've got another arm. You're a little bit jumpy, aren't you?"

I swallowed hard. "Yeah, sometimes my nerves get the best of me. I've been worried all day about dropping something, and just when I start to feel comfortable, bang! It catches up with me." *The story of my life.*

Before Keanu could respond, Hale thundered down the stairs and after throwing a curious glance in our direction, moved past us into the kitchen.

"Oh my God," I gasped. "I didn't have a chance to clean up the mess yet." I ran after Hale's retreating figure.

"Carrie, wait!"

Keanu called after me, but I paid no attention. If Hale saw that I'd left the shards of cup all over the floor—

"Miss Jorgenson!" Hale screamed.

My insides immediately turned to Jell-O. *That's it. He's going to fire me. Shortest work stint in the history of a server.*

I took a deep breath and with shaky hands, pushed through the doors. Hale was standing there, glaring at me and pointing toward the floor.

The older woman was watching the show with interest. She came around the counter and handed me a twenty-dollar bill. "Here, honey. It's a rough world out there, and you're going to need this in the unemployment line."

Keanu appeared with a broom between his hands. The woman glanced from him to me and grinned, then beckoned me closer with her finger. She was tinier than me, and I bent down so that her lips were level with my ear.

"I hope you got to see him with his shirt off at least."

My face must have turned at least ten different shades of red. The woman gave me a high five, then turned and exited the café.

Hale placed his hands on his hips, waiting for my response. I opened my mouth, but before the words could fly out, Keanu intervened. "Sorry, Hale. I wasn't paying attention."

What the—? I stared at him in disbelief.

Hale watched Keanu, clearly unconvinced. "*You* did this?"

"Guilty as charged." Keanu's gaze met mine. "Hey, Carrie, grab some paper towels and spray, will you? I don't think I'll need the mop for this."

"It's coming out of your check this week," Hale growled at him.

I stood there, my feet frozen to the floor, and Keanu shot me a warning look. "Now, okay? There's some in the back room."

I mumbled something that I think resembled a "yes" and flew into the kitchen, almost knocking Vivian over in the process. I found the spray and towels and hurried out front. Keanu took the dustpan outside and dumped the remains into the trash bin. The incident already forgotten, Hale was walking amongst the guests outside, shaking hands and most likely asking how their service was. Great. I was still probably doomed.

I waited until Keanu came back inside. "Why did you do that? It was my fault, not yours."

He shrugged, but his mouth formed a sly smile. "Look, it's your second day here. What do you think Hale would have done if he'd known you'd dropped that cup?"

"Fire me?" I asked.

"Good guess," Keanu said. He leaned over the counter, the ocean-like eyes watching me intently.

"I don't know what to say. That was really nice of you. Let me reimburse you for the cup at least."

He flashed a genuine grin that warmed me from head to

toe. "It's no big deal. I'm guessing you need the job pretty bad."

"You'd be right." I noticed a couple approaching a vacant table outside and gathered some menus and table settings together. "I don't think he likes me."

Keanu frowned. "Oh, he likes you all right. That's why you *got* the job. He'll be hitting on you before long."

I looked up at him, horrified. "Please tell me you're joking."

He shook his head sadly. "I wish. Did he ask you if you had a boyfriend?"

"No."

"No you don't have one, or no, he didn't ask?"

I laughed. "He didn't ask, and, yes, I do have one. Brad came to the island a few months back, but I've only been here a few weeks."

Keanu reached for a coffee packet and placed it in the holder underneath the machine. "What does he do?"

"He teaches surfing at the resort." I didn't want to talk about Brad anymore. I was still upset about last night. He'd returned home sometime after I'd fallen asleep, showered, and then left for work before I'd woke this morning. I'd been so exhausted that even if he'd lain next to me all night and blown a conch shell, I still would have been dead to the world.

There had been a text on my phone from Brad earlier. Two words—*Miss you.* Yes, that was Brad's best attempt at an apology. He could be genuinely sweet and affectionate at times, but his communication skills did leave a bit to be desired.

Keanu grabbed some silverware packets from under the counter. "You guys must be serious if you followed him out here?" It was in the form of a question, not a statement.

"We've been dating for almost a year." I realized I hadn't given him an answer but chose not to elaborate. Instead, I changed the subject. "How about you? Do you have a girlfriend?"

Before he could respond, the door of the café opened, and two elderly women entered and walked in our direction, nodding politely at us. They were both slender with gray hair. The shorter one wore hers in a tight curly bob, while the other woman's hair extended past her shoulders and was almost as long as mine. They were dressed in slacks and short-sleeved Hawaiian print blouses. The one with the curly bob clutched a clipboard to her chest.

"Hi, ladies. What can we do for you?" Keanu flashed a gleaming smile.

"We're wondering if we could see Mr. Akamu for a moment," the woman with longer hair asked.

"Certainly." Keanu started in the direction of the patio, but at that moment, Hale surprised us when he pushed open the kitchen doors.

He glared at the both of us. "Why are the two of you standing around? We have customers waiting outside!"

Keanu narrowed his eyes but chose to ignore Hale's statement. "These two ladies would like to see you."

Hale stared at them with an impatient air. "Yes, what is it?"

The woman with curly hair extended her hand, but Hale only nodded in return. She looked startled but spoke anyway. "Mr. Akamu, we're volunteers at Hopeful House. It's an organization for children and young adults who suffer from cancer. We were wondering if you'd care to make—"

Hale rudely cut her off. "Sorry, ladies. Not interested. Have a good day." With that, he disappeared into the kitchen without a backward glance at them.

The two women stood there for a minute, flustered and exchanging shocked looks. My heart went out to them. What a crappy thing to do. Even if Hale wasn't going to give them any money, he could at least have been civil. That didn't cost anything.

I reached into my apron pocket. I only had thirty dollars in tips so far for the day, but they were welcome to them.

The women smiled at us and without another word, headed for the door. Keanu saw me draw out the bills but shook his head at me.

"Ladies?" They turned around and watched as Keanu reached into his wallet and then stuffed several bills into their outstretched hands. I couldn't see all of the denominations but knew that at least one had been a twenty. "With compliments of Loco Moco Café."

The woman with longer hair handed Keanu a receipt and hugged him. He seemed faintly embarrassed by her actions.

"What a dear boy you are. God bless you and your family," she said.

A shadow passed over his face, and I found myself curious if this cause might have personal meaning for him. I didn't feel it was my place to ask though.

Both women thanked him again, waved at me, and departed. Keanu's expression was somber, and I wondered what had changed. I opened my mouth to say something, but he interrupted.

"I'll take these silverware packets outside. Why don't you see if Poncho has some orders ready to go? You've got to learn how to handle the food sooner or later." He gave me a playful nudge. "Just don't think of it as coffee."

Like a noble gentleman, he didn't want to talk about the gallant act he'd performed, so I smiled and didn't press. "Okay, wise guy."

I went into the kitchen, where Poncho was putting the finishing touches on a couple of sandwich wraps. He placed a healthy side of mango and pineapple on each plate. "For table five. When you come back, I will have the poi ready for table three."

"Got it."

"You'd better hurry up there, *ho'aloha*." He chuckled at my bewildered expression. "Do not worry. It means my friend. I would never say anything dirty to a nice girl like you, Miss Carrie. Now the big kahuna, on the other hand…" He clucked his tongue in disapproval.

"Are you talking about Hale?" I whispered, my eyes darting around the room in fear that he might appear at any second.

Poncho nodded while he added spices to the mixture he was stirring on the stove, which looked like some type of salsa. "*Kahuna* means several things. In ancient Hawaii, they refer to it as an expert. I tend to think of it myself as the one in charge. Both terms describe Hale. He is an expert at making money without doing anything at all. He is like that man who turned everything to gold. King Muffler, yes?"

I burst out laughing. "I think you mean King Midas. Speaking of nicknames, is Poncho one?"

He shook his head. "It is my given name. I was born in Mexico, and my family moved here when I was very young. My mother is of Hawaiian descent. My father, rest his soul, insisted I be named for a Mexican Revolution general. Most people, though, they think that I am named for a shawl. Big difference, no?"

"Yes." He seemed a bit eccentric, and Vivian had told me that he was majorly OCD about his kitchen, but I already liked the man.

I delivered the order and managed not to drop one item. Maybe I was getting the hang of this. I'd probably worried for nothing—this was going to work out fine. A tropical breeze, I laughed to myself.

As I turned from the table, my sneakered foot connected with the patron's sandaled one. I tripped and went flying into table four.

Fortunately, there were only drinks on their table, but they toppled quickly into the sand. A few patrons laughed, and some unkind children pointed and called names, but at least the patrons at the offending table were nice enough to help me up. My face burning, I kneeled down to clean up the mess.

"I'll bring new drinks right away," I promised.

Lola appeared at my side. Like Vivian, she had blonde hair, but hers was darker, more of a dirty shade, like Brad's. It fell in soft, perfect waves around her shoulders. She had a voluptuous-looking figure and soft brown eyes with long, thick lashes that reminded me of Bambi. Her mouth was sullen as she stooped beside me to help.

"Nice going. Hale saw you," she hissed.

"That's great," I said. "Where is he?"

Lola pointed toward the building. He was standing at the upstairs office window, arms folded across his chest, staring down at us. Even at this distance, it was quite obvious he didn't look happy.

"You take these into the café," she said. "I'll get table two's order. Bring out number three's. Don't rush. Take your time. It's all a balancing act. You'll get the hang of it by tomorrow."

"If I'm still here tomorrow," I reminded her.

She glanced upward at Hale again but said nothing.

Keanu stopped me on my way back inside the building. "Hale wants to see you upstairs."

I struggled to breathe normally. "Oh God. I'm doomed."

He stared at me, expression grim. "If I could take the rap again, I would. But he saw the whole thing. Make up something. Say that your contact lens fell out. Be prepared—he likes to lord it out over people, especially women. You saw what he did to those two volunteers earlier. Hale has no feelings at all—like a regular snake."

"Some snakes have feelings, don't they?" I tried to squelch my fear.

Keanu shook his head. "Not boa constrictors. I don't know why his wife stays with him."

"He's *married*?" By the way he had leered at me yesterday, I'd assumed he was a single, older guy on the prowl.

"Going on twenty years." He gave me a pat on my shoulder. "Good luck."

My legs were like dead weight as I trudged through the kitchen, ignoring the sympathetic look from Poncho. I climbed the stairs slowly and noiselessly. As I reached the top landing, I could hear Hale's voice resonating through the walls and froze in panic. Oh yeah, I was finished.

"I'm cutting you off without another dime. Yep, you heard me right." There was a pause, and then Hale laughed, the sound echoing in my head. "Please. Do you think you're the first person who ever said they wanted to kill me? Get in line."

I waited for him to continue but heard nothing. I looked up and caught sight of Hale standing there watching me, hands on his hips.

"Well hello, Miss Jorgenson."

I swallowed nervously. "I…um…didn't want to interrupt but heard you wanted to see me."

Storm clouds brewed in those bone-chilling eyes of his, and I longed to be anywhere else but here.

Hale pointed at the leather couch in the center of the wood-paneled floor. "Have a seat. There are a few things I need to say to you."

CHAPTER THREE

———

I forced myself to move forward, feet shuffling across the floor. I wondered if there was a tactful way to ask for a job recommendation.

Hale gestured toward the couch again. "Sit."

I bristled inwardly at the word. Did the man think I was a dog? "Um thanks, but I think I'll stand."

Hale cocked one fine, arched eyebrow at me, obviously not used to people defying his requests. "Miss Jorgenson, do you want to keep working here?"

"Yes."

A muscle ticked in his jaw. "Yes, what?"

Who the heck does this guy think he is? Did he get his jollies by making everyone jump through hoops like trained seals? As badly as I needed the job, I wasn't about to grovel at his feet. I had *some* pride left. "Yes, Hale."

He appeared startled for a moment, and then his mouth twitched into a smile. "You're spunky, Miss Jorgenson. I like that. But the fact remains that I don't think you're cut out for this job. You're about as graceful as a pig at a luau."

Lovely. I would have preferred the cliché bull-in-the-china-shop reference. I paused, trying to tame the anxiety growing from within. "Please, I'm trying. It's going to take me a little while longer to get the hang of it. You'll see."

His smile was evil and foreboding. "Tell you what I'll do, Miss Jorgenson. I'm going to give you one more chance. But there's a condition attached."

Of course there was. Even though I'd only worked here two days, I already had an idea of how this guy operated. I braced myself. "What is it?"

He licked his lips, and his smile widened while a wave of nausea rolled through me. "Tomorrow night after work, you'll go to dinner with me."

I knew it. This guy had no morals, hitting on his employees. "I'm sorry, but I can't have dinner with you. I have a boyfriend."

Hale laughed. "Let him get his own dinner."

Footsteps sounded on the stairs, and a petite Polynesian woman appeared. She was dressed in a white silk suit, and her bare, tanned legs donned an expensive pair of strappy sandals in the same color, with Silverstone studs that bore the distinct trademark of Versace. She carried a white Gucci leather bag that was larger than my bathroom sink. Her narrow face was pretty, with high cheekbones, and she had short, black hair cut in a blunt style that was striking with her features. Dark eyes that were slanted and focused on Hale quickly shifted their gaze to me. I watched her expression change and nostrils flare as she scanned me up and down.

Uh-oh. This must be wifey poo.

"What's going on here?" She addressed Hale while continuing to glare at me.

Hale leaned down to kiss her on the cheek. "I was chatting with a new employee, sweetie." He gestured to me. "Carrie Jorgenson, this is my wife, Alana."

I extended my hand. Alana narrowed her eyes, and I saw something in them that unnerved me. It was a calculating, all-knowing look. This woman was sharp and nobody's fool. I guessed that she knew exactly what her husband was.

"It's very nice to meet you." My hand was left dangling in midair and finally, having no choice, I returned it to my side. Talk about your awkward moments.

Alana's face turned crimson as she stared at her husband. "You never change, do you? This is why we can't get back together. You promised you would stop fooling around. As usual, your word means nothing."

Hale held up a hand in protest. "It's not what you think, babe. I hired Miss Jorgenson because of her exceptional customer service skills."

Oh yeah, he was definitely stretching the truth with that

one.

"Don't give me that," Alana snapped. "How stupid do you think I am? I have my spies. I know that you're fooling around with someone else besides this floozy too." She thrust a French manicured nail in my direction. "How much more am I supposed to take?"

First a pig at a luau and now a floozy? Really?

I started to say something then thought better of it. I backed up toward the stairwell until I caught Hale's eye. He nodded at me.

"You can leave now, Miss Jorgenson. Keep up the good work."

Before I was completely down the stairs, I heard something crash overhead, and then Alana started shouting. Hale yelled back, "You're nuts," and then another loud crash ensued. Unnerved, I wasn't watching where I was going and plowed right into Vivian at the bottom of the stairs.

"Whoa." She laughed. "You look like you've seen a ghost."

I pointed upward. "Call the police. I think they might kill each other."

She waved her hand dismissively. "It happens all the time—believe me. She'll run out of here crying in a minute. Just watch." She pulled me by the arm over to the prep table. "Better get out of the way, or she'll mow you down."

A minute later, I heard the sound of high heels clicking on the stairs, and Alana appeared. She sobbed as she ran past us, and despite her nasty attitude, my heart filled with pity for the woman. "Why does she stay with him if he cheats on her?"

Vivian shrugged. "They're actually separated at the moment. And she stays with him because of the money. What else could it be? He's got tons."

Poncho rang a little bell by the counter. "Yoo-hoo, Viv. Take this cheeseburger out to the man at the front counter, please."

Vivian grabbed the platter and hummed a little tune low in her throat. Lola, the other full-time waitress, laughed with Poncho at some private joke and then disappeared into the café. I was the only one upset by the brawl, while it was business as usual for everyone else.

"Did you get an order pad yet?" Vivian asked.

I shook my head, and she gestured me to follow her through the double doors. After Vivian placed the plate down in front of a man who grunted "thank you," she reached down under the counter while I took the opportunity to peer at the contents on the shelves. There was a bottle of dill pickles about two feet tall, supplies for the two-burner coffeemaker station, and packets of silverware already made up. There was also a box filled with order pads. She thumbed through them for a minute, selected one, and handed it to me. There was a series of numbers on the top right-hand corner identifying each check, and at the bottom it said *Pad Two*, with *Have a nice day!* scrawled underneath it.

"What does that mean?" I asked, pointing at the number on the bottom.

"See…" Vivian removed her order pad from her apron pocket. "Mine is pad one. You got Carmen's when she was fired. Lola's three. We have a couple of other part-time servers who only work on weekends, and they use numbers four and five. If Keanu takes orders, he uses number six. This way, Poncho always knows who the order belongs to." She hesitated. "And Hale, if there are any problems with the service."

Lovely. "Are you full-time?"

She nodded. "Full-time and then some. Yeah, me and Lola. The restaurant is closed on Mondays, and we both usually have Sundays off. Poncho's off on Sundays as well. That's when Leo, our backup cook, comes in. He's also in most mornings to get breakfast started. Then Poncho takes over. Poncho likes to work alone. Let me tell you—he's amazing. If he gets really behind, Lola does some light cooking as well, but he hates anyone messing around in his kitchen. Poncho's a bit neurotic when it comes to people touching his stove. And don't even dream about opening the fridge. He becomes a complete psychopath then."

"I heard that," Poncho yelled.

Vivian laughed. "The other two girls, Sybil and Anna, are in college, so they don't want many hours, but they're cool about helping out if Lola or I need time off. I'm guessing you'll be full-time too and probably work noon to closing, like me. Lola's shift fluctuates. If Anna comes in for the morning, Lola works the same shift as me."

I stared at her for a full beat, wondering if I should tell her. I needed to confide in someone. "Hale asked me to have dinner with him tomorrow night."

Her eyes widened. "Really?"

"What should I do? I have a boyfriend and no interest in dating my boss, especially someone like him. He can't fire me if I don't go out with him…that's harassment."

She clucked her tongue. "Don't worry. Maybe nothing will come of it, now that the old ball and chain has been in to check up on him."

I caught the note of sarcasm in her voice. "You don't like her?"

Vivian stared at me in disbelief. "She doesn't love him and vice versa. Alana's a spoiled, pampered princess who's afraid of losing her meal ticket. I think they're going to end up divorced anyway."

Wow. It was like walking into a real-life soap opera.

Vivian touched my arm. "Come on. There's a table of six outside. Help me take the orders. It will be good practice for you. Poncho likes neat printing, but you can abbreviate. Look at your pad. There're already some items listed there. SD is for soda, CF is for coffee, and HHBRG is for Hale's Hamburger Platter. So you only have to circle these items instead of writing them down. And of course POI is self-explanatory."

I followed her outside and watched as she took down the first two orders with ease then gave me a gentle push forward. "Hey, guys. This is Carrie. She's new, so go easy on her."

An elderly man with silver hair smiled at me. "Carrie, I'll take a chicken salad wrap with no tomato, fries, and a piña colada, please."

I wrote down *Chk wrap, no tom, fry, piña.*

Vivian looked over my shoulder and nodded. "Not bad." She took the rest of the orders with great precision, and we went back to the café together to fill the drink orders.

"If people want specialty drinks, we call The Lava Pot," Vivian explained. "It's a tiki bar at the resort that we have on speed dial. Since we're so short staffed, it's easier to have them prepare the drinks. Sometimes Casey, the bartender, brings them over himself. God, that man is so hot." Vivian stopped to fan herself. "They bill Hale, and he settles up with them weekly. Poncho has some piña colada mix in the fridge, so you don't need to bother this time."

I turned my order in to Poncho, who had burgers going on the grill along with fries and something else I couldn't identify. He moved to the counter and began slicing open a pineapple with a sharp butcher knife. He saw me watching and gave a conceited smile. "You see? This is why I use so many pineapples. Everyone comes here for my famous salsa. There is never enough." He whacked the fruit with vigor, and I jumped. "But will Hale give me a raise? No. Unappreciative jerk." He glanced at my order. "Not bad, girlie. You may work out after all."

I flashed him a smile of relief.

The rest of the evening went smoothly. The café closed at nine, but we weren't finished cleaning up until almost ten. Poncho was a compulsive neat freak when it came to his kitchen, and the only thing I was allowed to do was sweep the floor and empty the dishwashers. Since we had no busboy, Vivian and I cleaned tables, both the inside and outside ones. Lola was in the kitchen with Poncho.

"Bet she leaves before us," Vivian whispered to me. "That's all right. I'll ream her butt out when she gets home."

"Are you guys roommates?" I asked with interest.

Vivian shook her head furiously. "No way. She's only staying with me for a few days. Lola has a basement apartment, and one of her rooms got flooded in a recent storm. I felt sorry for her and stupidly offered her my place to crash for a few days, but now I'm sorry I did. Lola's a slob, and she brought tons of stuff with her, afraid some of it might get damaged if left behind. Hello, storage locker anyone? My place is tiny. Plus she brought her cat." She wrinkled her nose in disgust.

Her face looked so comical that I fought a sudden urge to laugh. "Are you allergic?"

"No, but I hate cats. My father had one when I was little, and she bit me when I tried to pet her. I even had to get stitches.

Forget that crap. Give me a goldfish any day."

I chuckled as I listened to her, hoping it would divert my thoughts from the searing pain in my legs. I had thought today might be a bit easier on my feet, but no such luck. Still, I would need to learn how to adapt if I wanted to keep the job. My head pounded, and I was starving. How the heck did Vivian and Lola make this work look so darn easy?

Loud, angry voices were heard coming from Hale's office. Vivian ran into the kitchen and a minute later came back out to report. "Poncho's up there, and he doesn't sound happy."

Lola emerged from the kitchen, a large leather bag slung over her slim shoulder. "Time for me to head out. I'm meeting Jack for a quick bite. Then I'll be home. Should I bring you back some Chinese food?"

"Yeah, that would be great," Vivian said. "It would have been even better if you'd helped me and Carrie clean off the tables though."

Lola cut her eyes from Vivian to me, as if I was responsible for Vivian's sarcastic remark. "Look, I was cleaning out the fridge, okay? By the way, Poncho said there's a pineapple in there in case anyone wants to take it home."

"Why isn't he using it tomorrow?" Vivian wanted to know.

Lola rolled her eyes. "Said it felt a bit soft to him. You know how he is. Everything has to be perfect. Bring it home, and we'll use it to make daiquiris."

Vivian sighed. "Not tonight. I'm too tired."

"Suit yourself. Later, girls." Lola turned and exited through the patio door.

Vivian snorted. "She makes me nuts. Sure, we could have daiquiris if *I* made them, and then *I'd* get stuck cleaning out the blender. Too much effort. I'm going with wine and TV reruns tonight, thank you very much."

Before I could respond, we heard someone running down the stairs. A second later, Poncho pushed his way through the swinging doors, backpack in hand. He didn't even bother to acknowledge us as he charged past at a fast and furious pace. The glass front door that led to the lobby slammed so hard I was positive he must have broken it.

"What was all that about?" I asked.

"I only heard bits and pieces," Vivian said. "He told Hale he wanted more money *or else*. Poncho should know by now it's a losing battle. I don't know why he stays here. A man with his talent could go to any five-star restaurant." She lowered her voice. "I think Hale has something on him."

I was intrigued. "Like what?"

The doors to the kitchen opened, and Keanu appeared. "You ladies all set out here?"

Vivian picked up her purse. "Yeah. I'm hightailing it out. See you both in the morning." She winked at me. "Good job today, kiddo. You're doing really well."

I smiled. Maybe I could do this after all. "Thanks for your help."

Keanu and I were alone. He smiled at me, almost hesitantly. "I've got my moped outside. Do you live close?"

"Our apartment is in town," I said. "It's only about a fifteen minute walk."

"Is your boyfriend coming to meet you?"

I wondered why he seemed curious about Brad then reminded myself that it didn't mean anything. He was probably just being sociable. "No. He's gone out with some friends."

Keanu frowned. "You shouldn't be walking by yourself. I know the path is well-lighted to town, but it's no trouble to give you a ride."

I was tempted to say yes. My legs ached and could use a rest, but it probably wasn't a good idea, especially if Brad happened to see us. I didn't know if he'd actually be jealous because I'd never given him a reason to. Still, if I saw Brad arriving home on the back of an attractive girl's moped, *I* would not be very pleased.

"Actually, I'm looking forward to the walk. I think it will help me sleep better."

He smiled but didn't argue with me. "Well, okay. Are you working tomorrow?"

"No idea. I guess I'll have to check with Hale."

He leaned forward on the counter. "Tomorrow's Friday, and since it's a popular day at the resort, I'd say it's a safe bet. If Hale's got you working the same shift as Vivian, it will be twelve to nine. He may ask you to come in a little earlier though. Probably the same with Saturday. That's our busiest day of the week, especially with the band and karaoke hour during dinner."

My heart started to pound against the wall of my chest. "You have karaoke here?"

I must have sounded a bit too excited, because Keanu grinned. "You like karaoke, huh?"

I emitted a high-pitched squeal. "Love it." I was relieved that he didn't ask if I was any good, because the jury was still out on that one. I loved to sing, period. Books and music had kept me occupied as a child when I'd had no one else to turn to. I longed to have a career in theater, maybe even a star part in a Broadway musical someday. Okay, I realized that was stretching things a bit, but it was a dream that had provided solace and comfort to me during many lonely hours while growing up.

We heard footsteps on the stairs, and a minute later, Hale emerged from the kitchen. He nodded to Keanu as he punched a code into the register, and the drawer opened. He started scooping bills into a zippered bag. "See you in the morning, Keanu. Miss Jorgenson, you're scheduled from twelve to nine tomorrow, like today. Lola is working from eight to five, so she'll cover lunch breaks for you and Vivian."

"Okay."

"Before you leave tonight, go over to The Lava Pot and bring me back a Mai Tai. They'll charge it to my account. Make sure you use the back entrance when you return. I'm locking the doors so that no one from the resort will be able to enter. Or, you can come in from the patio entrance. I always leave both doors unlocked until I leave."

"I'll grab the drink for you," Keanu offered.

Hale glared at Keanu. "Is your name Miss Jorgenson? No, I don't think so." He turned his full attention back to me. "Don't be long. I think we'll need to have another little chat when you get back."

Oh no. Me, alone with that sleaze? Now what was I going to do?

Keanu was silent as he opened the patio door for me, and didn't even bother to say good night to Hale. Apparently no one was off-limits when it came to Hale's humiliation tactics.

When we were outside the café and out of earshot, Keanu touched my elbow. "Come on. I'll show you where The Lava Pot is. I have to go in that direction anyway. Are you sure you're going to be okay?"

The truth was no, but I nodded anyway. I didn't want to be alone with Hale. "Wh-what do you think he wants to talk to me about?"

Keanu ran a hand through his hair. "I'm not sure, but I did overhear him tell Poncho that the register came up short by a hundred dollars."

My mouth went dry. "I'm no thief, Keanu."

He nodded. "I believe you. Seriously, who knows with him? Hale may have made it up so he could be alone with you. Look, I can wait around outside the café if you need me."

What a sweet gesture, and I almost took him up on it. "It's all right. No job is worth being in constant fear of your boss. I'll bring him his drink, and if he tries something, I'll take off."

Keanu drew his lips together in a thin, firm line as he reached into his jeans pocket and pulled out a pen and an Aloha Lagoon business card. He jotted a number down on the bottom of it and handed it to me. "This is my cell. Call if you need anything, okay?"

Despite the fact that my insides felt hollow, I managed a smile. "Well, do you happen to know anyone who's hiring? But seriously, thanks. If I don't see you again, it was nice working with you, albeit briefly."

Keanu started to say something then stopped. He continued to watch me with a thoughtful expression. "I hope I *will* see you again, Carrie."

He walked down the path to a small parking lot, got on his moped, and then turned and gave me one last look. The engine roared to life, and the bike sped off out of sight.

I exhaled a long, nervous breath. *All right, let's get this over with.*

There were a few people sitting at The Lava Pot's outside tables on the boardwalk, laughing and enjoying themselves, drinks in hand. I didn't see any staff around, so I went through the glass-paneled doors that led to the inside bar area. There was a young man behind the bar filling an order, and others were waiting.

I blew out a sigh and shifted my weight from one sneakered foot to another, trying not to be impatient. I already knew that Hale didn't like to be kept waiting. Oh well. He was probably going to fire me anyway, so what difference did it make?

After a few minutes, the bartender smiled at me. He was cute, with light brown hair, and probably a few years older than me. "Hi, I'm Casey. What'll you have?"

Ah, this was the guy Vivian had been drooling over. You had to love a man with an English accent in Hawaii. "Hi, I need a Mai Tai for Hale Akamu. Could you charge it to the Loco Moco's account?"

Casey's smile faded. "Are you a new employee there?"

"Yes, I'm Carrie."

He shook my hand and then grimaced. "Well, you have my sympathy."

Good grief. Was there *anyone* who liked my boss?

I had my drink shortly afterward, scribbled a signature on the receipt Casey placed in front of me, mumbled a thank-you, and then shuffled my way back down the boardwalk and through the sand. I made it a point to be extra careful so as not to trip and upset the almighty's beverage.

The urge was great to stop and watch the palm trees swaying in the warm breeze, but I knew that wasn't a good idea. I glanced at my watch and figured that Hale was probably already steamed I'd been gone fifteen minutes. My hands began to shake, and I quickened my pace. Was Hale planning on firing me because of the money, or simply looking for an excuse to be alone with me? The thought was enough to make my skin crawl.

As the rear of the café came into view, I noticed the lights were out inside. A shiver crept down my spine as I stepped onto the patio and reached for the door handle. Maybe I should just keep walking back to my apartment. What if he grabbed me when I went in? I poised myself, ready to throw the drink in his face, and cautiously pushed open the door. Hale was inside no doubt, waiting to pounce on me in the dark. *Sick pervert.*

I stood in the doorway. "Hale?"

There was no answer.

Goose bumps dotted my arms as I flicked the switch on the wall, and the main room of the café became flooded with light. Still, Hale was nowhere to be seen. Well, if he thought I was going upstairs to his office, forget about it. I didn't need any job *that* badly. I'd leave his beverage by the register and take off.

I walked behind the counter and placed the glass next to the napkin holders and salt and pepper shakers. It was then that I noticed that one of the swinging doors to the kitchen was slightly ajar. I squinted closer, trying to determine what was holding it open.

A man's black moccasin was in plain view, resting on its heel. Part of a black pant leg could be seen as well.

Maybe Hale had gotten sick? Had he slipped on the wet floor that Vivian had mopped before leaving? No, that was more like something *I* would have done. I drew closer and peered around the edge of the door into the kitchen. I gave a sharp gasp, and my clammy hands gripped the wood for support.

Hale was lying on his back inside the door, a steady stream of blood flowing from his chest. There was blood spattered on the walls as well. A page from an order pad had been pinned with a butcher knife to his chest. Directly above the *Have a nice day!* someone had scrawled *PIG* in large block letters with a black marker. A piece of pineapple hung out of his open mouth, while his vacant eyes were open and staring upward at the ceiling.

I looked down at my feet and whimpered. The blood was starting to pool around my white sneakers, and the bottom edges were turning red as a result.

The café turned upside down, and I lost my footing. A hysterical cry left my mouth as I fell and landed hard on the tiled flooring. I scrambled to my feet in an instant, between jags of crying and screaming then glanced down at my hands. My palms were red with Hale's blood. Agitated, I rubbed them frantically on my jeans, trying to cleanse them while my stomach threatened to explode.

This must be some sort of a bad dream. Things like this didn't happen in paradise. There was no rocket scientist needed to figure out that my boss—aka, the big kahuna—was dead. With the exception of funerals, I'd never seen a dead body up close before. A million thoughts and questions flooded my brain, and one stood out from the rest.

I wondered if I had met a killer today.

CHAPTER FOUR

My lungs screamed and begged for me to pay attention. *Air. I need air.*

I fought against the urge to pass out as nausea stirred through my body. The Mauna Loa Volcano was due for an eruption, but I was fairly certain I was going to beat it. I burst through the patio entrance and started running toward the water.

Someone grabbed my arm, but I shook the person off, not even stopping to look and see who it was. A male voice yelled "Carrie," but I paid no attention and plowed on. I ran toward the waves that seemed to beckon me with reassurances that everything would be fine once I reached them.

I fell to my hands and knees, crawled to the edge of the shore, and proceeded to vomit. The night was still, and the waves continued to whisper softly to me as I lay there on my side, gasping for air.

Please let me wake up from this nightmare now.

A cool hand pressed against the back of my neck, steadying me as I retched again. When I had finally finished, I managed to weakly turn my head and saw Keanu's worried face next to mine. He gently helped me to my feet as I stumbled against him.

He forced me to look at him. "What happened?" Then he stared down at my hands in disbelief. "What the… Did you cut yourself?"

I pointed toward the café and found myself babbling like an idiot. "Call them."

Keanu's face was puzzled. "Call who?"

"9-1-1. Dead. Blood." I trembled as the bile rose in the back of my throat again.

Keanu's expression changed from confusion to shock. "Who? Hale? What happened?"

"Dead," I repeated, the insides of my stomach still flipping around like a gymnast. I moved away from him and sank down into the sand. "S-someone stabbed him."

He gave me a sharp look and then turned and ran inside the café. Despite the warm breeze that whipped through the palm trees, I was chilled to the bone, and my teeth began to chatter. I glanced down at my hands. There were still remnants of Hale's blood on them. I let out a low moan and submerged them in the shallow water, rubbing them together in a neurotic frenzy. Then I vomited again.

My head reeled as I lay back on the sand with my feet submerged in the water, listening to the tide rushing in. For a moment I was too ill to care that I couldn't swim and one vicious wave might carry me off into the endless dark ocean. I sighed and closed my eyes.

Keanu found me again, and without a word, lifted my soaking-wet body effortlessly into his arms. He placed me in one of the restaurant chairs and wrapped a towel around my shoulders. His eyes were dark with worry as they stared into mine.

"The police and medics are on their way. I told them to come in through the rear entrance. Hopefully the guests inside the resort won't notice anything." He lifted a can of ginger ale from the table and placed it against my lips. "Drink this. It will help settle your stomach."

I shook my head. "I can't."

He narrowed his eyes. "Please don't argue with me, Carrie."

I took a sip, afraid that I might be sick again, then leaned back in the chair. Keanu placed the can on the table and stared out at the water.

"Who did this?" I asked.

He shook his head. "No idea."

A thought occurred to me. "I thought you'd left. Why were you outside the café?"

Keanu's gaze met mine. "I was worried about you, so I came back. And no, I didn't kill Hale, Carrie."

"I never said—"

"You were thinking it though."

"No." I placed my aching head in my hands. "I really don't know what to think."

He reached for my hand. "You're in shock. For the record, I know you didn't do anything either. I figured I'd stick around to see if you needed a ride home. I had no idea if he'd fire you or maybe try to come on to you. It's rotten to speak ill of the dead, but the guy wasn't exactly one of my favorite people."

I wondered what he meant but didn't ask. I was too overcome with emotion to say anything. Then the tears started to roll down my cheeks. Keanu reached an arm out toward me as if he was going to embrace me then stopped himself. He continued to pat my hand lightly.

After another minute, we heard the unmistakable sound of sirens approaching in the distance. I started to rise from my seat, but Keanu held up his hand. "No, I'll go talk to the police. I'm sure they'll want to speak to you as well, but stay here for now and rest."

I nodded mutely while my teeth continued to chatter again at a noisy but steady rate. A couple of EMTs rushed into the café, and a man in a red Hawaiian shirt followed them at a more leisurely pace. Another man in a policeman's uniform was right behind him. Keanu approached the patio door, but the policeman said something to him, and Keanu hung back. He stared over in my direction but didn't move toward me.

I wondered who the man in the Hawaiian shirt was. Maybe a relative of Hale? Surely he couldn't be in law enforcement, not dressed liked that.

I felt guilty leaving Keanu to deal with all of this, so I slowly rose to my feet, surprised at how unsteady I was. As I approached the café, the two EMTs exited the building and got back into their vehicle. Why had they left Hale in there? Was he not really dead? Had I been wrong?

Some people had started to gather on the beach, and I caught the low murmur of voices as they watched the scene unfold before their eyes. So much for the resort guests not finding out.

My mind had overfilled to capacity with the vision of Hale's body, the paper pinned to his chest with the knife, and that ridiculous piece of pineapple hanging out of his mouth.

"Carrie." Keanu interrupted my thoughts. "This is Detective Ray Kahoalani. He'd like to ask you some questions about Hale. Are you feeling up to it?"

The truth was no, but what choice did I have? I glanced at the man with apprehension, and he nodded at me, face expressionless. He looked like a native of the islands and close to Poncho's age.

The detective gestured back to the table. "You don't look very well, Miss Jorgenson. Would you like to sit down?"

I shook my head. "No thank you. I'm fine. Detective Kahol—er..." Darn, I botched his name big-time. I still couldn't believe this man was a detective. Talk about your casual attire.

He smiled. "You can call me Detective Ray. Everyone does."

"Why is Hale still in there?" I asked. "Isn't he dead?"

Detective Ray gave me an odd look. "Yes. We're waiting on the coroner's office to take his body away. The EMTs have already pronounced him dead. This is a crime scene now, and he will not be moved until photos are taken and the coroner's staff arrive."

"Oh." It was all I could think to say. I must have been wowing the detective with my intelligence.

"When was the last time you saw Mr. Akamu alive, Miss Jorgenson?" The detective wanted to know.

"It was about fifteen minutes before I found him. He asked me to run over to The Lava Pot and get him a Mai Tai. When I came back, he was lying on the floor, so I ran back outside."

"Was there anyone else inside the restaurant?" Detective Ray asked.

I shook my head. "Hale was alone. Keanu walked over to the bar with me and then took off on his moped."

Detective Ray eyed Keanu curiously. "But something made you come back."

Underneath the lights from the café, Keanu's face colored slightly. "I-uh, was worried about Carrie being alone with him. Hale had a reputation. There was a rumor going around about an incident with a former employee, so I wanted to make sure she'd be okay."

The detective focused his attention on me again. "I see. Was today your first day on the job?"

"My second." What did that even matter?

He wrote something down on his pad, and my nerves tingled. Great. Did the man think I might be a suspect too?

"Did you touch the body at all?" Detective Ray wanted to know.

I thought that was a strange question, but it wasn't like I could argue with him. "I slipped in the blood when I found Hale. I didn't touch him though."

"What was Hale doing when you left to go get his drink?"

I swallowed hard and reminded myself to breathe. "He was emptying out the register." Nervously I stared at Keanu and wondered if I should say something about the money shortage. Keanu frowned back in return. I figured he understood my silent question.

Detective Ray addressed Keanu. "How long were you outside before Miss Jorgenson came out?"

"I parked my bike at the rear of the café by the dumpster," Keanu explained. "I'd just reached the patio entrance when Carrie rushed out the door. I tried to grab her, but she kept on running toward the water."

The detective had a great poker face. I couldn't tell if he believed Keanu or was getting ready to take both of us down to the station for mug shots. "We're going to secure the restaurant tonight. No one will be allowed in or out while we search the place. Would you happen to know Mr. Akamu's next of kin?"

Keanu reached into his jeans pocket for his phone. "His wife, Alana. I have her number on my cell. As a matter of fact, I have numbers for all the employees if you need them."

Detective Ray nodded with approval. "That would be a big help. If we can collect all of the necessary evidence by tonight or early tomorrow, we'll release the crime scene. I will probably question everyone here instead of down at the station. I wouldn't plan on being open for business tomorrow though. I'll take the wife's number if you have it handy."

"Hey, Detective." The policeman I'd seen entering the building a few minutes earlier approached us. He had brown hair in a buzz cut and appeared to be in his late thirties. His build was stocky, and he sucked on a lollipop.

Detective Ray sighed. "Yes, Billings, what is it?"

The policeman stood there for a minute, wearing a puzzled expression, as if he'd forgotten his reason for interrupting us. He didn't seem to have much to work with in terms of brainpower.

"Oh! Now I remember." Officer Billings grinned. "You don't need to phone the wife, boss. A call just came in over the radio. Apparently Mrs. Akamu phoned the station and asked if the rumors about her husband were true. Officer Hudson wouldn't confirm anything but did tell her you were at the café if she'd like to speak to you. She started crying and said she'd have a member of the staff bring her right over."

"Wait, she's already here?" Detective Ray asked.

"Yes, sir." The officer bit down on the lollipop and made a crunching sound. When he finished chewing, he elbowed Detective Ray in the side. "Said she was over at The Lava Pot having a drink when someone told her that her husband had been hurt. Funny her being so close by, huh? Do you want me to book her, Dano?"

We all stared at the man in confusion.

Detective Ray gave him a strange look. "Who the heck is Dano?"

"You know…" Officer Billings laughed. "They used to say that all the time in the original *Hawaii Five-O* show." When none of us responded, he lowered his eyes to the ground. "Sorry. Bad joke, I guess. But I always wanted to use that line."

Detective Ray rolled his eyes toward the star-filled sky and growled. "Go back inside the café, Billings. I'll meet you there in a minute."

"Roger, sir."

"It's Ray, not Roger."

"I knew that."

In the meantime, Keanu had been scrolling through his phone and writing down names and numbers on a piece of paper Detective Ray had given him from his notepad. "This is everyone except for Carrie. I don't have hers yet."

I recited my cell phone number for Detective Ray, who then folded the paper in half and placed it in his shirt pocket. "I'll call everyone when I get back to the station and arrange times to meet with them tomorrow. Of course, it will be up to Mrs. Akamu if she wants to reopen the café or not. You can both leave now. I have a couple of other officers on their way to help me go over the crime scene. I'll be in touch."

My legs were numb as I walked back over to the table for another sip of ginger ale. I was ashamed that my thoughts had shifted from Hale's dead body to the fact that this might be the end of my new career. What would Vivian, Keanu, and Lola do? Heck, for that matter, what was *I* going to do?

I drew out my phone and called Brad. The call went directly to voicemail. I sent him a text. *Can you give me ride home?* My brain was fuzzy, and I couldn't remember what he was doing after work tonight. If he was out for drinks with friends, it might be a while before he checked his messages.

Detective Ray nodded at something Keanu said then turned and went back inside the café. Keanu strode over in my direction and took my hand.

"What are you doing?" I asked.

"I'm taking you home," he said and guided me to the back of the café where his moped was parked.

"I'll be fine," I said. "There's no reason for you to bother."

"No, you're not fine. You're white as a sheet, and you just puked your guts out."

"But I don't want—"

Keanu narrowed his eyes. "Did anyone ever tell you how stubborn you are?"

I smiled. "Yeah, lots of times."

He put a helmet on his head and handed me an extra one. "Please get on the bike, Carrie. No more arguing."

I shot off another quick text to Brad, explaining briefly what had happened, and positioned myself on the bike. I had a little trouble adjusting my hair inside the helmet, but Keanu waited patiently until I was ready. "I'm all set."

"Okay, put your hands on my waist."

I edged close to him on the seat and waited for him to start the engine. Instead, he tensed visibly against me, and I wondered what he was thinking.

I spoke softly in his ear. "Keanu."

He seemed startled at the sound of my voice. "Yeah?"

"What's going to happen to me, to my job? They're going to think I'm a suspect."

Keanu moved into action, and the bike came to life. He looked back over his shoulder at me. "I don't know, Carrie. It really isn't looking good for any of us employees. Everyone I can think of had a reason to want Hale dead."

His statement took me by surprise, and before I could stop myself, two words tumbled out of my mouth. "Even you?"

Keanu was silent for a beat. Then he revved the engine and stared down at the ground. "Yeah, even me."

CHAPTER FIVE

I'd never ridden on a moped before. Any other time I was certain I would have enjoyed the experience more. Hey, I was in tropical paradise, on a star-filled night in January with temperatures hovering in the seventies. Things couldn't get much better, right?

Unfortunately, several things were wrong with this scenario. My boss was dead, and everyone at the café where I worked was a suspect, including me *and* the guy who was driving me home. I shut my eyes and let myself experience the warm breeze upon my face. Although exhausted, I doubted sleep would come easily tonight. The vision of Hale's dead face appeared in my mind and refused to leave.

Before I could attempt to make any further sense of the situation, Keanu pulled the bike up in front of my apartment building. There were three units on each floor of the four-story stucco building. Brad and I lived on the bottom floor.

I got off the bike and handed Keanu back his helmet. "Thank you for the ride."

He smiled. "I'll call you if I hear anything. The police will probably phone you as well, but like I told Detective Ray, I'm the contact person for employees. Hale preferred to leave that part of the job up to me."

I hated to ask, but it seemed necessary. "Um, do I still have a job?"

His bright eyes lit up the darkness. "That seems to be the question of the day, doesn't it? I doubt that Alana will close the place down permanently. It's a popular attraction at the resort and a great moneymaker. Hale's owned it since he was barely out of his teens."

I saw his jaw clench suddenly and wondered if something else was bothering him. I didn't feel I knew him well enough to ask, so instead I tugged on my braid, a compulsive gesture I always performed when worried. "Alana doesn't like me. She caught me with Hale in his office and probably figures we were carrying on."

"Don't worry about it," Keanu said. "When I get a chance to speak with her, I'll set the record straight." He glanced around. "What time will your boyfriend be home?"

I shrugged. "I'm not sure. He might have gone out with some friends after work."

He studied me for a moment. "Carrie, can I ask you something that's really none of my business?"

Here was my chance. "If I get to ask you something in return."

He smiled. "Fair enough. I was wondering if you had another reason for coming to Hawaii…besides wanting to live in a tropical paradise and being with your boyfriend."

His words rendered me speechless for a moment. "Why would you ask that?"

Keanu watched me closely. "I don't know. It's a feeling I have."

This guy was good. I tried to laugh it off. "What other reason do I need? I'm young and wanted to start a new adventure in my life. I'm hoping to become a singer someday, so why not start here?"

He continued to stare at me with an expression that said he didn't quite believe me, but he only nodded in response. "I'll wait until you get inside."

I tried to make light of the situation. "Hey, no fair. I didn't get to ask my question."

Keanu grinned. "Go ahead."

I wondered if I actually had enough nerve to go through with it. "What did you have against Hale?"

The smile faded, and when he looked away, it seemed almost as if he was struggling for composure. When Keanu's eyes locked on mine again, his expression was veiled. "It's nothing. Hey, you need some rest. This has been a long, crazy day. I'll see you tomorrow."

Crap. As usual, I'd gone too far. I hoped he wasn't angry with me. I already considered him a friend and looked forward to seeing him tomorrow. "Okay, sounds good. Thanks again for the ride."

"No problem."

I unlocked the front door and glanced over my shoulder. He waved, revved the bike, and then disappeared from sight.

"Brad?" I called, although it was obvious that he wasn't home yet. There weren't clothes strewn all over the floor. I went into the small eat-in kitchen, annoyed to see he had left his dishes in the sink as usual. I always did them, but right now was still weak from my recent stomach mishap. I filled a cup with water and a tea bag then nuked it in the microwave. I glanced inside the refrigerator. There was some leftover pizza, soda, and of course, beer. Cripes. It looked like the inside of a college dorm fridge.

Brad had changed since he'd come to the island. For the first few months in our relationship, he'd been kind and sweet. Once the job in Hawaii had materialized, so had a different person, and he'd started to show his selfish side. Now that we were living together, you'd think this would have drawn us closer—but instead, I felt almost like we were virtual strangers.

I'd come here intending to take control of my life, but instead it was spiraling out of control right before my eyes.

I settled on the small, blue floral-patterned loveseat with my tea and clicked the remote to the television. Nothing looked interesting. My thoughts returned to Hale, and I shivered, pulling a blanket around my shoulders. I didn't want to but forced myself to remember how I'd found his body. The pineapple in his mouth made me think of Poncho. Could he be a killer? No, I couldn't see it. And the server pad? What number had been on the bottom? Holy cow. I hadn't even thought to check. I prayed it hadn't been mine.

My cell phone rang, startling me. I glanced down at the screen, but it was an unknown number. "Hello?"

"Carrie?" It was a woman's voice, distinctly familiar. "It's Lola from the Loco Moco. I just heard. Are you all right?"

I stared at the phone in confusion. "How'd you get my number?"

There was a pause on the other end. "Jeez, don't get so defensive. You gave it to Vivian and me earlier, remember? And the detective, what's his name—Roy? He just called me."

I exhaled deeply. "Detective Ray. Sorry. I'm a bit on edge."

"Well, that's understandable. Are you all right? That had to be horrible for you to find him like that."

I shivered. "It was awful. Who could do such a thing?"

Lola sighed. "I hate to say this, but I think we all saw it coming. I mean, the guy had more enemies than Hawaii has pineapples."

I took a sip from my mug and closed my eyes. "We're all suspects, you know. What did Detective Ray want?"

"He wants me to come over to the café for questioning tomorrow. When I asked why, he said all employees would be coming in at some point. He'll probably call you too."

As she spoke, my phone buzzed, and I saw that I had a new voicemail. "Lovely. I think that he just did."

I heard Lola talking to someone in the background. "Viv's home, and she's freaking out. Hang on—I'll put her on."

"Care?" Vivian's voice was strained. "Omigod, I don't believe it!"

My voice trembled. "It doesn't seem real."

"You poor thing," she crooned. "Do you want us to come over?"

"I'm not going anywhere," I heard Lola yell, "except to bed." A door slammed in the background.

"Don't stay in that bathroom forever!" Vivian shouted as I cringed and moved the phone away from my ear. "God, she's so annoying. Is your boyfriend with you? I'll come keep you company. What's the address?"

I wrapped my hand around the mug for warmth. "Thanks, Viv, but I'm okay. I only wish I could get the image of his face out of my head."

"Yeah, talk about freaky," she agreed. "Hey, I know this sounds insensitive of me, but my biggest concern right now is money. Did you hear anything about when the café might reopen?"

I leaned back against the couch wearily. "Keanu said it's up to Alana. He doubts she'll close it down for long."

"Oh, heck no. That's the last thing that money-grubbing wench would do. Wow, this bites. It was bad enough to work for Hale, and now I have to work for *her*? She's probably thrilled he's dead."

I remembered Alana crying earlier and wondered if it could have all been for show. "Why would you say that?"

"Well, they're still legally married, so I'm sure she'll inherit everything," Vivian said. "He had to have been worth a fortune. Think about it."

I honestly didn't want to. This was too much for one day. I heard a key tumble in the lock and knew Brad was home. "Viv, I have to go."

"Okay, maybe I'll see you tomorrow. Get some rest, hon."

I clicked off as Brad entered the room. He closed and locked the door behind him, strode over, and gave me a kiss on the top of my head. "Hey, babe. Anything to eat?"

Nice to see you too. "Didn't you get my message?"

"Hmm." He stripped off his shirt and deposited it on the floor. "I've got to take a shower. I'm all sand and sweat."

I rose from the couch and blocked his way to the bedroom. "Do you think you could listen to me for a minute?"

He sighed with impatience and then stroked his finger down the side of my face. "You're cute when you're mad."

"I'm being serious."

He glared at me. "Can't we talk later? I'm beat."

Gee, join the club. Brad was all about himself these days, and I was growing tired of it. "You didn't even read or listen to my messages, did you?"

He pulled his phone out of his pocket and then stripped his shorts off, throwing them on top of the shirt. Even now, with anger surging through me, it was difficult to look away. His body was as close to perfect as one could get, and it was easy to see why women stared at him whenever we went somewhere together. To make matters worse, Brad knew how good-looking he was. If his job had required that he come to work naked, he wouldn't have had a problem with it.

Brad examined the screen. "Oh, sorry. I didn't know you needed a ride. We had a party down at the beach after work. Good thing I got a lift home. Had one too many." He grinned. "But don't worry. I'm all yours for the night, babe."

I sighed in frustration. "Read the next text, please."

He stared at the phone, and I watched as his expression changed to shock, then mild amusement. "No kidding. Well, no great loss. The guy was a major tyrant. I went in there once, and he was ticked off at me for getting sand all over his precious floor. Doesn't he know the customer is always right?"

"Brad, I found his body! They're looking at me as a possible suspect."

He examined his face in the mirror above the bathroom sink and frowned. "Nah. You just started there. Why would anyone think that? You worry too much, dollface."

"Maybe, but I do need a job, and after only two days, I might find myself unemployed again. You did remind me that I'm a freeloader, after all."

He put his arms around my waist and nuzzled my neck. "I'm sorry, baby. Are you okay?"

I let out a long breath. "Yeah, I'll be fine."

He drew back, lifted my chin, and kissed me, but nothing stirred inside for me like it used to. My mother had always told my sister, if you really want to get to know a man before marriage, live with him. It was the one useful piece of advice she'd ever given.

Brad's hands made their way up inside the back of my shirt, and I stiffened. He stopped and looked down at me, a confused expression on his face. "What's the matter now?"

"I told you—I found a dead body tonight. I'm not exactly in a romantic mood."

Brad released me and reached for the glass-enclosed door of the shower. "Yeah. Whatever." He removed his underwear, winked at me, and flung the briefs across the room, where they landed at my feet. "Care to join me?"

I gave him what I hoped was an incredulous look. Brad closed the door behind him, and I heard him chuckle over the spray of the water.

I went outside to the small porch we shared with the other first-floor tenants. The sky was dotted with stars, and a warm breeze drifted in from the water. I watched the nearby palm trees swaying in the breeze as they softly whispered amongst themselves with their own stories to tell.

I leaned against the pillar and closed my eyes. Where had things gone wrong for us? I thought my moving here to join Brad would make everything perfect in my life. Instead I had started to realize that I was living with a man oblivious to my needs and who didn't care about me as much as I'd originally thought. *So what am I doing here?*

I glanced at my cell phone. It was after midnight, six o'clock back home. The new day was not lost on me. At the very least, I could call and wish her a happy birthday. What harm would it do?

Defeated, I scrolled through the contacts in my phone and dialed the familiar number. She'd be heading off to work soon—well, if she hadn't been hitting the bottle all night. Might as well get it over with.

A scratchy female voice answered after the second ring. "Yeah?"

"Happy birthday."

She gave a snort. "How nice of you to spare a moment for me."

There was never any winning with this woman. "What do you have planned for the day?"

She ignored my question, like she'd been ignoring me for most of my twenty-four years. "I thought you were going to send me some money?"

I shut my eyes tight. "I just got a job. I'll send some when I get paid."

She blew into the phone, an indication that she was sucking the life out of a cigarette. "I need it for rent. Thank God for Penny. Your sister is the only one who's ever cared about me."

"That isn't true, and you know it." We were almost five thousand miles apart, but as I listened to her cold, uncaring voice, I knew it wasn't far enough. It would never be far enough.

"Was there anything else you wanted? I'm very busy here. Some of us can't afford to run off to paradise. Some of us have responsibilities."

"No, that's all." Tears filled my eyes, and I brushed them away. I wasn't crying because of the way she'd talked to me, because after all these years I was finally used to it. It was the realization that I was cutting off all ties with this woman. I'd send the money because I made a promise, but that would be the end of it. You couldn't help someone who had no desire to be helped.

I thought of Keanu and what he'd said earlier. The man barely knew me but had surmised that I wasn't here for palm trees or to escape the white stuff back home. Keanu wondered if there was another reason, and he'd been correct.

She still blamed me for my father leaving all those years ago. I'd tried in vain to make her love me and pay attention to me, but the efforts had been useless. I wondered if the dull ache in my chest would ever completely go away. The two words that I was about to speak held more meaning than she knew.

"Good-bye, Mother."

CHAPTER SIX

As I'd suspected, the voicemail message on my phone turned out to be from Detective Ray. He wanted me to come by the Loco Moco at 12:30 the next afternoon for further questioning. I mentioned it to Brad that morning before he left for work.

"You know," Brad said as he worked his finger around the inside of the peanut butter jar while I still lay in bed after a restless night of sleep, "that's how they do it on the cop shows. This way you can't hear what the other suspects are saying and vice versa." He tapped the side of his head. "Maybe I should have been a cop."

Okay, as long as we were indulging in fantasies, I wanted to be Julie Andrews. "Sorry. I can't see it."

"Hmm." Brad nodded in agreement. "Who wants to get shot at all the time anyway, you know?"

As I approached the café for my appointment, I spotted Keanu sitting by himself at one of the tables on the patio. He caught sight of me and waved me over.

"Get any sleep last night?" Keanu asked. He was wearing black cargo shorts and a dark blue Loco Moco Café T-shirt. The pleasant smell of his cologne drifted through the air to me—a crisp fragrance that was a combined woodsy and musky scent. His blue eyes shimmered in bright sunlight that surrounded us.

I shook my head and wished I'd taken some aspirin. My head was pounding. "Not really. How about you?"

"Not much." Keanu gestured toward the patio door of the café. "Detective Ray's not done with Vivian yet, but when he is, go through the patio entrance. We're trying to avoid attracting more suspicion inside the resort itself."

"Have you spoken to the detective yet?" I asked.

Keanu nodded. "Yes, I was the first one. I've been busy for most of the morning trying to keep people away." He took a healthy sip from the Starbucks cup in front of him. "You missed the earlier crowd."

"What crowd?"

"The 'lookie-loos' is what we call them," Keanu explained. "People who heard about the murder and are curious for more details. There were tons of them standing at the café's entrance off of the lobby this morning. All resort guests, I think. Anyway, when Alana decides to reopen the restaurant, the place will be jam-packed, and we'll all be running our tails off. Poncho's a fantastic chef, but they won't be coming here for the food—believe me."

The patio door opened, and Vivian appeared. She looked delicate and pretty in white shorts and a pink lacey tank top. She waved and walked over to us.

"Hey, Care. Are you up next?" she asked.

I nodded. "Should I go in?"

Vivian shook her head. "Detective Ray's gathering his notes together. Better wait till he calls for you. If you ask me, the guy's pretty disorganized. I'm not sure that he could find a K-cup in a Keurig machine. No, he'll come get you when he's ready, like he did to me when he finished with Poncho."

I glanced around. "Where's Poncho now?"

"Gone home, I guess." Vivian took her sunglasses off the top of her head and adjusted them on her face. "He didn't speak to me on the way out, but I will say that he wasn't looking happy."

"What did Detective Ray say?" Keanu asked.

Vivian lowered her face toward the ground. "Uh, he said I wasn't allowed to discuss it with anyone. Oh shoot, I don't see why I can't—"

The door to the patio opened again, and Detective Ray stuck his head out. He frowned when he saw the three of us talking. "Miss Jorgenson, I'm ready for you."

How I dreaded this meeting. What was the point? Hadn't we been over everything last night?

"Good luck," Vivian whispered.

Keanu watched me without a word, the expression on his face intense. I trudged slowly toward the door, wondering what the man was after. And why was he questioning us here instead of down at the police station?

Today Detective Ray was wearing a green Hawaiian shirt with little blue flowers and tan-colored khakis. I wondered if he owned a police uniform—or even a suit—for that matter. He pointed toward the table where his coffee cup and pad were strategically placed. "Make yourself comfortable, Miss Jorgenson."

To my surprise, there was no crime scene tape, like I'd always seen on television shows. Even though I could no longer physically see Hale's body, the vision of him lying on the tiled floor, with blood splattered on the walls, would be forever ingrained in my head. I even knew the exact spot he'd been lying in.

As soon as I sat down, Detective Ray picked up his pen. "Did you happen to notice anything of interest about Mr. Akamu's body last night?"

"Other than his being dead, you mean?" *Shoot.* I hadn't meant to sound so insolent.

He shot me a grim look. "The sheet of paper from the server's pad. Were you able to get a good look at it?"

"No, Detective. I wasn't thinking about it at the time." My mind had been filled with the image of blood—and pineapple. Panic set in. "Wait, was it mine?"

"It had a number six on the bottom," Detective Ray said. "Vivian said it wasn't hers. Did it belong to you?"

Keanu's. "No."

"Do you know who it belonged to then?"

Uh oh. I didn't want to get Keanu in trouble. I was having a difficult time believing he might be a killer. "I'm new here and not sure who it belongs to."

He gave me a shrewd look. "Miss Banks said that it belonged to Keanu Church."

Well, so much for trying to help a fellow out. This man was deliberately trying to trip me up, and I was starting to get annoyed with him. "If you already knew who it belonged to, then why ask me?"

Detective Ray shifted in his seat. "So you didn't see anyone else on the premises when you found Mr. Akamu's body?"

I thought I'd already answered that question last night. "That's right. The lights were off, and the café was dark when I came back with Hale's drink."

Detective Ray checked his notes. "You came in through the patio entrance?"

"Yes."

"What did you do then?"

"I called out to him. When he didn't answer, I decided to leave the drink on the counter and go home. So I went around behind it, and that's when I saw Hale's shoe propped against the door."

Detective Ray scribbled some more notes on his pad. His handwriting was atrocious and resembled that of a doctor writing a prescription. "Mrs. Akamu said that she found you upstairs with her husband earlier that evening. He told her he was assisting a new employee. Was that the truth?"

My eyebrows rose slightly in disbelief. I had found a dead body. I was new in town, had no ties to the victim, and it was only my second day of employment. Did they honestly think I could have been the one to do this? "No."

He frowned. "Please explain."

I blew out a breath. "Well, Hale told me he didn't think I was cut out for the job. I had spilled some drinks outside, and there was an incident in the café with coffee too. I'm a bit of a klutz sometimes. I asked him for another chance, and then Hale said that he wanted me to go to dinner with him—the next night, I mean, tonight."

Detective Ray's eyes widened. "I see. What did you say?"

Man, this was uncomfortable. "I explained that I had a boyfriend, but Hale didn't seem to care. I had no interest in Hale romantically." *Who could?* "Then Alan—er, Mrs. Akamu came up the stairs, and I left the room right away. After that they started throwing things and shouting at each other."

The detective's smile was thin. "Getting back to when you found Mr. Akamu's body. Did you notice anything else about it that seemed off?"

"Well, the word *pig* was written on the paper," I said. "But you already know that." *Was this another trick question?*

He gave me a sharp look. "Miss Jorgenson, do you have any idea why I'm doing the questioning here instead of down at the police station?"

Clueless, I shook my head. "No, sir."

He started doodling on his pad. "Sometimes people who are present at the crime scene—like you—can offer certain insight to things we might normally miss. For example, the pineapple that was sticking out of Hale's mouth. I checked the fridge after you and Mr. Church left last night. There was a pineapple in there that had a small chunk missing from one side. It was about the size of the piece that was found stuffed down his throat. Did you open the fridge last evening?"

What was he getting at? "No. I had been told that Poncho didn't like the rest of the staff messing around in the kitchen, especially with his fridge. Lola was allowed to use the fridge since she helped with the cooking sometimes."

"Really." Detective Ray made another note.

Oh good grief. I clamped a hand over my mouth. Now I was throwing Poncho and Lola under the bus. "Um, I didn't mean…"

Before I could say anything further, the doors of the kitchen were pushed open, and Alana Akamu barreled in, a five-foot fireball on stiletto heels. She click-clacked her way angrily over to the table where we were sitting and thrust a finger at Detective Ray.

"I need to speak with you, Detective."

Detective Ray rose to his feet. "Please, Mrs. Akamu, you need to wait outside while I finish questioning this woman."

Alana folded her arms across her chest. "No. I need to talk to you this minute, and it can't wait." She shot me a look of defiance. "I'm sure Miss Jorgenson would be willing to wait a few minutes—if she wants to keep her job here, that is."

Why was this woman so nasty to me?

Detective Ray gave me a resigned look. "I'm sorry, Miss Jorgenson. Would you mind waiting outside for a second?"

"Sure, no problem." I rose to my feet and walked past Alana, who raked her eyes over me, nostrils flaring. Jeez. Maybe I shouldn't plan on staying here. Then again, if I left, that might make me appear even guiltier.

Keanu was using a handheld calculator and jotting some figures down on a ledger. I slid into the chair across from him. "Balancing the payroll?"

He smiled. "I'm trying to help Alana out as much as I can regarding the daily receipts. She knows nothing about running a restaurant. So how'd it go? That was pretty quick."

"I'm not finished," I said. "She stormed right in and gave me the evil eye. Why does she hate me so much?"

"Because she's aware her husband was interested in you." A muscle twitched in Keanu's jaw. "Alana's no fool. She knows exactly what Hale was capable of."

Great. A woman scorned and out to get me. "But she's okay with my working here?"

Keanu nodded. "I had a talk with her earlier. I explained you have a boyfriend and had no designs on her husband. She agreed to let you stay on. Try to take what Alana says with a grain of salt. She's grieving and doesn't know what she's doing."

I thought about what Vivian said yesterday. Was she *really* grieving though? My gaze locked on Keanu's, and his mouth formed a thin, hard line.

"I can guess what you're thinking."

"She was nearby last night," I volunteered. "Maybe…"

He held up a hand. "Don't get involved, Carrie. Let the cops handle it."

I pointed at the café. "Detective Ray was asking me questions and deliberately trying to trip me up. He thinks I could have killed Hale."

Keanu nodded. "He did the same thing to me. That's what the police have to do, Carrie. They can't assume anyone is innocent. Stay calm, and don't give them any reason to suspect you. In the meantime Detective Ray said we can reopen for business again tomorrow. Alana was all for it, especially since it's a Saturday, and that's the biggest moneymaking day of the week."

Interesting. Alana had to be sitting pretty right now. I wondered how much in life insurance policies Hale might have had as well.

As if her ears were ringing, the door slammed, and Alana trotted toward us at a rapid pace. I half expected to see her tiny legs topple off those five-inch heels. She glanced at Keanu. "Do the receipts look okay?"

He nodded. "Don't worry. I'll put everything in order."

Alana's face softened. "I don't know what I'd do without you, Keanu." Then she noticed me watching, and her expression immediately soured. "The café will open late tomorrow, and we'll have a staff meeting with everyone first. Carrie, plan on coming in at ten thirty. We'll open at eleven. Customers will be allowed to order breakfast until noon."

"All right, Mrs. Akamu," I replied. "I'm sorry about your husband."

"Sure you are," Alana snapped as she stomped away from us and got into a black Porsche that was parked on the side of the building.

"So you really think she's okay with me working here, huh?" My voice was tinged with obvious sarcasm.

Keanu's eyes twinkled. "Try to keep in mind everything she's going through."

Detective Ray appeared in the doorway and crooked his finger toward me, and I rose.

Keanu walked over with me and addressed him. "Is it okay if I run these back upstairs? I'll be in and out within thirty seconds. Scout's honor."

Detective Ray nodded. "I was an Eagle Scout myself, so how can I argue with that? Plus, you've already given your statement."

We waited until Keanu had returned outside, and then the detective nodded at me. "Miss Jorgenson—"

"Carrie," I interrupted. "Please call me Carrie."

"Very well." Detective Ray walked behind the front counter and motioned for me to follow him. He pointed down at the floor where Hale's body had lain. "Did you happen to notice anything in Hale's pockets last night?"

Another weird question. "I didn't get close enough to look. Plus, there were other things that grabbed my attention, like the blood and the—"

Detective Ray produced a plastic bag from his pocket and held it up for me to see. There was a slim, silver bracelet inside. "Is this yours?"

I studied the bracelet. It did look vaguely familiar, and then I remembered why. "I'm pretty sure Vivian was wearing it yesterday."

I'd done it again. This was no way to make friends with your fellow coworkers. Meet Carrie Jorgenson, the world's biggest stool pigeon.

Detective Ray observed me carefully. "Alana thought the bracelet was yours. I wondered if it might have fallen off your wrist when you bent over him."

I shook my head. "I told you—it's not mine. When I found Hale, I tripped and fell down in the blood and then ran out of there. I didn't bend directly over him. You found it in his shirt pocket?"

"Yes," the detective replied. "Upper left lapel one."

I tried to remember what Hale had been wearing yesterday. Black pants and a short-sleeved denim shirt that had actually looked good on him, until it had become covered in blood… "I probably didn't notice the bracelet because all I could see was the knife—and the blood, of course."

Detective Ray blinked at me. "What knife?"

How had this guy ever made detective? "The knife that was sticking out of his chest when I found him, of course." *Duh.*

Detective Ray shot me a disbelieving look. "We didn't find a knife, Carrie."

CHAPTER SEVEN

––––––––

For several seconds, Detective Ray and I continued to stare at each other in silence. Finally, I forced my jaw to move. "There was a knife sticking out of Hale's chest. The page from the order pad was pinned to his shirt with it." Had I been hallucinating? No. "You *must* have seen it."

Detective Ray wrote something down on his pad. "We found the page to the order pad. It was sitting on top of Hale's chest. There was blood on it and a tear in the middle that a knife could have gone through. But we did *not* find a knife. Please describe it for me."

The blood thundered in my ears until I thought I'd pass out. I must have looked pretty bad because Detective Ray led me by the elbow to the table we'd previously been sitting at.

"You're as pale as a ghost, Miss Jorgenson. Sit here, and I'll get you a glass of water."

I had definitely seen a knife, but for the life of me, couldn't remember what it had looked like. I continued to rack my brain to no avail. I must have managed to block out certain details of the murder scene.

Detective Ray handed the glass to me, and I brought it to my lips. He waited until I'd returned it to the table. "Better?"

No. "Yes, sir."

"Can you give me a description of the knife? Was it one that you used here at the café?"

I shut my eyes for a few seconds but continued to draw a blank. "I can't seem to remember what it looked like. But there was definitely a knife."

He made more notes and grunted. "We knew Mr. Akamu had been stabbed. The killer may still have the knife in their possession, but it might be in the café as well. They could have easily washed and replaced it."

What he really meant, but was too polite to say, is that an employee killed Hale, washed the knife, and then maybe chopped up some pineapple with it. Someone like—

"I'll have to get some of my men over here to make another pass through the place." Detective Ray observed me closely. "Thanks, Miss—er, Carrie. If I need any further information, I'll call you."

My insides quaked with fear. What if the knife did show up at the restaurant? Would one of us be arrested? "Um—"

Detective Ray waved me off. "That's all. Have a good day."

It was obvious he wasn't going to discuss any further aspects of the case with me. Having no choice, I rose to my feet and exited through the patio. Again, I tried to remember specific features of the weapon, but the only knife I could mentally picture was the one Poncho had used to slice pineapple earlier that day...a pearl-handled butcher knife. Had that been the one I'd seen?

"Hey." Keanu was waving to me from the table. "What's wrong?"

I sat down in the chair opposite him. "Nothing. I'm fine."

He gave me a sharp look. "You're not fine. Go ahead—spill it."

I glanced toward the door of the café, as if afraid Detective Ray might start yelling and running toward us. "He's going to have a cow if he sees us talking."

Keanu shrugged. "We work together. What, we're not supposed to speak to each other ever again? Come on. You look like you're about to burst."

I was impressed that he could read me so well, but still hesitated.

Keanu's voice was gentle. "Carrie, you can trust me. I won't repeat what you say. Honest."

Trust had always been a difficult issue for me. However, when I looked into those hypnotizing blue eyes that were as cool and calm as the ocean, I believed him. In one day he'd saved my job and also held my head while I'd gotten sick. I found myself wondering if Brad would have done the same thing. A few months ago my answer would have been a resounding yes. Now I wasn't so sure.

Then again, Keanu had a reason for wanting Hale dead too. Oh, for goodness' sake. He was right. I had to have someone to confide in, so I leaned in close. "Last night, after I got sick, you went back inside the café and found Hale. Then you called 9-1-1."

He nodded. "What about it?"

"Do you remember the knife that was sticking out of his chest? What it looked like, I mean?"

Keanu stared at me, confused. "There was no knife. Just the check from the order pad lying on his chest with *pig* written on it. Did you see a knife?"

My mouth was dry. "Yes, it was holding the page pinned to his chest."

"Are you sure?" he asked.

I blinked at him, annoyed. "Of course I'm sure! Keanu, I think I'd know if I saw a knife or not."

"Okay, okay." Keanu held up his hands. "Let's think this through for a minute. If there was a knife when you found him, and then no knife when I went inside a couple of minutes later…"

We both stared at each other, reaching the same conclusion.

"That means the killer was inside the café when I found Hale." I gave an involuntary shiver. The killer must have been hiding, perhaps in the kitchen or maybe upstairs in Hale's office. What if I had gone upstairs after I'd discovered Hale? I'd probably be dead too. "Why would they take the knife?"

Keanu pressed his lips together tightly. "Maybe it was incriminating to them. What if they didn't wear gloves? Do you remember what the knife looked like? Was it from the kitchen?"

"No, I'm drawing a complete blank. All I remember was that the check had said *pig*, the blood, and that silly piece of pineapple hanging out of his mouth. It's like it was meant to be symbolic." I paused for a moment. "Vivian said that Poncho was already questioned."

Keanu nodded. "Like she also said, he wasn't too happy when he left. I've seen everyone today except Anna. She's one of the part-time servers."

"When is she coming?" I asked.

"She never showed up for her appointment," Keanu said. "And Detective Ray was *not* happy."

I'll bet. "Getting back to the knife for a moment. The person who stabbed Hale grabbed the knife before you went inside. Or maybe they were still hiding in there when you went back in. So why didn't we see them leave?"

Keanu forced a smile to his lips. "Well, you were sick, and I was a bit distracted by that. They must have used the back entrance where my moped was parked. Too bad there's no security camera out there. It had to have been someone who was familiar enough with the place and had been here before."

Someone like an employee.

"Yoo-hoo!"

We both jumped. A man with silver dyed hair was approaching us, a large plastic bag slung over his shoulder. He was about our age or maybe a few years older. He blew the hair off his forehead and winked at Keanu. "Who's the pretty lady, K?"

A grin formed at the corners of Keanu's mouth. "Carrie Jorgenson, this is Tad Emerson. He works for Lovely Linens. Tad, Carrie started with us yesterday."

Tad and I sized each other up. He was tall and slim, with green, catlike eyes that looked like they were afraid to miss anything. He was dressed in a pink Hawaiian shirt, white cargo pants, and flip-flops. He puckered his lips together. "Aren't you a little doll. But don't get any ideas about stealing my man here."

Keanu rolled his eyes at Tad. "I'm not your man and never will be."

Tad placed his hands on his hips and made a face. "Oh, you sure do know how to hurt a guy, K." He looked around at the empty tables. "How come there's no one eating outside on such a divine day like this? It makes me want to burst into song." He started to sing the opening strands to "Oh, What a Beautiful Mornin'."

Keanu and I exchanged glances. So apparently everyone *didn't* know. "Dead," I whispered.

Tad cocked his head to one side. "Come again?"

"Hale's dead," Keanu said. "He was stabbed to death last night."

Tad looked from me to Keanu and clamped a hand over his mouth. "Is this some kind of a joke?"

"Afraid not." Keanu sighed.

I thought maybe Tad would scream in horror or shudder, but instead he smiled. "Whoa. My psychic abilities are incredibly spot-on. I knew someone was going to take the big kahuna out one of these days."

Keanu gave him an incredulous stare, while I raised my eyebrows in unison.

"Look, I know he wasn't a nice man, but no one deserves to die like that," I said.

Tad pouted openly. "Honey, that man was vile. All I ever tried to be was nice to him. A few months back, I had two tickets for *Sweet Charity* at the Hana Hou Theater, so I invited him to come along. I confess that I'd always admired him, what with his arrogant, confident air, and he wasn't exactly shabby to look at either. But I only asked him as a friend."

I exchanged glances with Keanu.

Tad was in his element and didn't notice. The color rose in his cheeks. "Do you know what nasty name he called me?"

I again stared at Keanu, who gave me a look as if to say *you're on your own with this one.* "I think I can guess."

"Word, girlfriend. Word. So, K." His voice took on a high-pitched whine. "I guess you won't be needing fresh linens today?"

Before Keanu could respond, our attention was distracted by an elderly woman approaching from the boardwalk. She was toting a rolling cart behind her that was filled with white bakery boxes. She had short, brown hair and was tiny in stature and a bit on the plump side. Her face was pleasant as her eyes darted back and forth from me to Keanu. She extended her hand and patted him lightly on the cheek.

"Six today, honey," she said. "I'm guessing you might not need them though. We heard about Hale." She made a *tsk-tsk* sound under her breath. "I'm so sorry."

Tad clucked like a chicken. "I knew it was going to happen." He gave the woman an air kiss and then a quick once-over. "By the way, Ellen darling, you look fab."

Ellen flushed with pleasure but continued to stare at me with unabashed interest. "Thanks, Tad." She grabbed Keanu's arm. "Come on—give me all the dirt. Who do you think did it?"

Keanu sighed heavily and then gestured at me.

"No!" Ellen shrieked. "She doesn't look like a murderer."

Keanu hid his smile. "I only wanted to introduce you to our newest server. Ellen Bentley, this is Carrie Jorgenson."

Ellen took my hand between her two tiny, warm ones. "Nice to meet you, dear." Then she nudged Keanu again. "My, she's just your type! Now tell me all about Hale."

Keanu's face turned crimson, while I tried to look anywhere but at him. "There's nothing to tell. We don't know who did it."

"Do you think it was a fellow employee?" Ellen asked. "If you want my opinion, I'd go with…"

Keanu raked an agitated hand through his dark hair. "What kind of pies did you bring?"

Ellen held up six fingers. "Two chocolate, one strawberry rhubarb, a pumpkin, and two pineapple filled."

"My favorite!" Tad squealed.

Keanu craned his head toward the sky, as if asking for God and heaven above to help him out. He sat down at the table and reached for a leather-bound checkbook that was buried in the midst of all the paperwork. In record time he filled out a check and handed it to Ellen. "Here you go. Thanks for bringing them over. I appreciate it. Please thank Liam as well." Then he bent his head over the paperwork again.

Ellen seemed disappointed that she wasn't going to find out any more details. "If you hear anything—"

Tad had a compact mirror in front of him and was admiring his reflection. "Yes, we know where you live, darling. As a matter of fact, the entire town of Aloha Lagoon knows where to find you."

Ellen's gaze came to rest on me again. "Nice meeting you."

"Likewise." I smiled.

As she took off down the path with her cart trailing behind her, I sat down opposite Keanu. "Is she a delivery person?"

Keanu shook his head. "Ellen and her grandson own a bakery in town. It's not open to the public, but they're always great about getting baked goods to us whenever we need them. Poncho's so busy with the main entrees he doesn't have much time to handle dessert as well." He picked up two of the pies. "Perhaps Detective Ray would like to take one home."

"Isn't he a prince?" Tad asked as Keanu walked into the café. "He's got it bad for you, girlfriend. I can tell."

My heart skipped a beat. "What are you talking about? I have a boyfriend, and Keanu knows that. His name is Brad."

"Ooh," Tad squealed. "I *love* names that rhyme with my own." Then he tapped the side of his head. "Uh-uh. Honey, I know these things. I swear that I was a psychic during a previous life."

This guy was something else, but even though we'd just met, I already liked him. He had a zest for life that I found so appealing. I needed to surround myself with positive people like him. It was almost like chatting with an old girlfriend from high school.

Tad studied his reflection in the mirror again then blew himself a kiss. "Taddy, you're gorgeous. You ought to be in pictures."

"Speaking of pictures," I said, "where is this theater you were talking about? What was it called?"

He beamed. "You like the theater?"

"Are you kidding? I love it. My dream is to go to New York and be on Broadway someday."

"No fooling?" Tad clasped his hands together in awe. "You are so coming with me on Sunday night to the Hana Hou."

"What does that mean in English?"

"The Encore Theater. They're holding auditions for *Little Women*, the musical. Ever heard of the book by Louisa May Alcott?"

I made a sound low in my throat. Okay, it was more like a shriek or maybe a full-fledged scream. "Oh wow. I loved that book as a kid! Where is the theater located? I live in town but don't have a car."

Tad's eyes resembled giant emerald jewels. "It's too far of a walk from town, but I'll tell you what. How about I give you a lift? I'm auditioning too."

"Seriously? You wouldn't mind?"

"Anything for a girlfriend." He took a business card and a pen out of his pocket. "Here, love. Write your address down on the back. I'll pick you up at six o'clock sharp."

"This is so nice of you." My hand shook as I wrote out the information. As a child, I had been known to bury my head in a book on more than one occasion. It was my one escape and solace from real life. I loved classical literature, ranging from books by Louisa May Alcott to Laura Ingalls Wilder to E. B. White. Okay, so maybe it was a bit optimistic to think I'd be cast as Jo March, the lead and tomboyish sister of the four girls, but you had to reach for that brass ring when you had a chance, right?

"What about you?" I asked. "What are you auditioning for?"

"Well, I'd love to play Laurie," Tad said in a matter-of-fact tone. "Of course every male who auditions will want that part. At least they know me there. I did manage to snag a bit part in *Grease* last year, so I think I have a good shot. Do you have a lot of experience?"

"I was in a few plays in school," I admitted, "but I don't have any real musical experience. I'm going to sing karaoke at the café tomorrow night, if they'll let me."

He made a face. "Oh, honey, they'll let *anyone* sing. I've been to the Loco Moco on karaoke nights. Your boss—well, former boss, that is—would go upstairs to his man cave and put his earplugs in. The only reason the big kahuna went along with it is because the more that people sing, the thirstier they get, and that means more *kala*—er, money—for him. He didn't care who made a spectacle out of themselves. You could have Madonna wriggling around up there, and it would have made no difference to him."

Keanu returned from the café empty handed, and it seemed a safe assumption that Detective Ray liked pie.

He held two boxes out to me. "We can't keep these until tomorrow. Poncho hates us to serve day-old anything. Do you want to take a couple home with you, Carrie?"

"Sure. Thanks." I hoped I didn't sound too eager, but there wasn't much to eat back at the apartment, besides some peanut butter and a few canned goods. Plus I wanted to hold on to as much money as possible. Alana could still decide to fire me at any moment.

Tad raised his hand in the air. "Me too, K. That pineapple pie has Taddy written all over it." He smacked his lips. "Delish. I can't wait to indulge in some while I watch *Pretty Little Liars* tonight."

"Do you live in town?" I asked Tad.

He took the pie from Keanu's outstretched hands. "Yes, I have a fabulous little place above the linen store. My uncle owns the building, so the rent is dirt cheap for me. Or should I say, sand cheap. Ha-ha."

Great. Hawaiian shtick, anyone?

Tad's face twisted into a genuine frown. "I almost ended up losing both my job and apartment, thanks to that miserable boss of yours."

Keanu and I exchanged glances. "What happened?" I asked.

"When I invited him to attend the musical with me, he called up my uncle, who's also my boss, and told him that I was coming on to him. Can you believe it? Like I couldn't do any better than him!" Tad's nostrils flared. "He told Uncle Simon that I'd been acting inappropriately in front of his customers, which was a bunch of horse pucky. Do you want to know what really happened?"

Keanu raised his eyebrows at me.

"Uh, *yeah*," I said. "Of course we do."

Tad brushed his hair off his forehead. "I went up to Hale's office to ask him about the show. He called me some terrible names and then punched me right in the face."

"That's awful," I said.

Keanu folded his arms across his broad chest. "That was the day when you came down the stairs with a bloody nose and said that you'd tripped and hit the wall?"

Tad lowered his eyes to the ground. "Yeah, I was afraid to rock the boat at the time because Hale might have given his linen order to a competitor. I didn't want my uncle's business to suffer because of me. I could have filed assault charges but decided not to. Then the next day my uncle called me into his office and said Hale demanded that I either be fired or he receive a permanent discount for my 'coming on to' him. Hale's one of my uncle's largest accounts, so he agreed to lower his rate. The man was a full-fledged jerk to me."

"Wow." It was all I could think to say. I felt sorry for Tad. No one deserved to be treated or judged like that, especially by Hale.

He winked at me and picked up his pie. "Lovely to meet you, Carrie hon. I'll see you Sunday night. Stay handsome, K."

Keanu smiled and shook his head. "You're something else."

Tad blew him a kiss. "I am. Remember the saying, guys. You know, when someone gets what they deserve."

Perplexed, I stared at him. "You mean what goes around, comes around?"

Tad's eyes gleamed as he shook his head. "Nuh-uh. That's an expression for the mainland, silly girl. Here we say, 'Karma is a beach.'"

CHAPTER EIGHT

———

The buzzing from the alarm clock awakened me. I reached my hand onto the nightstand and fumbled to find the shut-off button without sending it crashing to the floor like I'd done the day before. I sat upright, blinked the sleep out of my eyes, and turned to my left, but Brad wasn't there. In fact, it was obvious from the undisturbed sheets and blanket that his side of the bed had not been slept in.

Brad didn't usually work Saturdays at the resort, so I wondered if he'd spent Friday night partying, and God knows where or whom he was with. Some days I felt like his mother instead of his girlfriend. I checked my phone, and there was a text that had come in about midnight, shortly after I'd fallen asleep while watching a rerun of *Seinfeld*.

Babe, staying with friends tonight. Pies were great. Everyone loved them. Bring more tomorrow.

I was so enraged that I almost threw the phone against the wall, but stopped myself in the nick of time. That wasn't an option since I couldn't afford a new one.

What a selfish jerk. I hadn't even had one bite of either pie—and I'd been looking forward to a large piece for breakfast this morning. Brad must have come home briefly while I was downstairs in the laundry room last night and then left with both pies before I'd returned. He hadn't bothered to leave a note. I had no idea where he had gone.

While I showered and dressed, that little voice of doubt started to creep into my head again. Had Brad really been out partying with friends? And why was I never asked to join them? I wanted to trust him more than anything. Back home, he'd never given me a reason to doubt him. Brad had been a devoted boyfriend then, sweet and complimentary, and we'd seen each other almost every night after work. Several of those glorious and fun evenings had been spent at his apartment.

As I made my way toward the café that morning, I wondered again why I was even trying to save this relationship. Brad and I had first met at a local ski resort in Vermont. He had recently moved there from California, where he'd lived his entire life. His parents were wealthy and had sold their home and relocated, leaving their youngest son to fend for himself. That should have been my first indication that they wanted to be rid of him too.

Brad had an older brother in Vermont who'd informed him that a local ski resort was looking for an instructor. While growing up, Brad had spent several posh vacations in Colorado, where his parents owned a condo, and he was as comfortable on skis as on a surfboard. However, it wasn't long before Brad realized he wasn't cut out for the frigid Northeastern climate.

Maybe I should start putting money aside for my own place. Then again, I wasn't even sure my job was permanent, so it seemed I was stuck for the time being.

When I arrived at the restaurant, I grabbed the *Aloha Sun* off the counter and idly skimmed the rental section.

"Looking for new accommodations?" Poncho was standing behind me, grinning, meat cleaver in his hand.

"Cripes," I muttered. "You'd better put that down before Detective Ray walks in."

He muttered something indistinguishable underneath his breath. "That man. I am not certain how much faith I have in his credentials. Pretty sure that he could not find the murderer if he was standing right in front of him."

Voices could be heard coming from upstairs. "Who's up there with Alana?"

"Keanu," Poncho said. "Apparently she was in early this morning, looking over the books and questioning him about some discrepancies."

I followed him into the kitchen. "What, does she think he's embezzling money or something crazy like that?"

Poncho shrugged as he started slicing vegetables on the pristine counter. "Who knows with that woman? She is not concerned about us or the customers. In all the time I have worked here, she has never once inquired about me or my family's welfare. All she cares about is herself and those expensive purses she likes to lug around."

Okay, obviously a touchy subject for him. "What day is Hale's funeral scheduled for?"

Poncho gave a palms up. "No idea." He started to say something else, and then we heard the tapping of Alana's heels on the stairs. He wiped his hands on a paper towel. "You can ask the queen herself. She wants to meet with all of us."

I'd forgotten about the impending meeting. In a moment, Alana came into view followed by Keanu, whose eyes instantly locked on mine. Embarrassed, I turned away and then chided myself silently. Why had I done that?

"Everybody into the restaurant." Alana practically spat the words out of her mouth. No *good morning, nice to see you, hope you die like my husband*—nothing. Since I was closest to the door, I pushed it open and held it for Alana, who was directly behind me. She glared at me and didn't even bother to say thank you as she passed by.

Vivian and Lola had arrived and were deep in conversation until they caught sight of us and then separated, guilty looks upon their faces. It didn't take a mastermind to guess what—or whom—they'd been talking about. They sat down together at one of the tables, and I joined them. Poncho and Keanu remained standing on opposite sides of the counter, while Alana took center stage.

Alana looked crisp, cool, and very businesslike in a pink silk suit and a silver pair of stiletto sandals on her tiny sized-five—I guessed—feet. Despite her small stature, her presence was powerful, and my palms started to sweat.

"I will speak to Sybil and Anna during their shift tomorrow, as well as Leo," Alana announced. "I believe all of you here are always scheduled off on Sunday, is that correct?"

Lola nodded, a sly smile on her face. "And Monday."

Alana surveyed her employee with visible contempt. Lola returned the stare, obviously unintimidated. She was a tough one to figure out—nice one moment and then distant the next. As far as brains, the jury was still out on that detail.

Alana's nostrils flared. "I'm aware that the café is closed on Mondays. So that would mean *everyone* has to be scheduled off that day. How come I didn't know that you were a brain surgeon, Lola?"

Lola snapped a piece of gum in her mouth and giggled. "Sorry. I wasn't sure if Hale had ever told you. I realize he kept you in the dark about *a lot* of things."

The entire room was so quiet that you could have heard a napkin rustle to the floor.

"You should be careful what you say, sweetie. I'm your boss now." Alana took a step toward our table and glared down at Lola. And you won't keep your job by offering to sleep with me, either."

Whoa.

Lola watched her with genuine surprise. "Not me. Hale was a pig. Guess that honor was reserved for you, *boss*."

I exchanged glances with Vivian, who immediately lowered her eyes to the table. This incident was about to turn into a screaming, hair-pulling debacle that neither one of us wanted to witness.

Alana stood stock still, her face pinched with anger. She took a step toward Lola, and Keanu suddenly rushed forward from behind the counter to put a hand on her shoulder.

"Okay. We're all upset. Let's fill Alana in on some of the procedures she might not know about."

"I'm familiar with *all* the procedures," Alana snapped back at him. "I plan to run a tighter ship than Hale did. If extra help is needed with serving, I can step in. I've waited on tables many times."

Keanu nodded. "Alana and I will be upstairs for most of the morning, going over past sales records and such. We expect the place will be very busy, especially with the curiosity factor figured in. If anyone needs help, don't hesitate to call us. As everyone but Carrie already knows, Saturday is generally the busiest day of the week around here."

Alana eyed me sharply. "I will help out the part-time staff tomorrow too if needed. I plan to be off on Tuesdays. On that day I will entrust Keanu to run the café, and expect all of you to obey him as you would me."

Vivian kicked me under the table, and I flinched, hoping Alana wouldn't see.

Alana caught my reaction. "Is there a problem, Carrie?"

I shook my head. "Not at all."

Her cheeks were bright red. "When we are finished, I'd like to talk to you upstairs. *Alone*." She glanced at Keanu. "We will carry on the café in Hale's memory. He was always so proud of the establishment, and I—"

Her voice broke, and she dabbed at her eyes with a tissue. Everyone squirmed in their seats with obvious discomfort. "That's all."

"Wait, I have a question," Vivian said.

Alana stared at her in surprise. "Yes?"

"When is the wake and funeral?" Vivian asked.

A tear ran down Alana's cheek. "He's going to be cremated, and the service will be private. Now get back to work." She turned on her heel and disappeared through the swinging kitchen doors.

Lola gave a loud snort. "Crocodile tears. She's got more money than God. If I was her, I'd sell the place and spend all my time sunning on a yacht."

Before Vivian or I could reply, Lola slid out of her seat and went behind the counter to put together silverware packets for the tables. Poncho had already returned to the kitchen, and Keanu was starting a pot of coffee.

Vivian nudged me. "She's lying."

"Who? Alana?"

She shook her head. "Lola. I think she did sleep with Hale."

Gross. "Get out. How do you know?"

Vivian rose to her feet and adjusted her apron. "There's a rumor that Hale was seen with one of his female employees at The Lava Pot, tying one on—or twenty. I never actually saw them myself, but someone started spreading the rumor around. A few of the customers have even come in and asked if it was me! Talk about scary. This was right before Alana and Hale separated—well, one of the times. There are too many to count. Anyhow, the woman was so drunk that night I heard she could barely stand. Then there was talk that they checked into a room afterwards. When Alana found out, she moved out of their house and into a suite at the resort."

"When was this?" I asked.

She paused to consider. "A couple of months ago, I believe."

I watched as Lola, oblivious to our conversation, made her way out onto the patio to check the tables. I could not imagine anyone needing a job that badly, or perhaps I didn't want to. Sure, the man had been good-looking and wealthy, but his overall attitude and shabby treatment of others made him repulsive to me.

Keanu walked over to us and motioned at me. "You'd better get upstairs. Alana doesn't like to be kept waiting."

My insides quaked with fear. "What do you think she wants?"

He looked at me sympathetically. "I think your job is safe. She probably wants to ask you about what happened with Hale the other night. I noticed that she came in right after you went upstairs to see him."

I groaned. "Nothing happened, and she knows that. Why does she insist on tormenting me?"

"It's not just you," Vivian said. "Alana's always been suspicious of any female around Hale, and I can't say I blame her, having heard about his track record. The guy cheated on her too many times to count."

"But not with me," Poncho yelled from the kitchen.

We all laughed.

"Time to lower my voice, I guess," Vivian muttered.

With a sigh, I pushed through the doors and slowly made my way up the stairs to the office. Alana was sitting at Hale's desk, a pile of papers in front of her as she entered information into the computer.

She looked up and scowled. "Took you long enough."

I decided to cut to the chase. "What is it you wanted?"

Alana narrowed her eyes. "I'd like to know what my husband said to you the other night."

Ugh. "Mrs. Akamu, I really don't think—"

She slammed the desk drawer shut. "It's Alana. And I don't care what you think. Tell me what he said. Did he ask you to sleep with him?"

Good grief, this was humiliating. "No. He asked me to go to dinner with him, and I explained that I had a boyfriend."

Alana snorted. "Like that made a difference to him." She stared down at her hands in her lap and then wrung them in obvious frustration. Her gaze searched mine. "Look, I'm aware of what my husband was capable of. I caught him cheating on me before. Right in the middle of the act too."

Why would she possibly want him back then? Was it for the money?

It was as if she'd read my thoughts. "It wasn't about money. I did love him. He was a kind and gentle soul when we first met over twenty years ago."

Okay, were we talking about the same person here?

"There were things that happened in his life that changed him," Alana went on. "It doesn't excuse what he did to me, but I was willing to take him back. I thought we loved each other enough to overcome our problems. And then he cheated again with that—" She sighed. "A leopard doesn't change its spots, I guess."

But how could you possibly love a man like that? For a moment I felt a twinge of pity for Alana. I was starting to have my own doubts about Brad and the "friends" he visited too often. If it turned out the friend was female, we were finished as a couple. I would never tolerate a man cheating on me.

"When I told him I had a boyfriend, he laughed. Then you came upstairs."

She focused on the wall behind me and nodded. "It doesn't matter. He would have taken you out to eat and then got what he wanted from you. Women were like putty in his hands. He was seen with a female employee a couple of months back, and I know who it was. I have plenty of spies around. The lookie-loos are always happy to bring me up to date on Hale's latest conquests."

"What are you talking about?" I asked, trying to play dumb.

"I'm talking about Carmen. She's the woman Hale fired the day before he died. Her number was in his cell phone, right at the top of recent calls that night. She's the one who killed him—I'm sure of it."

CHAPTER NINE

———

I stared at Alana in confusion. Would Carmen have killed Hale just because he had fired her? A possibility, I guess, but it seemed a bit farfetched to me. "Why would Carmen want to kill Hale?"

"Because she was in love with him," Alana explained. "I saw the way she always looked at him. She flirted with him shamelessly, even when I was around. Obviously her world was devastated when Hale fired her. I need to find a way to incriminate her."

I couldn't help but wonder if Alana's real reason for incriminating Carmen was because she thought her husband was fooling around with the woman.

Alana eyed me suspiciously. "Now that Carmen's gone, that will be more difficult to do. You could help me. Get chummy with Lola. She was friendly with Carmen, and I bet they still keep in touch. Ask her out for drinks, and suggest Carmen come along. Take Carmen out after work tonight and get her drunk. From what I hear, that's easy enough to do."

I was too stunned for a moment to say anything. In the first place, there was no reason for me to trust Alana. She'd been nasty to me since the moment we'd met. What if she was setting me up, along with Lola and Carmen? As much as I wanted to learn who the killer was, I had no plans to go along with this crazy scheme of hers. "Sorry. I don't want to be involved."

Her mouth twitched. "I should have known I couldn't count on you. Maybe you were even in on it too. You, Vivian, *and* Lola might have plotted this with Carmen."

This woman gave new meaning to the word *whackadoodle*. Anger rose from within me and to the surface, threatening to boil over at any moment. "Hold on a second. I'm sorry your husband died. He wasn't a very nice man, but I had no reason to want him dead. Plus, I'm brand new to the café. You're way out of line." I untied my apron and flung it on her desk. "No job is worth this much aggravation."

I whirled around and started for the stairs, but she placed a hand on my arm. "Wait a second. Please don't leave. I can't deal with hiring any more help right now, on top of everything else."

I blew out a sigh and turned to face her.

The color rose in Alana's cheeks. "I apologize. This isn't easy for me."

"I'm sorry for your loss," I said quietly. "But the fact remains there's a killer out there somewhere." I hated what I was about to say next. Even though my need for money was great, it seemed necessary. "Maybe it would be better to shut the place down for a while."

Alana leaned her head back in the chair and closed her eyes. "No. Hale wouldn't have wanted that. Plus, the money it brings in is too hard to pass up. Between you and me, I'm not sure of my financial status going forward. Hale's will won't be read for a few days."

"Carrie!" Poncho yelled from the foot of the stairs. "They need you out front."

I glanced at Alana, who gave me a dismissive wave. "Go. Today will be busy. All the guests from the resort and the locals will be here, trying to find out what happened. Remember what I said earlier. If anyone asks, tell them you know nothing. And our little conversation is to remain confidential, if you get my drift."

Oh, I got her drift all right. Her words and cell phone rang out simultaneously in my ear. She turned her back to me while she answered the call, and I in turn tried to get my bearings together. The brief flash of humanity Alana had shown seemed to have disappeared in the blink of an eye.

I started down the stairs, and something shiny caught my eye on one of the steps. I stooped down and picked up a key. It looked like it might belong to the front door. I shoved the key into the pocket of my pants. I'd find out who it belonged to later.

When I stepped off the bottom stair, Poncho caught my arm and drew me over to the stove. He was surrounded by a myriad of dishes on the counter, which included a stone casserole containing a side of pork, burgers for the grill, and bowls of coconut and shrimp. There was also a pitcher of what looked like margarita mix.

"What did she say to you?" he whispered. "Does she know who did it?"

I thought of her threat and shook my head. "She wanted to know what Hale said to me the other night. I kind of felt sorry for her."

Poncho's face suffused with anger. "Do not *ever* feel sorry for that family, *ho'aloha*. They have no feelings. She is just like her husband. They force people to—" He turned away from me suddenly and started chopping onions with a vigor. "Go out front. The vultures have descended."

I stared at him, puzzled. "What were you going to say?"

Again, he shook his head stubbornly and pointed in the direction of the café. "Go!"

Yikes. I hurriedly pushed through the doors and noticed that there were already people seated at the tables outside and a small crowd waiting by the front door. I glanced at the wall clock. We didn't open for another fifteen minutes.

"It looks like a stampede forming," I whispered to Keanu.

Keanu's expression was grim as he tied an apron on. "I think it's safe to say that I won't be helping Alana upstairs today. You ladies are going to be buried. Lola may need to assist Poncho with some cooking too."

"Leave me alone," Poncho shouted from the other side of the door.

Vivian rolled her eyes. "Be nice to everyone, and if they ask, just say you have no idea what's going on. You never know who you might be speaking to. That Detective Ray's probably got some of his coworkers posing as customers."

"Look," Keanu said. "There's no proof it was anyone who worked here. Hale had a bad habit of not locking the back door until he left. There have been times when I've come in first thing the next morning to find that the alarm was not set either."

"That wasn't Hale's doing." Vivian glanced at me. "Leo closes on Sunday nights, and he always forgets to set the alarm. Sometimes the place stays like that until Tuesday morning. Hale always yelled at Leo, but he should have fired him for being such a dope."

"Like I said," Keanu continued, "there's no proof it was an employee. Anyone could have come in through the back or patio doors."

I knew he was trying to make me feel better, but I was still convinced we were all at the top of Detective Ray's suspect list.

"Is that what the police think—that the killer came in through the back?" Vivian asked.

Keanu nodded. "The only security camera is by the lobby's entrance. They had to have entered through the patio or back kitchen door."

"So it was someone familiar enough with the place who knew they didn't have to worry about being on camera," I pointed out.

"True," Vivian admitted. "But all people had to do was look up when they entered the restaurant from the lobby and they would have seen the camera. It's not exactly hidden. Anyone could have cased the joint, so to speak, and they'd have learned that there wasn't one in the rear of the building."

"Whoever did this didn't think we were coming back the other night," Keanu said, his eyes pinned on me. "They thought we'd left for the evening when you went to get Hale's drink."

Vivian lowered her head, but I caught the hint of a smile. "Maybe they thought the two of you were going out. You know, *together*."

Okay, I liked Viv, but at that moment I was seriously thinking about choking her. Talk about your awkward moments.

Without another word, Keanu turned and went to the front door to unlock it.

"Thanks a lot," I whispered to Vivian.

"What'd I do?"

I gritted my teeth together. "That was embarrassing for both him *and* me."

She grinned. "Aw, get off your high horse. He likes you. I can tell."

I was certain she must be imagining it. Before I could muster a reply, the café was suddenly filled with customers, several jostling each other for a prime place at the counter. It wasn't long before the dozen or so tables and seats at the counter were filled. I was in panic mode because even though I had a couple of days under my belt, I still had no idea what the heck I was doing. Vivian handled the tables out on the patio, while Lola, Keanu, and I rushed back and forth from the café area to the kitchen. Poncho kept yelling at everyone to stay out of his "work space," but eventually he let Lola come back to help with some simple orders, such as burgers and fries.

The room grew silent when Alana walked past me with an apron on. Without a word to anyone, she went outside to help Vivian with the crowd.

"Hey, girlie." An older lady at the table against the wall tugged on my arm. "Tell me what really happened to that little weasel Hale."

I was stunned at the words and fascinated by the sight of her well-lined, leathery face. She reeked of cigarette smoke, and the smell made my head ache. "There's nothing to tell."

She snorted and punched her seatmate in the arm. "Do you believe this? They're not gonna let us in on the dirt. People have been waiting around for years to see that creep get what was coming to him."

Egads. I stared at her in disbelief. "I'm sorry, but I really don't know anything." I ran to get them water, but when I returned, she grabbed hold of my arm again, refusing to let me leave.

"Look, honey," she said. "I've been coming here since Mr. and Mrs. Akamu bought the place over twenty years ago. Hale was a punk kid back then. So you're not even going to tell me what happened? Rumor has it that he was stabbed."

"I don't know anything," I lied again.

Keanu came over and laid a hand on my arm. "I'll take this order, Carrie. Why don't you see if the entrees for the two men at the counter are ready?"

I uttered a silent prayer of thanks, relieved that he had saved me from the tight grip of the old gossip, but her words left me thinking. There was no proof that an employee from Loco Moco Café had committed the crime. Like Vivian said, anyone could have come in through the back door. But how would they know that the waitstaff had already left for the night?

Goose bumps dotted my arms. What if someone had been watching the Loco Moco employees that evening, waiting for everybody to leave? Maybe it was someone who'd even been a customer earlier in the day. I wondered if Detective Ray had thought of this.

I grabbed the plates from Poncho and set them in front of two men at the counter.

"Got any ketchup?" one man asked.

"Oh, of course." I reached under the counter and handed it to the man, who began to pour it all over his burger and fries. My stomach growled at the smell. I hoped I'd get a lunch break sometime today, but it didn't look promising.

I was waiting for Poncho to gather an order together when I heard the familiar clacking of high heels approaching. Alana stormed into the kitchen and slammed a piece of paper down on the order wheel that sat on the counter near Poncho. He checked it, grunted, and removed more vegetables from the stainless steel fridge.

When Poncho finished with an order, he left the order paper next to the plate. The server who took the order was then responsible for bringing it to the customer and keeping track of it until the customer was ready to leave. It was an old-fashioned way and required a great deal of organization—on his part at least—to keep everything straight. Many of the restaurants back home had computerized systems, but Keanu had told me Poncho preferred this way, and no one wanted to rock the boat. An unhappy chef was never a good thing.

"Hey." The old lady at the table waved some bills at me. "Can you cash us out?"

"Certainly." I went over to take her money, and she rose from her seat. She gave me two twenty dollar bills. The check had come to $29.15 for her and her friend. "I'll get your change."

"Keep it, honey." Her voice was raspy. "I'm sorry if I made you uncomfortable before when I asked about your boss."

"It's fine, really," I said.

She adjusted her large canvas bag over her skinny shoulder. "They say what goes around, comes around. Serves him right for what he did to that girl so many years ago."

Was she talking about Alana? "What girl?"

"Care," Vivian yelled. "Can you get that couple in the corner? They've been waiting for about ten minutes."

By the time I had taken the order, the older woman and her friend had left.

"Shoot."

Vivian was standing next to me. "What's wrong?"

"Did you see those two women I was waiting on?" I knew I wouldn't be able to get her statement out of my head for the rest of the day.

"Paige and her sister Lorna? Yeah, they're regulars. Why?"

"She was starting to tell me something about Hale," I said.

Vivian snorted. "Don't pay them any mind. Those two are the biggest gossips on the island."

"Do you know where they live?"

She shook her head. "Somewhere in town, I guess. They're not resort guests—I can tell you that much."

I waited on a table of four, a family that was staying at the resort. They'd heard about Hale and tried to pump me for information, but when I explained that I was new, they seemed content to leave me alone.

*   *   *

By the time six o'clock rolled around that night, my legs ached so badly that I could barely stand. And there were still three hours to go.

I'd received a brief lunch break. I didn't know the policies for eating at the café, but Vivian explained that Hale had allowed employees one free meal a day. Poncho had been very accommodating when I'd asked for a burger and fries—okay, two orders of fries actually.

At six thirty, a couple of crewmembers began to set up for Benny and his Ukulele Wahines, the band that played at Loco Moco Café on Saturday nights. Lola explained to me how the band had been brought over from Maui after Kauai had experienced a sudden crisis of sorts while dealing with a lack of ukulele musicians. The band was a family affair that consisted of Benny, his wife, sister-in-law, and daughter.

I loved live music and couldn't wait to watch them perform, but my biggest rush of excitement came when I noticed the karaoke machine being carried onto the makeshift stage. A cloth tent had been erected overhead. Suddenly I didn't feel so tired anymore. There was a lull for a few minutes while Vivian, Lola, and I all stood around watching the crew set up.

"Still want to sing?" Vivian grinned.

"Definitely," I said.

"Girl, you must have nerves of steel," Lola said. "You could never get me up there. Maybe to dance, but no singing."

"Oh, I love it." Since I was a child, performing had always been a passion of mine, whether it be singing or acting. When I was about nine or ten, a friend's mother was nice enough to take me to see *Into the Woods*. I instantly fell in love with the stage and the character of Rapunzel. Afterward, whenever I wanted to escape my childhood, I would go to that magical place in my head far, far away and pretend that I too was a princess locked up in a tower, waiting for my Prince Charming to come along. Or at the very least, someone who actually cared about me.

Sure, my singing needed a little work, but if I kept practicing, I'd have to improve at some point. Hey, no one expected karaoke singers to be perfect, right?

"Tad's taking me to an audition at the Hana Hou tomorrow night. I'm so excited."

Lola snorted. "I'd stay away from him if I were you."

Vivian gave her an incredulous look. "Ah, he's harmless."

"I'm not sure about that," Lola said. "Remember the night he came out of Hale's office with a bloody nose? He was real upset. I wouldn't blame Tad if he wanted to even the score in some way. And Hale was always making fun of him, even with other customers when he thought that Tad couldn't hear them."

"Tad's no killer," Vivian said.

Before I could reply, two men sitting at a nearby table waved me over.

"Can we get our check?" The male who spoke was probably midfifties or so, bald and stout, the fat sloping over the sides of his chair. The other man was about the same age but rail thin with a full beard, shaggy brown hair, and yellow-tinged teeth. Talk about your complete opposites. The thin man winked at me, and I took an abrupt step backwards.

I tore the page out of my pad and handed it to the bald man. "Sorry if I kept you waiting."

He handed me a fifty. "Keep the change, pretty lady."

Holy cow. A twenty-dollar tip. "Thank you very much." I smiled gratefully.

"I'm Tim, by the way. This is my buddy Sam."

"Carrie. Nice to meet you."

Sam leaned back in his chair. "Hey, Carrie, do you happen to have a boyfriend?"

Oh jeez. "Yes, I do."

"That's too bad." Tim's eyes raked over me, and I suddenly longed for a cleansing shower. "I just got a new ski boat and was wondering if I could take you for a ride sometime."

This guy needed to think of a more original pickup line, and use it on women closer to his own age. Still, he was a paying customer, and I didn't want to drive his business away. "Ah, even if I didn't have a boyfriend, I wouldn't go. I can't swim."

Tim rocked back in his seat and hooked his thumbs into the pockets of his jeans. "Bet you'd look good in a bikini, even with a life preserver over it."

Ew.

"Excuse us, gentlemen."

I whirled around. Lola and Vivian were both standing behind me.

Vivian put her hand on my shoulder. "Carrie needs to go take her medication now. They just let her out of the facility last week. She's looking well, don't you think?"

The two men gave me a funny look and rose to their feet. They nodded curtly toward us and then quickly left the patio.

"What the heck did you do that for?" I was laughing so hard that I was afraid I'd drop my tray.

Lola grinned. "They pulled the same stunt on me last week. Viv came over and told them I had six kids at home. I thought that would have kept them away forever."

"What can I say—I'm a born storyteller." Vivian grabbed my hand. "Come on. Time for me to introduce you."

There were eight tables full of people on the patio, and the jitters were starting to take hold. *Don't be silly. You've done this plenty of times.*

"Aloha, everyone," Vivian spoke into the microphone. "Thanks for coming out for Loco Moco Café's weekly karaoke night, to be followed by the fabulous Benny and the Ukulele Wahines! We've got a special treat for you tonight. Our newest employee, Carrie, is going to start us off. So come on—put your hands together for her."

A few appreciative whistles and clapping followed while I took the mike from Vivian and the machine started from behind.

"What am I singing?" I whispered, having forgotten to make a selection.

"Aretha Franklin's 'Respect,'" she shouted into my microphone.

Not one of my favorites, but hey, I could handle this. I drew a deep breath and dove right in. It was only a few seconds before I lost myself in the entire song. Vivian started dancing next to me, and then Lola jumped up on stage and started bumping me from the other side. I stared out across the patio and saw Keanu standing there with his arms folded, grinning at us. His eyes locked on mine, and there was a message in them that I couldn't quite figure out.

Then I missed a word. Great. *He needs to go away.* I shut my eyes for the rest of the song.

"*R-E-S-P-E-C-T,*" Lola and Vivian shouted, thereby drowning me out. I actually thought I sounded pretty good for once. Maybe all the practice was finally paying off.

There was a smattering of clapping, and I opened my eyes. Keanu was applauding, the smile still in place. All of the tables but one had emptied out.

I stared at Lola and Vivian, who were high-fiving each other in honor of their great performance. "Hey, guys, was I that bad?"

Lola wiggled her hand back and forth. "Eh. You need some work on those high notes, hon. They kind of went right through me. But no worries. It's all good."

I stared at her, puzzled. "What do you mean?"

Vivian grinned. "She means we should be thanking you."

"For what?"

Vivian jumped off the stage and slumped into one of the now vacant chairs. "Because everyone left. This is the first time I've been off my feet all day, and I owe it all to you."

CHAPTER TEN

————

Like the rest of the full-time staff, I was scheduled off on Sunday. For some reason, Vivian said, the café did the least amount of business that day. I thought that was strange, what with it being the weekend and all, but didn't question her explanation. I wondered, though, in light of Hale's death, if the staff would be run into the ground with nosy tourists like the day before. Vivian assured me if it was that busy, I could expect a phone call. She then informed me that she never answered her cell on Sundays.

The café was closed on Monday, so I had two full days to myself and a nice pile of cash to look at, thanks to my tips the day before and the partial check I'd received from Alana, since the staff was paid on Saturdays. The tips had been better than I'd hoped for, as we'd been busy all day. All of a sudden I felt very wealthy. I sent off a Western Union check to my mother, picked up a few groceries, and made plans to put the rest in my bank account.

Vivian had warned me that the tips weren't always that generous. Maybe the customers had felt sorry for us, thinking one of us might be wearing orange soon. Despite the eager questions and interest, I had not seen one customer shed a tear over my boss's death. And some of them had known him for years.

My mind was now preoccupied with the audition that night. In order to keep busy and not let the nerves take over, I spent most of the day cleaning the apartment. I reminded myself I was not doing this to please Brad. Neat by nature, I had no desire to live in a pigsty.

Brad had texted the night before to say he was going to a party at a friend's house and wouldn't be home. He worked Sundays at the resort, so he mentioned that he'd see me later in the evening and then we would "catch up." That usually meant he'd come home with romance on his mind.

I was ready at six when Tad knocked on the door. He had on a pair of tan shorts, a purple polo shirt, and matching flip-flops. He looked at me in my white skirt and red silk blouse and frowned.

"Love, you look like you're going to a job interview instead of an audition."

I cursed under my breath. "I knew I was overdressed. But I really want to make a good impression. Is it that bad?"

Tad glanced around the room. "Where's your closet?"

I led the way to the bedroom, and he thumbed his way quickly through my sparse wardrobe. "Keep the skirt. You've got cute legs. But wear these flat sandals and swap the blouse out for this yellow tank top. It looks good with your dusky complexion."

I wrinkled my nose. "It's a Mediterranean skin tone."

"Whatever. I prefer the term dusky. Yellow is a great color for you."

I had to admit this was better than what I'd originally picked out. I ran into the bathroom to change and then met him outside by his white convertible.

I studied him curiously. "How do you know so much about fashion?"

Tad moved his Gucci sunglasses from the top of his head and settled them in front of his eyes as he started the engine. "I *live* for fashion, girl. I'm originally a New York City boy. I even graduated from the Fashion Institute of Technology."

That actually explained a lot. He seemed more like a big-city guy to me, although I had no doubt he would manage to fit in anywhere. "Hey, that makes us practically neighbors!"

Tad fist-bumped me, eyes still pinned on the road. "I actually majored in jewelry design. I created some pieces for my cousin's bridal party. After I met her wedding planner and consulted with her a few times, I decided that was what I really wanted to do." He stopped for a red light and when I didn't respond, glanced over at me with curiosity. "What, did you think only women can be wedding planners?"

"I wasn't thinking that at all. I love David Tutera and *My Fair Wedding*. I can picture you arranging some five-hundred person affair at the Aloha Lagoon Resort someday."

He sniffed. "Word, girlfriend. And you can bet it would be like no other wedding that place has ever seen. But I'm in no hurry. I like working at the linen store. The customers are great to deal with—well, all besides your former boss, that is. Plus I get to cruise around town in gorgeous weather for most of the day."

"In a nice sports car too," I teased.

"Darn straight. The store's been in the family for over thirty years. Great Uncle Jack ran it before Uncle Mickey took over. I was sick of the city and needed a change, like a tropical one, so I begged him for the chance. Plus, some of his biggest clients are hotels and resorts, like the Aloha Lagoon. And what happens at hotels? *Hello*, weddings!" He launched into a chorus of "I Love to Cry at Weddings" from *Sweet Charity*. "That's from one of my favorite musicals."

I laughed. "I know the show well. You're a wonder."

"Hmm, I am, love. I truly am." Tad checked his reflection in the rearview mirror. "So, any leads on who did away with the big kahuna?"

I shrugged. "No idea. It's not like the cops are sharing details with us. We're all considered suspects. Even me because I found him!"

His tongue was practically hanging out of his mouth. "Shut up. You poor love. How could they think that? You just started there!"

"Yes, but for all the police know, I could have committed the crime and then pretended to find him."

"I did see that happen on a crime show once," Tad mused.

"Plus the murder weapon is missing."

I hadn't realized I'd spoken the words out loud, then immediately wanted to pinch myself. "I probably shouldn't have told you that. Please don't say anything to Detective Ray."

Tad stopped for another light, and his jaw dropped so far I thought it might hit the floor of the car. "If that turns up in someone's possession, they'll get arrested for sure. Face it, darling. Everyone at the Loco Moco disliked the guy, and I'm sure there were others too. Maybe people who worked at the resort that he wronged, customers—heck, there could even be a business connection to his shopping mall. From what I heard he outed tenants left and right from there with little warning. The guy wasn't exactly a fan favorite."

We pulled into a small paved parking lot behind a light blue stucco building and got out of the car as I recalled the customer from yesterday. "There was a woman who came into the café and said something about Hale and what an awful thing he did to a girl years ago. She left before I could get any more information out of her. Do you have any idea what she meant?"

Tad wrinkled his nose. "Well, I can't be positive she's referring to the same incident, but my uncle did mention that Hale was once involved in a horrible car accident. Seems the car he was driving hit another one for no specific reason. His parents and a woman in the other car were all killed. Hale was the only survivor."

"Oh right. I googled him on Brad's laptop the other night and saw that. When did it happen again?"

Tad tapped the pen he was carrying against his chin. "Twenty years ago? I can't be sure. Now, to be fair, even though the man was a jerk, he must have carried a load of guilt around since that day. I believe my uncle said it wasn't alcohol related either. Maybe he lost control of the vehicle. His parents were wealthy, respected people and well liked—the total opposite of him."

If Hale had been carrying around guilt from that horrible accident, he certainly kept it well hidden. In the brief amount of time I'd known him, I hadn't seen him perform a nice gesture or say a kind word to anyone. "What about the woman in the other car?"

Tad opened the door for me. "No idea. You could probably track down some old newspaper records through the local library if you're that interested. Maybe even dig up some more dirt on the kahuna while you're at it. He had a lifetime of pissing people off on a daily basis, honey."

We entered the theater, which was blue on the inside of the building as well. The floors were polished concrete, the walls a teak color, and the padded plush seats a shade of navy.

"Maybe Blue Hawaii would have been a better name for the theater," I joked.

"Already taken. Haven't you seen the Blue Hawaii Wedding Chapel yet?" Tad asked. "It's right in Aloha Lagoon. Fabulous place, darling."

I scanned the rows and rapidly calculated in my head that the theater must hold about 300 people. A man wrote down our names and handed us sides, which were a portion of the script. He also gave us forms to fill out so that we could list our experience.

There were about fifty people seated in the various rows. We settled ourselves in the second to last row, and Tad leaned over. "There're two nights of auditions, so before you get too excited, double this crowd."

I thought back to the book. "There are about what—ten parts in all?"

Tad started counting on his fingers. "Marmee, Jo, Amy, Beth, Meg, Laurie—that's the role I want—God, I could totally rock that part—Father, John Brooke, Aunt March—" He paused. "Then again, it would be fun to play her too." He smiled like a Cheshire cat. "What part are you trying for?"

"Jo, of course."

He studied me for a second. "You seem more like the Meg or Beth type to me. But in the long run, it will all come down to your singing skills."

Great. That was what I'd been afraid of.

"Attention, everyone." A tall, powerfully built man, with dark hair in a buzz cut, greeted us. "I'm Jeff Temple, director of *Little Women, The Musical*. Thanks for coming out tonight. We'll be calling you up one by one, or in some cases in twos, for acting scenes. You can hand your sheet to me or my assistant director, Ben, on your way to the stage."

Ben, the man we had seen at the door, was now in the front row. Still seated, he turned around to wave at us.

Jeff went on. "If you have a certain musical number you'd prefer to do, please inform our pianist. Otherwise we'll ask you to sing a tune from the show. I'm trusting you're all somewhat familiar with the book, a version of the movie, or the musical itself. Well, if you want a part, that is."

Everyone laughed.

"Our performances are usually only six shows, two weekends in a row, but this one will have an extra week added on, either at the beginning or the end," Jeff continued. "I'll know for certain within the next couple of weeks."

An appreciative murmur ran through the crowd, and people started whispering in hushed tones.

"What's going on?" I asked Tad.

He leaned closer to me and spoke quietly. "I can't confirm, but rumor has it that a good friend of Jeff's is also a director in Hollywood. He'll be vacationing here in the next couple of months, and as a favor to Jeff, he's coming to see the show. There's always the chance he's on the lookout for a fresh new face too."

Oh man. It was settled then. I *had* to have a part in this show and would do just about anything short of pole dancing to get one.

Tad and I watched the auditions for about forty-five minutes until Jeff suddenly turned and pointed at me. "Next."

"Go get em', girl," Tad whispered.

Jeff nodded at Tad. "You too."

We made our way down the aisle and handed our forms to Ben, who was seated on the aisle and already had his hand outstretched to receive them. We climbed onto the stage and waited for further instruction.

"Carrie and Tad," Ben read from our papers. "You're going to be Jo and Laurie."

Tad pumped his fist. "Yes!" Then his cheeks colored. "Sorry."

Ben and Jeff both smiled at this.

"Okay," Ben said. "Whenever you two are ready. Start with the scene on page 155."

I had an idea which scene this might be, and my suspicions were quickly confirmed when I found the page. It was the one where Laurie confides his love to Jo and she refuses him. Okay, a tad bit uncomfortable—slight pun there—but I was actually more afraid I might burst into laughter. I barely knew this guy, but on the plus side, at least he wasn't a total stranger.

Tad gripped me by the shoulders and stared into my eyes, fully lost in the role. It took great effort on my part to hold the giggles back.

Tad stroked my hair with his left hand. "Really, Jo?"

As the script indicated, I reached my hand up to his cheek. "Really and truly, Teddy."

Tad huffed, turned, and stomped angrily to the rear of the stage.

"Teddy, where are you going?" I cried.

"To the devil!" At that moment Tad tripped over a fan cord with his flip-flops and went flying across the stage.

Everyone else burst into laughter and then applauded.

"Well, that's definitely one way to get our attention." Jeff crooked his finger at Tad. "Come on down here while Carrie sings for us. You'll go next. Carrie, if you have a preference, let Martha know."

Tad's face was beet red, and I was genuinely sorry for him because I knew what it was like to be embarrassed like that. During an audition back home, I'd accidentally elbowed the director in the face when he'd been reading a scene with me. Needless to say, he'd wound up with a black eye, and I didn't get the part.

I walked over to the little, white-haired old lady who was poised in front of the piano by stage left. She flashed me a reassuring smile, but I wasn't nervous. Singing gave me a certain freedom like nothing else ever could. For that matter, being on stage—in any capacity—was similar to wearing comfortable shoes for me. Growing up, I'd felt more at home there instead of my actual house.

"Could you play 'Better'?" It was a song that Jo March sang when she found herself conflicted about life and love.

Martha nodded happily and handed me the lyrics for the song, which I gratefully accepted. I knew them, thanks in part to some more googling the night before, but figured it would be a good idea to follow along, in case I forgot some of the words. I'd practiced earlier on my own, but there had been no one around to tell me how I sounded, with the exception of the tenant across the hall who'd asked what was wrong with my cat. Embarrassed, I didn't have the nerve to say I didn't own one.

When Martha started to play, I looked directly out into the audience. A trick I had learned years ago was to find an object to focus on, not a face. A light switch on the back wall worked well for this purpose. I then concentrated on the emotions Jo would be feeling at that particular moment. In truth, the song was kind of an ironic fit for me, not that I would ever admit it to anyone. Funny how art imitates life sometimes.

There was polite clapping when I finished, and Jeff scribbled something down on the paper in front of him then nodded to me. "Thank you, Carrie. That's all."

Flustered and annoyed with myself, I returned to my seat. I knew I'd been off-key. Maybe I should forget the whole crazy idea of ever becoming a performer. As much as I loved to sing, it was becoming apparent I possessed no talent for it. Sure, I knew long ago that I was never going to be a Celine Dion or Barbara Streisand, but I sincerely loved performing and the head rush I experienced from it.

I was so lost in my own thoughts that it took a moment to realize Tad was almost finished with his rendition of "Take a Chance on Me." He actually sang pretty decently, in a rich baritone voice that surprised me. However, the gestures he made and the extra drama he had inserted during our scene together didn't convince me personally that he was the Laurie type. Laurie—or Theodore Lawrence—was the rich, handsome male lead, a big brother model to the poor March girls and also hopelessly in love with the tomboy sister, Jo.

Still, maybe all was not lost. If given the opportunity, I thought Tad could have portrayed an excellent Amy March—the littlest sister who was not only spoiled but liked to whine about the injustices of the world. He even looked a little like her.

Tad slumped in his seat next to me, still red faced as he gulped a long sip from his water bottle. "Dang. I can't believe I was so clumsy up there. I have to stop wearing these flip-flops. But they are so comfortable." He examined his foot with admiration. "I do need a pedicure though."

"You sounded good," I said.

"I have a confession to make," Tad admitted. "Before I read the lyrics up there, I thought the song 'Take a Chance on Me' was Abba's." He groaned in frustration then settled back in the seat. "I could have done so much better."

I squeezed his hand reassuringly and waited for him to say something about my performance. He continued to sit there, watching the rest of the auditions, until I couldn't stand it anymore. "How did I sound?"

Tad still stared straight ahead, his movement not doing anything to encourage my confidence. "Your acting is divine, hon. Great facial expressions up there."

"Thanks," I said. "But what about the song? I didn't have much time to practice beforehand. How did I sound?"

Tad blew out a breath and turned to face me. "Darling, I adore you—really I do. I think your acting skills are superb."

"But?" I prodded.

He cleared his throat. "Okay, let me ask you this…how do *you* think *you* did?"

I sighed. "I was afraid of that."

CHAPTER ELEVEN

———

Tad and I stopped for a quick coffee on the way home, and when he dropped me off at the apartment, I noticed that it was after ten o'clock. I was tired and decided to snuggle into bed to watch some television before I fell asleep.

I figured Brad might not come home again, but it was obvious he had stopped by the apartment while I'd been at the audition. There were dishes in the sink, and his wet towel and dirty clothes were all over the bedroom floor. I started to pick the towel up and then stopped myself, throwing it back down. No. I wasn't doing that again.

My cell phone buzzed, and I glanced at the screen. The number was familiar, but I couldn't place it. "Hello?"

"Hi, Carrie, it's Keanu. How are you?"

A warm tingle spread through me, and I wasn't sure why. "I'm fine. How about you?"

"Never better." There was silence for a moment. "How did your audition go tonight?"

I hesitated. "Not very well, I'm afraid. But it's always fun for me to perform."

"I didn't get a chance to tell you, but you did a nice job last night with your Aretha Franklin number."

I almost burst out laughing. Even *I* knew that had not gone well. "You're such a liar."

He chuckled, a deep throaty one that was addicting to my ears. "I know the Loco Moco is closed tomorrow, but Alana asked me if I would call one of the servers to come in and spend a couple of hours doing some extra cleaning around the place. Things like dusting, waxing the floor, polishing table legs, etc.

She wanted me to pick one person, and to tell the truth, I thought you might really need the money."

"You'd be correct. But if I'm the only one working, how will I get in? Will she be there?" I prayed the answer was no.

"No, she has to go see the undertaker tomorrow. But she wants the place to be in top shape for Tuesday's opening. Between you and me, I think she's trying to prove something to everyone—that nothing has changed and she can handle the place as well as Hale did. I've got some receipts to go through and checks to write to vendors, so I'll be there while you're downstairs working."

The silence that stretched between us seemed to go on for an eternity, even though it couldn't have lasted more than a few seconds. "Okay. What time?"

"How about one o'clock? I know I always need a day to sleep in."

"That would be nice, but to tell the truth the time of day probably won't matter. I just had coffee, so I probably won't be able to sleep now." I sighed. "I'm not sure why I do these things."

Keanu's voice was low and sexy on the other end of the line. "You can't be trusted around coffee—I already know that."

I laughed, remembering the incident from the other day. "Oh, real nice."

He chuckled. "Sorry, couldn't help myself. Okay, don't drink any more caffeine tonight. See you tomorrow."

As I disconnected, a slight tap sounded on the front door. It was a little late for visitors. I opened the door a crack to find a voluptuous, bleached blonde standing there in a lime green, sparkly tank top that read *Princess* across her well-endowed chest. She had paired it with tiny jean shorts so tight they threatened to cut off her circulation. She seemed surprised to see me.

"Oh." She giggled. "I'm sorry—I must have the wrong apartment. I was looking for Braddy."

My girlfriend radar instantly zoomed into the fact that this was probably *not* a coworker. "Yes, Brad lives here. Can I help you?"

She smiled as recognition dawned. "That's right. I'm so ditzy sometimes. I forgot that Brad told me he was living with his sister."

I sucked in some air. "Excuse me?"

She let out an obnoxious giggle again and held a man's black wallet in front of her. "I'm Heidi. He left this at my apartment last night."

What an appropriate name. Heidi Ho, Heidi *the* Ho— take your pick. The options were endless. I stared at her, speechless.

Heidi seemed oblivious to my confusion. "I didn't notice it until late this afternoon when I went to make the bed up." The long eyelashes I was positive were fake fluttered wildly. "We had quite a bit to drink last night."

The room started to spin at a violent rate. I counted to ten, then reached out and snatched the wallet from her outstretched hand.

She gave me a sly little smile. "Will you make sure that Braddy gets it?"

I gripped the edge of the door so tightly that my knuckles started to turn white. I forced myself to meet Heidi Ho's gaze, and it took every effort of my being to keep from lunging for her throat. "Oh, he's going to get it all right."

With that, I slammed the door and locked it, almost catching her outstretched hand in the process. Enraged, I threw the wallet across the room, where it hit the wall, and the contents burst out all over the floor. I ran into the bedroom and started shoving clothes into my suitcase. Tears of humiliation streamed down my face and blinded me as I emptied out the two dresser drawers in which I kept some T-shirts and underwear.

I had been played for a fool. How could I have been so stupid? Brad never wanted me here. He tried to discourage me from coming, but I had been focused on making an escape—not realizing that Brad might be looking for one from me as well.

I couldn't blame Heidi. She probably had no idea I existed. The signs had been there for a while, even before Brad had left for Hawaii, but I'd chosen to ignore them. That was no longer an option for me.

The key rattled in the lock, and I groaned inwardly. I'd been hoping to escape before Brad returned. I hated confrontations of any sort, but the time had come.

"Yo, babe, you home?"

"Yes," I managed to rasp between my clenched teeth. I zipped the suitcase shut and went into the bathroom to get my personal items.

Brad was behind me now. He placed his hands on my waist, and without thinking, I turned around and punched him right in the nose. I had never hit anyone before in my entire life. It was a reflex action, I told myself.

"Hey!" He put a hand to his face. "What'd you do that for?"

I ignored him as I scooped up my toiletries and shoved them into my cosmetic case. Then I pushed past him to grab my Nike duffel bag in the closet. I removed the key to the apartment from my key ring and flung it at him. "Your girlfriend Heidi was just here to return your wallet. Maybe she'd like to be your new roomie, because we're finished."

Brad was holding a piece of tissue to his blood-soaked nose but reached out to run his hand up and down my bare arm. "Aw, babe. Don't be like that." He pressed his lips against my ear and ran a hand up inside my shirt.

My body shook with disgust and rage as I jerked away from him. "When exactly did you become so self-absorbed?"

He shrugged. "So I spent a night there. We were drunk, and it just happened. Nothing personal, sweetheart."

"I thought I meant something to you." My voice quivered. The last thing I wanted to do was cry in front of him.

"You do," he protested, grabbing my arm. "Let me show you."

Furious, I shook him off. "I can't believe I was such an idiot." I grabbed my purse from the kitchen counter and glanced around to see if I'd forgotten anything else. No, all my worldly possessions were in my hands. I opened the door to the apartment and then slammed it so hard behind me that the wood of the frame rattled. I ran down the steps of the porch and started walking at a rapid and furious pace.

I had no idea where I was going. My arms were full of luggage, I had little money, and now I had no home. Perhaps it wouldn't have been a bad idea to hold off until the morning. How would I ever find any accommodations this late at night? Maybe I could get a room at the resort. If I could even afford one, that is.

I walked on for the next ten minutes, my gait slowing while the ache in my arms from the luggage grew. My duffel bag knocked against my side, and my eyes started to fill. I considered my options, which were slim. I could call Vivian. No, wait— Lola was already staying with her. Maybe Keanu would know a place where—*no*. I refused to call him. I didn't want him to see me as some pathetic, needy co-worker. I knew he would have helped, but my pride was standing in the way.

The lighted tiki torches along the path welcomed me as the Aloha Lagoon resort came into view. As I stared at the lights, one clicked on in my brain. The key I'd found yesterday…could it possibly be to the café's door?

Of course, the place was closed tomorrow, and Keanu had mentioned that Alana was busy with more important matters, which meant she probably wouldn't be coming by. So who would know if I spent the night there? What harm would it do? I wasn't going to take anything. I just needed a place to crash. Hopefully I'd be able to find a more permanent situation in the morning.

I went around to the rear of the Aloha Lagoon resort, where I hoped there might not be any security cameras, and continued until I reached the door of the café's patio. I didn't want to go into the main resort building and enter the place from the lobby because someone would definitely see me then. All I needed was to have Detective Ray seek me out tomorrow with a warrant for breaking and entering.

As I approached the patio door, uneasiness surged through me. What if the killer returned? I reassured myself that Hale's death had been planned methodically and that there was no reason for someone to want me dead—or was there?

I looked around nervously at the large banyan trees rustling in the breezy, warm night. Laughter could be heard coming from the nearby water, and I spotted a couple embracing in the distance. They were probably guests at the resort, out for a romantic beach stroll. It was a beautiful night to walk hand-in-hand with the one you loved.

It was either curl up at one of the tables for the night or venture inside. I had seen Keanu set the alarm last night when we left and was certain the three-digit code was 007. Maybe Hale had been a James Bond fan.

I inserted the key into the patio door, praying, and as if by magic, it turned easily. The alarm panel started flashing, and my heart rate increased as I rushed over to punch in the code. Thankfully, it was the correct one. I switched on the light, hoping no one in the resort would see and become suspicious, but I needed to make sure that there was no one else inside.

After about five minutes, when I had scanned every inch of the place and decided that the boogeyman and Hale's killer had taken up residence elsewhere, I shut the light off and climbed the stairs to Hale's office. I set my suitcase and cosmetic bag next to the desk and kicked off my sandals. I spotted a small battery-operated lantern sitting on the bookcase in the corner and brought it over to the couch with me. I didn't think anyone would be able to see this from outside, and I hated sleeping in the total darkness.

That was, if I would be able to sleep at all.

The silence was deafening as I glanced around the room. I was thankful that the office was air conditioned because the humidity outside was pressing and had managed to drench me during my walk, along with the added weight of my luggage. Hopefully there was someplace I might be able to snag an inconspicuous shower in the morning—and not in the ocean.

As I lay on the couch, my nosy nature began to work overtime. I walked over to the desk, toting the lantern with me. Sitting down in Hale's chair, I reached for the main drawer. Locked. Then I tried the two drawers on the left hand side. Both opened easily. The reasonable side of my brain told me I had no right to go through the drawers. The naughty side of my brain told the reasonable side to shut the heck up.

At first there was nothing to hold my immediate interest. Some bills from the bakery, produce receipts, a checkbook that I glanced through. I noticed on the register that a check had been written to Carmen in the amount of five thousand dollars and thought that was strange. A payroll service created our checks—their name had been on my copy yesterday. Plus that was way more than any of us would make in a regular week. So what was that all about?

I reached back far into the drawer, and my fingers connected with a folder full of laminated newspaper clippings. There was one of a young Hale cutting the ribbon on the Loco Moco Café, smiling broadly at a couple standing nearby. I read the tagline underneath and discovered they were his parents and this had been when they bought the café. There was another photo of Hale graduating from business school with honors. Several articles also contained five-star reviews of the Loco Moco from food critics.

At the bottom of the pile, I spotted a newspaper article that featured a picture of a twisted piece of black metal next to a guardrail, and a wave of dread shot through me. The article was dated March 7, 1997. Before I even read the headline, I had a premonition what this was—the car accident Hale's parents had lost their lives in. My heart began to thump loudly against the wall of my chest as I read on:

Three locals were killed in a horrific car accident last evening along Route 22 in Oahu. Maya and Sampson Akamu were passengers in a 1997 BMW driven by their son Hale and died instantly when the car suddenly jumped the middle line and struck a 1990 Dodge Omni going in the opposite direction. The driver of the other vehicle, Elizabeth Peyton, was taken to a nearby hospital where she later succumbed to her injuries. Hale suffered a broken leg and severe contusions but is expected to survive.

I placed the clipping back inside the folder with trembling hands and thought back to Alana's words the other day. This in no way excused Hale's infidelity and the cruel manner in which he dealt with people, but it had to have affected him on many different levels. How could you possibly live with yourself when you had caused an accident that resulted in the death of your parents, plus another human being?

I opened the bottom desk drawer, and my pulse quickened when I noticed that there were manila files labeled with each employee's name, including me. Guiltily, I glanced around, then chided myself. No one was here, and there weren't any security cameras inside. If for some reason I was mistaken, I'd be searching for employment again tomorrow.

My folder was first, and I wondered if Hale had had any time to compile dirt on me from my references or if he'd scribbled any nasty notes. Negative on both accounts. All the folder included were copies of my W-2 and I-9 forms and my pathetic résumé. I rifled through the other employee files, feeling lower than dirt. What was I expecting to find? A written confession from one of my coworkers that they had killed Hale?

I lifted Keanu's file out with trembling hands and again cursed the bad side of my brain. I learned that he was twenty-six, two years older than me, and the address given for him belonged to a house in Poipu, a nearby town in Kauai. Tad had happened to mention the place earlier when he was talking about the best—and most expensive—areas to live in Kauai. It sounded like more than anyone who worked at Loco Moco Café—with the exception of the Akamus—could afford. So what was Keanu doing there, then?

The other files held nothing of interest. There were no clues in Carmen's file about receiving extra money. I wondered if Alana's assumption was correct and Carmen had been sleeping with Hale. I lifted out the last file, which belonged to Poncho. Like me, he lived in town. Well, up until last night I had anyway. Now I was too poor to even own an address.

There was another page in the file, which was an agreement of sorts. I examined it closely.

I, Poncho Suarez, do hereby agree to employment with Loco Moco Café as their head chef for a period of time not to end before August 1, 2020.

It was signed by him and Hale in July of the previous year and notarized by a Stephen Tamatoa.

So Poncho had worked at the café for over a year, and for some ridiculous reason had committed himself to another three years of torture working for the boss from hell. This was why he had not sought out another employer and had asked Hale for more money instead. The question was, why had he agreed to such a long-term status at the Loco Moco? Did Hale have something on him?

I put the file back in its proper location and closed the drawer, my body racked with shame over what I had done. I went over to my suitcase and dug out a sweater, draping it over me as I lay down on the couch. The temperature in the room was comfortable, but like Linus from *Charlie Brown*, I needed some sort of security blanket. I turned the light down as low as it would go without the room being in total darkness.

I lay there wide awake for a long time, thinking about my findings. It had become painfully obvious that everyone associated with Loco Moco Café had something to hide. Vivian had been vague when I'd asked her about her personal life and how she had come to work here. Tad had confided that he disliked Hale for humiliating him. Even Keanu had confessed to a reason for wanting Hale dead when he drove me home after the murder.

As much as I hated to consider the idea, it was very plausible that one of my coworkers could be Hale's killer. Maybe I should think about returning to the mainland. But how would I get there? I didn't have enough money for a plane ticket. Perhaps in a few weeks I could gather enough funds together. If I left, I might look even more suspicious to Detective Ray. Yes, for the time being I was stuck here.

I was determined to stay awake until I had my life and this crime all sorted out. However, weariness finally won the battle, and I closed my eyes.

When I awoke, sunlight was slanting through the upstairs window. It took a minute for recognition to set in and for me to remember where I was and how I'd gotten here. The café was silent, although I could hear the faint sounds of laughter coming from outside. There were probably some kids playing down by the water.

I glanced at my watch. Both hands were pointed at the twelve. I looked closer and discovered the hands weren't moving at all. Shoot. The battery must have died during the night. I reached out my arm and knocked my phone to the wooden floor with a loud thud. I'd forgotten that I had left it next to me last night—probably afraid I might have to call 9-1-1 in a hurry if Hale's killer showed up.

I rolled off the couch to grab my cell and saw from the screen that it was 9:30. I had a couple of hours to get ready before I needed to meet Keanu. Maybe I could go over to the resort and grab a shower first. For now, I decided that a little more sleep was in order. Exhausted, I lay back down and closed my eyes, pulling the sweater over my head.

I had started to doze off but then detected the sound of heavy breathing coming from nearby and was pretty certain it wasn't my own.

There was someone upstairs with me.

The blood pounded in my ears, and my heart knocked against the wall of my chest so violently I was afraid I might pass out from fear alone. With trepidation, I slowly lowered the sweater from my face and forced my eyes open.

Poncho was leaning over the couch, his face full of both shock and disbelief as he looked down at me. I in turn stared back mutely, as it wasn't Poncho's expression that held my attention.

In his outstretched hand, he held a large, sharp butcher knife that was pointed…directly at me.

CHAPTER TWELVE

———

Words lodged tightly in my throat, unable to escape, and made it difficult for me to breath. I put my hands in front of my face and whimpered like a frightened five-year-old.

"No. Please don't."

Poncho stared at me in confusion, and then his eyes darted to the knife he was holding. Sheepishly, he lowered it to his side. "My apologies. I did not mean to frighten you, *ho'aloha.* I heard a noise and came upstairs to investigate. I was downstairs chopping vegetables. It saves on prep time for tomorrow, and I like the quiet when no one else is around. At least, I *thought* no one else was around."

I sat up and rubbed my eyes, waiting for my heart rate to return to normal. "You gave me quite a scare." I eyed the knife, and then like an electric shock, my brain gave a nervous jolt. The knife that had killed Hale…I remembered now. It had a white pearl handle. This wasn't the same one.

Poncho frowned. "What are you doing here, Miss Carrie?"

I'd almost forgotten that I'd broken into the place. "I— uh." *Okay, how to get out of this one?* I stared into his dark brown eyes, but there was no anger directed toward me. Instead, I saw only kindness and compassion. Might as well come clean.

"I moved out of my apartment last night. It was kind of sudden, and I didn't know where else to go."

He gave me a puzzled look. "But how did you get in here? Only me, Keanu, and Leo have keys—well, besides Alana, that is."

"I sort of found one on the stairs yesterday." I realized this did not make me look endearing and attempted to explain.

"Please, I just needed a place to crash. I didn't take anything, honest."

He stared at me in silence, and I wondered if he would tell Alana. "Okay, but I have one more question for you."

Oh good grief. "No, I didn't kill Hale."

Poncho nodded. "That is good to know, but I was wondering if you might be hungry?"

His words took me by surprise, and I grinned back at him. "Starved actually."

Poncho turned in the direction of the stairs and waved his hand. "Come. We will get some breakfast in you."

I followed him down the stairs. There was something about Poncho that seemed fatherly, and I wondered about his own family.

"Do you have any kids?" I asked suddenly.

Poncho picked up a pair of plastic gloves and put them on. He added sesame oil to the frying pan in front of him and stirred it around absently before adding ground pork, egg whites, and onion. "Two boys, Pika and Piliki. They are five and seven."

I smiled. "Those are fun ages. I bet you enjoy them."

His eyes lit up. "I do. Family is everything to me. Even more so after—"

"After what?" I asked.

He added salt, pepper, and water chestnuts to the pan. My stomach was growling so loud I thought for sure he must be able to hear it. "Nothing. I have been through some situations in my life that have made me appreciate my family even more. You know what I mean."

Actually I didn't, since I had no real family to speak of, so I said nothing.

"Tell me." Poncho stirred the contents with a steel spatula. In another small pan he cracked a couple of eggs effortlessly with one hand then tossed the shells into the garbage over his shoulder without even looking back. *Score.* Not one speck of shell was in the eggs, either. Amazing. "Did you have a fight with your boyfriend, little girl?"

The thought of Brad made me want to wretch. "I found out he's been cheating on me."

Anger flashed through Poncho's dark eyes, making them foreboding and a little bit terrifying as well. "For shame on him. A nice girl like you does not deserve to be treated like that. He should have been counting his blessings instead. Someday the boy will be sorry."

I smiled. "Thank you, but I'll be all right. Maybe deep down I knew from the beginning we weren't destined to have some great, long-term relationship."

Poncho spooned out the hash and slid the eggs on top of it. He handed the plate to me. "Pork hash and eggs, one of my specialties. You go eat, and I will get us some coffee. How do you take yours?"

"With cream and two sugars, please."

I sat down at one of the tables against the wall. I chose one away from the windows, just in case someone from the lobby might happen to peer in and see me. I dug into the hash, which melted in my mouth. When Poncho arrived, I was already halfway through. "This is delicious. You really are an incredible cook."

He beamed as he placed the mug in front of me. "It is true. I am the best at what I do."

"Modest too." I laughed, but curiosity was already nagging away at me. "Why do you stay here when you could get a job anywhere?"

The color rose in his face, and he stared down at the table. Shoot. Me and my big mouth. What if he had killed Hale? No, I didn't want to believe that.

"So," he said, intentionally avoiding my question, "what do you have planned for the day?"

Don't push him, Care. "Well, I would just about kill—I mean—I would love to find someplace to shower. I'm supposed to do some extra cleaning around the café this afternoon."

Poncho took a long swig from his mug. "Who authorized that?"

"Keanu called me. He said Alana wanted him to find a server who could come in for a few hours to help out."

His mouth twitched under the moustache. "I see."

"You see what?"

Poncho rose to his feet with the empty mug in hand. "It is nothing."

"Come on," I pleaded.

"Maybe the boy likes you and that is why he asked. I can tell by the way he looks at you."

I was startled. "That's ridiculous."

He watched me closely. "Hm. I am pretty sure that it is *not* ridiculous. What is the saying? You should go for it."

"I'm sure he has a girlfriend." There was no way someone hadn't caught Keanu yet. He was gorgeous, sweet, and fun to be around. The complete package.

Poncho shook his head. "He and Tammy broke up. A few weeks back, I believe."

I could only hope that the circumstances hadn't been similar to my own. "How come?"

He extended his hands in front of him, palms upright. "Beats me. Why don't you ask him yourself?"

I cocked an eyebrow at him. That was not happening. "I don't think so."

Poncho shook his head. "The female mind—it works in such mysterious ways. What is the big deal? You want to know something, you ask."

Sure, I wanted to know. But if I asked, Keanu would think I might be interested in him. I was definitely attracted to him but had no intention of getting involved with someone else again—at least for a while.

Changing the subject seemed like a good way to go. "I would love to go take a shower. Is there any possible way I could have one at the resort?"

Poncho reached into his wallet and handed me a pass card, which looked similar to the ones that were inserted into hotel room doors. "I do not think you have been given one of these yet, but there is a locker room for the employees at the resort. This will get you in."

"Thank you so much. I'm going upstairs to get my things. Will you be here when I get back?"

He nodded. "Sometimes employees from the resort like to stop by for a snack around lunchtime, so I try to make myself available. I also like to put things in order for Leo the next morning. He handles the breakfast crowd until I come in at eleven, and let me say that he is not the most organized of cooks."

"You work a lot of hours." I thought about the agreement again.

"About fifty-five a week. But I love what I do and also need the money." He waved his hand dismissively. "Go, get your shower. Usually the facility is not too busy at this time of the morning."

I smiled gratefully. "Thanks for breakfast. It was terrific."

Poncho bowed slightly. "Anytime, Miss Carrie." He disappeared behind the double doors with my empty plate and the mugs.

With my stomach full and my mind a bit less stressed, I ran upstairs and grabbed a few things from my cosmetic case, along with a change of clothing and stuffed them into my duffel bag. This would hopefully look less conspicuous than dragging a suitcase behind me. After I let myself out of the patio door, I then made my way back around to the front of the resort.

I started in the direction of The Lava Pot, certain it wasn't open yet. I didn't want to go to the front desk and ask about the showers, but I might not have a choice.

While I stood on the boardwalk, staring at the building helplessly, a young woman approached me from the opposite direction. She was shapely yet slim, with short blonde hair and a pretty face. She was wearing an Aloha camp-style blouse with tan and black bamboo leaves scattered across it, black cigarette pants, and high heels. Although she wasn't dressed in the usual Aloha Lagoon uniform of shorts and polo shirt that I'd seen, I figured she must work here in some capacity.

"You look lost." It was a statement, not a question, and I caught the hint of a Midwestern accent in her tone.

"Kind of," I confessed. "Can you tell me where the locker room is?"

"Oh sure." She turned in the direction she had just come from. "Follow me." The woman surveyed me with interest as we walked along. "Are you an employee or guest?"

I shook my head. "Employee. I work at the Loco Moco. I'm Carrie."

She gave me a genuine, warm smile. "Nice to meet you, Carrie. I'm Gabby. Are you new to the island?"

I nodded. "Yes, I'm from Vermont originally."

"Ah, I'm from Chicago myself. Quite a bit of a difference here, isn't it?"

That was an understatement. I'd never encountered a dead body back home, but I chose to leave that detail out of our conversation. "Yes, it's *very* different from back home."

We went through an archway, and to our left. I spotted the glass door of the gym. I could see two men in there—one was running on a treadmill and another lifting weights.

"Here you go," Gabby said. "The employee locker room is on the other side of the gym. Go through the door next to the water cooler. You'll find the spa and saunas over in that direction too."

"Thanks so much."

She handed me her business card. "I own Gabby's Island Adventures. If you ever want to set up a tour of the island, please call me. I'd love to assist you."

I shoved the card into my pants pocket. "Sounds wonderful. I might just take you up on that." Since I was homeless at the moment, it was probably a safe bet that this wouldn't happen anytime soon.

Gabby gave a careless wave. "Tell my bud Poncho I said hello. He always takes such good care of me and my staff."

"Sure thing." I waited until she had walked away then slid the card Poncho had given me into the door. The gym was done up in bright colors and contained the usual amount of treadmills, elliptical machines, and bikes one would expect to see. There were also several flat-screen televisions mounted on the wall. I quickly discovered the water cooler Gabby had mentioned, next to another door. The two men didn't pay any attention to me as I casually strolled across the room to the door and opened it.

I spotted the spa quarters on the other side of a carpeted hallway. The place looked enormous through the glass-paneled doors, and I glimpsed a marble receptionist counter with a woman sitting behind it. I assumed there must be several massage rooms where they gave manicures, facials, and pedicures as well. Ah, to live in such grandeur.

After I found the door for the women's employee locker room and entered, I then stripped off my clothes. The lockers were built around a sitting area with rattan chairs cushioned in a seafoam green color. I grabbed shampoo, soap, and my razor from the duffel, then placed it back in one of the lockers. The resort was high end, and I knew my clothes would be safe. I entered the showers in the adjoining room.

The steaming hot water engulfed my body in a welcoming manner. If only I could wash away my problems so easily. I shampooed and rinsed my hair, then toweled off. There was no one around, but I went back into the cubicle for privacy to get dressed. Hair dryers were located by the mirrored counter section, and I was grateful, having forgotten mine in a rush to get here. I must have spent at least fifteen minutes on my hair alone. I bent forward at the waist and flipped it in front of me. Because my hair was so long and thick, it took forever to dry.

I'd been fed, and now I was clean. Funny how I'd never really appreciated the bare necessities in life up until now. I was already thinking ahead to where I would spend the night. Leo and Anna, the part-time server, would be in the café the next morning at six o'clock—or perhaps even earlier—to deal with the breakfast crowd. So unless I could manage to be out of there at five, I needed to find a new place to crash. But where would I go after I finished my work at the café today? I didn't want to tell Keanu what had happened. It was embarrassing enough that Poncho knew.

"How did you make out?" Poncho asked after I'd returned to the café and started to make my way back up the stairs. He motioned me to come into the kitchen. I stuffed my duffel bag into one of the lockers and then joined him by the stove. He was beating fresh, sliced pumpkin together with an egg and sugar mixture. With the other hand he lined a tray with parchment paper. Chefs were such wonderful multitaskers. I could barely boil water myself.

"I never knew a shower could be such a luxury. Sometimes it's the little things I take for granted, you know?"

A shadow passed over his face. "Yes, I know something about that."

My mind kept going back to the agreement I'd found upstairs. I wondered if there was a tactful way I could bring it up. Probably not.

"What time is Keanu meeting you?" Poncho asked as he added cinnamon and flour to the mixture.

"At one." I still had almost an hour to kill, but I could get started on the cleaning before he came along. "What are you making? That smells wonderful."

He nodded in agreement. "Pumpkin roll. I will leave it in the fridge after baking. Then I will add the cream cheese filling so it will be fresh for the customers."

"Oh, yum. I've definitely got to try some. Is that a popular dessert here?"

Poncho turned off the mixer and stirred the contents with a perfected hand. "Islanders eat a great deal of pumpkin. It is not all about the pineapples and mai tais, *ho'aloha*. We also eat a lot of fish. You need to stop thinking like a tourist." He winked. "So what made you decide to come to Hawaii? Was it to be with that dog turd of your boyfriend and attempt to keep a leash on him?"

He had such a way with words. "No, there were other reasons. It isn't something I want to get into right now."

Poncho's face was unreadable as he rolled out parchment paper onto two more cookie sheets and then divided the pumpkin mixture evenly between all of them. "Come on. Pretend that I am like your dad."

My head jerked up, and our eyes met. I gritted my teeth and spoke in a bitter voice that was unlike my usual tone. "I don't have a dad, so that won't work, thanks."

"Oh my, I am sorry," Poncho said. "Is he dead?"

We *really* needed to change the subject. "That's something else I don't want to discuss."

"Come on, little girl," Poncho urged. "You look like you need someone to talk to."

He was right. Since moving out of the apartment, I was feeling lost and friendless, not to mention lonely.

"All right," I conceded. "I'll tell you my secret, but you have to tell me one in return."

"Deal," Poncho said. "You go first."

I blew out a breath and began talking very fast, wanting to get this over with. I hated talking about my life back home. "I don't have a real family to speak of. My mother has ignored me for as long as I can remember. I could never quite measure up to my perfect older sister, Penny, in her eyes. So I decided it was time to forget my past and move forward with my future. When Brad said he was going to Hawaii, I decided to hitch a ride. As soon as I had saved enough money for the plane ticket, I was out of there."

Poncho was quiet as he loaded the trays into a wall oven and then wiped his hands on his apron. "I am so sorry for your troubles. If you were my daughter, I would treat you like a jewel. Children are a gift from God. Maybe someday your mother will feel differently."

My answer came without hesitation. "No. She doesn't care about me. My father left when I was four, and she's always blamed me for it."

His face was full of sympathy. "What a terrible load for a young woman like you to bear."

I bit into my lower lip. "I'm used to it. Time to move on." I didn't want to feel sorry for myself anymore. What would it solve? "Okay, your turn."

He gave me a wry smile. "What would you like to know?"

Why you made a deal with the devil, for starters. "Tell me your deepest, darkest secret. Nothing is off limits," I teased.

"All right." Poncho put the mixing bowl in the sink and squared his shoulders as he turned around to face me. His eyes, dark and ominous like a starless sky, hypnotized me into oblivion. "I killed a man once."

CHAPTER THIRTEEN

Okay, I must have heard him wrong. For the second time today, Poncho had managed to reduce me to a quivering mass of Jell-O, complete with extra fear on top. "Wh-what do you—who was it?"

Poncho's expression was somber as he rinsed the dirty bowl and placed it in the dishwasher. "It was not intentional, *ho'aloha*. This was back in my drinking days. Another fellow jumped me at a bar one night. He claimed I had been looking at his girlfriend the wrong way."

"Go on," I urged.

Poncho set out three packages of cream cheese and butter for the filling. "He punched me in the face several times. No one would help me. A bunch of men stood around, cheering him on and calling me some very bad names. They insulted my heritage. I lay there on the floor, all bloody and angry. When he went to hit me again, I grabbed my beer bottle and smacked him in the back of the head with it."

I was starting to feel sick. "And that one blow is what did it?"

Poncho nodded and stared down at his hands. "He died the next morning, and I was arrested."

"But it wasn't your fault," I protested.

He shrugged. "The dead man's family was wealthy. I believe they had friends in the district attorney's office. The court appointed a lawyer to represent me, as I could not afford one any other way. To this day I believe he thought I intentionally planned the whole thing. I was convicted on a manslaughter charge and sentenced to two years in jail. They tried to get me put away for longer, but thankfully that did not occur."

"When was this?" I asked.

Poncho added some lemon juice to the mixture. "About five years ago. Soon after Piliki was born."

The look on his face when he mentioned his son's name tugged at my heartstrings. How awful it must have been for him to leave his family, especially a wife who needed him, plus two small children. "I'm so sorry. I can't even imagine how terrible that must have been for you."

"We all learn from the events in our lives," Poncho said. "Tragedy can shape us sometimes. I like to think that my experience in prison has made me a better person. I know what it is like to go without a shower. To sleep in a cell with iron bars every night. I was an alcoholic back then and not the best husband to my dear Makani. I stopped drinking when I went away to prison. I now have a good life with my wife and sons and would not trade it for anything. I treat every day like it is my last one on earth because we are never promised tomorrow."

I laid a hand on his arm. "I think I could learn a thing or two from you."

"Perhaps." He nodded in understanding. "You have had your trials too, *ho'aloha*. I am sorry about your father."

"Wow, this sounds like a deep discussion."

Something inside me tingled as I recognized the voice and turned around to see Keanu's attractive tanned face. Poncho and I had been so engrossed in our conversation that neither one of us had heard him come in.

He had his sunglasses pushed up on the top of his head and was dressed casually in dark green khaki shorts and a white Adidas T-shirt that may have been painted on him. He looked terrific, as always. I noticed Poncho watching us, a hint of a smile beneath the moustache. I scowled, and he immediately turned back to his pumpkin-roll filling.

"So what are we talking about?" Keanu asked.

"It's nothing." My face warmed as I turned in the direction of the café. "I'll start waxing the floor."

Keanu followed me into the café and reached for my arm. I turned around to meet his gaze. "What happened to your father? Is he dead?"

This place was starting to feel like Grand Central Gossip. Still, it was nice to know he cared as I stared into those concerned blue eyes that hinted at an even more beautiful soul underneath. "It's not something I really want to talk about right now."

He smiled, but I thought I detected a flicker of hurt in his eyes. "No problem. I'll be upstairs if you need anything." With that he pushed through the kitchen doors, and a moment later I heard him jogging up the stairs to the office.

Wonderful. I hadn't meant to be a jerk to him, but I hated reliving that part of my life. I wanted to forget all that, but it seemed like everyone wanted me to continue drudging it back up. There didn't seem to be a happy medium for me.

In a panic, I remembered my luggage upstairs. I had shoved the makeup case and suitcase behind an armchair in the corner of the room before I left, thinking I might have time to retrieve them before Keanu arrived. Great. Now how would I get them out of there? I prayed that somehow he wouldn't notice them.

I worked in silence for the next hour, with only my thoughts to keep me company. Poncho left, and then there was only Keanu and me. After I finished the floor, I cleaned underneath tables, polished chairs, and even knocked down a couple of cobwebs that were hanging from the lights. One of the light fixtures was slightly higher than the rest, so I grabbed a chair and stood on it to reach the dust.

"Jeez, we don't need it *that* clean."

Startled, I shrieked and lost my balance. The chair toppled to the side, and I landed face down on top of Keanu. He let out an *oof* and lay still underneath me.

"Are you okay?" I stared down at his handsome face, and something stirred from within me.

Keanu opened one eye to look at me. Neither one of us moved or said anything. Heat flowed through my body, and for a moment I let myself wonder how those lips would blend with mine.

He reached out to me, and I was paralyzed by the sudden movement. *Oh my God, he's going to kiss me.*

"I can't breathe," he choked out.

Embarrassed, I rolled off of him. "I'm sorry. I didn't mean to hurt you."

A slow grin spread across his face as he stood and righted the chair. "You were fine. Actually I would have been quite happy to lay there for a while longer."

I wondered what he meant by that statement and waited for him to continue, but he busied himself with examining the chair to make sure it wasn't broken.

My hair had come loose from the ponytail, and I stopped to adjust it. "Oh great. My hair must be a sight."

"It is," Keanu admitted. "A beautiful one."

He spoke so low I didn't believe he thought I'd heard. When our eyes met again, I was the one who turned away this time. This was crazy. I had just broken up with my boyfriend. Was Keanu attracted to me? I liked him, and he was a sweet guy, not to mention gorgeous, but what did I really know about him? Not all guys were like Brad, right? Good grief, the self-doubt anxieties were really starting to kick in at an alarming rate.

Keanu broke the uncomfortable silence. "I'm starting to wonder if you might be bad for my health. I mean, in a couple of days you've given me first-degree burns and almost cracked my head open on the floor. I can't wait to see what you've got in store for me next."

The teasing smile reassured me that he was kidding, much to my relief. *It's a good thing you can't read minds, Keanu.*

Keanu placed his hands on his hips. "So...here's a question for you. Why is there a suitcase upstairs?"

Okay, this was going to be awkward, so I drew a slow, deep breath before answering. "Well, it's kind of complicated."

"Try me."

I bit into my lower lip, hating this part. It would sound like more self-pity. "I moved out of the apartment I was sharing with Brad. I spent last night here because I didn't have any other place to go. Please don't tell Alana—she'll kill me."

Keanu's expression was puzzled. "Your secret is safe with me, but why did you move out?"

Poor little Carrie. I tried to make light of the situation. "I found out that he was cheating on me."

Keanu's mouth set in a thin, hard line. His eyes locked on mine and resembled cold steel. "What a loser."

"I hope you mean Brad," I quipped.

"Of course I mean Brad. God, what a fool that guy—" He stopped and didn't finish his sentence. "Is there anything I can do?"

I sighed. "Not unless you know of a place where I can stay for next to nothing. Maybe a tent on the beach somewhere? I'm guessing that the resort is out of the question cost-wise for me."

"Those rooms don't come cheap." Keanu traced a pattern in the floor with his sneaker, obviously trying to analyze my situation. "But I think I can help you out. It just so happens that—"

"Carrie can stay with me tonight," a small voice said behind us.

We both turned around to see Vivian standing at the double doors of the kitchen, watching both of us with a bemused look upon her face. This was the second time someone had come into the café without me hearing them. I wouldn't make a very good watchdog.

"What are you doing here, Viv?" Keanu asked.

She lowered her eyes to the floor. "I uh—was meeting someone at The Lava Pot and—"

Keanu smiled, and I saw a flash of his dimple. "Mooning over Casey again, huh?"

Vivian scowled. "Oh shut up." She turned and winked at me. "I saw the lights on as I walked past and was curious what was going on." She cut her eyes back to Keanu. "So what are *you two* doing here?"

Keanu managed to sidestep her question. "By the way, did either one of you happen to find a key on Saturday? Alana called and said hers was missing. She thought it might have fallen off her key ring." He watched me closely. "Carrie, you didn't happen to see it, did you?"

Great, he knew. The jig was up. "Um, as a matter of fact, I *did* find a key. I meant to give it to Poncho earlier." I dug into my jeans pocket and handed it to him.

Keanu opened his wallet and dropped the key inside. "I'll stop by Alana's place and drop it off to her. Well, ladies, if you'll excuse me, I have to finish my paperwork. Carrie, it looks like you're all set here, so feel free to leave whenever you like. I'll bring your suitcase downstairs."

He gave me one long, last look and then disappeared into the kitchen.

Vivian grinned. "Sounds like I might have interrupted something intense. And what's this about a suitcase? Did you sleep here last night? What happened with your main man?"

I held a hand up in front of me. "Okay, way too many questions. Brad's been cheating on me. I was so angry that I punched him in the nose and walked out on him last night. I really didn't have time to think the situation through and ended up spending the night here."

Her nostrils flared. "Good for you. I'd never let a man treat me like that. Did Keanu ask you to come in here to clean?" Her mouth turned upwards into a sudden smile. "He's never asked *me* to come in and clean."

"Oh, cut it out," I growled. "He knows I need the money and was just being nice."

Vivian rolled her eyes. "Oh yeah, that's definitely it. Well, if you're done, we can shove off now."

"Viv, I don't want to inconvenience you. Is there a hotel around here where I could get a room? A cheap one?"

She looked at me like I was an alien. "Honey, one thing you should know by now is that there's *nothing* cheap in Hawaii. I don't mind you bunking with me for a couple of nights until you find a place. I only have a one bedroom apartment, but you're welcome to stay there."

"What about Lola?" I asked.

"She's been crashing on my couch," Vivian explained. "I have a sleeping bag, if you don't mind the floor. We'll look through the real estate section of the paper and see if we can come up with something for you. What time is your shift tomorrow?"

"I'm down for noon until closing," I said.

"Yeah, same with me. Tuesdays usually aren't real busy, so hopefully we'll have time for a lunch break. I need to get off my feet for at least a little while during the day." She glanced up as Keanu brought my suitcase and cosmetics bag into the café and placed them down next to me.

"So, you girls are all set?" Keanu asked.

Vivian nodded. "Care's coming home with me. We're going to grab a pizza and have a regular slumber party."

I picked up the suitcase. "Sounds like fun. I haven't done anything like that in ages." It made me miss Kim from back home.

Vivian shot Keanu a coy look. "Want to crash the party, K?"

He grinned. "Ah no, Viv, thanks. I think I'll pass." He turned to me. "I'm glad you won't be combing the streets late at night. If I find anything decent for an apartment, I'll give you a ring. See you ladies tomorrow."

Vivian picked up my cosmetics bag. "We'll pretend we're in high school again. I'll make up a pitcher of margaritas, and we'll talk about boys and everything." She watched as Keanu disappeared through the swinging kitchen doors, and lowered her voice. "Maybe one *particular* boy."

CHAPTER FOURTEEN

―――――

"So," Vivian said. "How are you holding up since you found out about your boyfriend? God, I hate men some days. Well, all except Casey, that is."

We were devouring pizza on the floor of Vivian's small living room, using the coffee table as our eating surface. Vivian said she ate this way most of the time. Since there was no room for a dining table, it worked out fine. The place was comfortable and homey, with a couple of pieces of modern art on the light green walls that mixed well with the beige carpeting. She had a small kitchen, a bathroom, and bedroom.

To me, it looked like a palace. When Vivian told me what she paid for rent each month, however, my heart sank. It might take forever for me to afford a place like this. Lola's cat, Benny, a big fluffy orange and white feline, was sprawled out next to me. I took bites of pizza with one hand and petted him with the other while he purred up a storm. As a child, I'd always wanted a pet, but my mother had claimed they were just something else for her to take care of.

"It was a shock," I admitted, "and pretty stupid of me since I never really suspected anything until the last few days. But I'm dealing with it. What else can I do? Curl up in a ball and cry my eyes out?"

"That's probably what he's hoping you'll do." Vivian refilled her glass and gestured at mine, but I declined. I was a cheap drunk, and after one alcoholic beverage, it was time to put me to bed. "No great loss. This island is filled with hunks."

I snorted. "No thanks. It's probably a good idea if I don't get involved with men again for a while. I've been burned enough lately."

She winked at me. "Are you sure? We do happen to have a major hunk working at the café."

"Poncho?" I teased, and we both burst out in laughter.

Vivian was still smiling as she muted the channel on the television. "Keanu's a hard one to figure out. I've only been at the Loco Moco about five months, but I can tell you he's one of the nicest guys I've ever met."

"Really? So how come you two never hooked up?"

She chewed her pizza thoughtfully. "I don't know. He's a good-looking guy and all, but there are no sparks for me when I'm around him. And I'm a big believer in sparks. Now when I see Casey the bartender, my whole world becomes a Fourth of July display."

I rolled my eyes at her, and then we both giggled again. "Ask him out then."

She made a face. "I wish. I heard he's into one of the surfing instructors. Just my luck."

"Interesting. Must be one of Brad's co-workers." Okay, I had to stop thinking about him. It was time for me to put Brad out of my head and heart—forever.

"So tell me about your family." Vivian reached for another slice. We'd ordered two small pies—one with bacon and pineapple, which I was drooling over, and the other with pepperoni and sausage.

I shrugged and tried to keep my voice on an even keel. "There's not much to tell. My father ran off when I was four. He used to send my mother money once in a while, but I haven't seen him in twenty years. I have an older sister, Penny, whom my mother adores. Mom's pretty much tried to ignore me my entire life."

Vivian's eyes grew wide. "Wow, that really bites. If it makes you feel any better, I don't have much of a family either. My father raised me. My parents were never married, and from what I understand, neither one wanted to be. I was the accident waiting to happen."

I raised my hand. "I know something about that."

She continued. "My father was always super overprotective. He didn't even let me date until senior prom rolled around. Finally I couldn't stand being under his thumb anymore, so after community college I moved here. I worked in an office then got a job waitressing at a place similar to the Loco Moco."

Her voice took on a wistful tone. "My father got married two years ago, and he and his young wife—who's like five years older than me—have a one-year-old baby, my half sister. He's too busy with his new family to spend any time with me anymore. The last time I heard from him was at Christmas."

My heart went out to her. "I guess we're more alike than I thought."

She lifted her glass in the air and clinked it against mine. "To making it on our own."

"Here, here." I was already feeling a bit tipsy but drained my glass anyway.

Vivian watched as Benny found his way into my lap. "He likes you, and it appears the feeling is mutual. That fur ball never comes near me. Guess animals are more perceptive than I give them credit for."

I stroked his soft fur. "I've always wanted a cat. Maybe I'll get one when I find a place that I can afford." *If that ever happens.*

It was so nice to have a girlfriend to talk to. I stretched out on my back, and Benny lay himself down on my chest. "So where's Lola?"

Vivian made a face. "She's staying at her boyfriend's tonight. I texted her while we were at the café and told her you were sleeping over. She said to be careful we didn't knock her boxes over. I swear—she's a little cuckoo in the head about the whole personal-space thing." She pointed to the neat stack of cardboard boxes in the corner of the tiny living area. "You should see my closet. She's got so much stuff crammed in there that I couldn't even find my shoes this morning."

"Can't she move in with her boyfriend instead?" I asked.

She did a palms up. "He's got a roommate, but I guess the guy is away tonight. I think Steve's planning to move into her place eventually. She's supposed to be going back home tomorrow or the next day. Let me tell you—it isn't soon enough."

I felt comfortable enough with Vivian to ask her opinion on the murder. "So, who do you think killed Hale?"

She blew out a sigh. "Who knows? I bet you anything that Detective Ray will be back again tomorrow, surveying the place like a vulture looking for his prey. Seriously, there are suspects galore, so why is he tormenting us? And don't let that wench Mrs. Akamu fool you. She's watching all of us, waiting for somebody to screw up. I know she's been going around saying Carmen did it. She thinks Hale slept with her."

"I thought you said Lola slept with him?" I asked.

"I don't know for sure," Vivian admitted. "Alana has her own ideas about everything anyway. That woman is nuts."

"How long did Carmen work for him?"

Vivian grabbed a pillow from the couch, punched it a couple of times, then lay on her side, propping it underneath her. "I'm not sure. She started before me. It sounds terrible to say this, but I think Carmen had major problems."

I raised an eyebrow. "What sort of problems? You mean with Hale?"

"Carmen was acting really weird for a long time. Then she was out sick a couple of weeks ago for four days. I thought for sure Hale would fire her then, but he didn't. And when she came back—" Vivian hesitated. "I went to put my stuff in a locker one day and didn't notice Carmen's bag already there. I accidentally knocked it to the floor, and a bottle of prescription pills fell out."

"But a lot of people take prescription drugs," I said. "That doesn't mean anything."

Vivian gave me a shrewd look. "True, but maybe she was abusing them. She acted weird all the time. One day she'd be over-the-top happy and then the next day all weepy. Personally, I don't think Hale fired her because of the tip situation with the customer. I think he was sick and tired of her strange moods and it was an excuse to be rid of her."

But why was he paying her money, then? Could Carmen have killed him, and if so, for what reason?

"It looks like Keanu was right." I didn't realize I'd spoken the words out loud. *Me and my big mouth again.*

"Oh really?" She shot me a coy look. "What exactly was Mr. Hottie right about?"

"The night of the murder, Keanu gave me a lift home. He told me everyone had a reason to want Hale dead—" I stopped suddenly. "Keanu's not a killer. I'm sure of it." At least I didn't think so.

She sighed. "I don't think he is either. And please don't lump me into that category. Sure I disliked Hale, but not enough to kill him. This whole thing totally bites."

"Did Lola ever actually tell you if she slept with Hale?" I rubbed Benny behind the ears, who didn't seem to care that I was saying nasty things about his owner. The purring was so loud it resembled a V-8 engine.

"Lola's pretty private about most things. When she does open her mouth, her tongue tends to get her in all sorts of trouble. Even though I can't stand having her here, she's okay to work with. She was pretty friendly with Carmen too."

I couldn't stop thinking about my heart-to-heart with the Loco Moco Café chef earlier. He had killed once—could he have done it again? I hated to think the worst of him. "What about Poncho? Do you like him?"

"Poncho's a great guy. I'm amazed at how organized he is in the kitchen. It all comes so naturally to him. Outside of the kitchen, he hasn't—" She stopped suddenly. "Let's just say his life hasn't been easy."

She knows. "Poncho and I had a talk today—about his life."

Our eyes met. "He told you about the killing?" Vivian asked.

It was a relief to talk to someone about this. "Do you think Hale was forcing him to stay there?"

Vivian's expression was puzzled. "Why would he do that? I'm sure a lot of people on the island were aware of his track record. Poncho even told me and Keanu over drinks one night at The Lava Pot."

I couldn't mention the agreement, because then she'd realize I'd been snooping. "I just wondered if there was another reason why Poncho didn't leave the Loco Moco."

She sniffed. "To tell you the truth, I'm surprised he's still there, especially after the stunt Hale pulled a couple of months ago."

I sat up eagerly, and Benny jumped off me. "What are you talking about?"

She attempted to hold back a yawn. "After I started at the restaurant, one of Poncho's kids got sick. I guess they found out he had a heart defect, and the poor little guy needed emergency surgery. Imagine Poncho's surprise when he found out Hale had cancelled his health insurance without warning."

I sucked in some air. "Please tell me you're joking."

Vivian raised an eyebrow at me. "This is Hale we're talking about, remember? Yeah, I'm afraid it's no joke. Poncho is the only one of us who used the insurance. I can stay on my dad's policy for a couple of more years, so it's cheaper for me that way. I think Leo has coverage through his wife. I'm not sure what Keanu does, and I believe—"

"Wait a second," I interrupted. "How could Hale do that? Isn't it against the law?"

She shook her head. "That's what I thought too, but turns out that if you have a business with fewer than twenty people, you don't have to notify your employees before cancelling their coverage. Can you imagine doing something so vile?"

No I couldn't. Sure, it was horrible to speak ill of the dead, but in my eyes Hale had just been reduced to lower than pond scum.

When Vivian's eyes met mine, she immediately lowered her face to the floor. "I guess it's a real good motive if you wanted to—"

"No," I said sharply. I didn't want to believe Poncho was a killer. For some reason he had signed the paper and agreed to work for Hale. Hale must have known about his past prison time and used it to his advantage. Maybe Poncho feared he couldn't get another job if Hale disclosed this to other potential employers. Could Poncho's anger and frustration have skyrocketed out of control when Hale cancelled his health insurance? But what would killing Hale have solved at that point?

Even though I liked Poncho a great deal the man did have a temper, plus this was an unbearable situation for him to be in. Poncho was a very proud man. My thoughts returned to the story he had told me about the bar killing. True, it hadn't been deliberate, and Poncho had also been humiliated and pushed to the breaking point first. Could something similar have happened with Hale too?

I didn't want to think about this scenario any longer. Shivering, I pulled the blanket off the couch and around my shoulders.

Vivian stretched. "I'm beat and going to turn in. Do you want to shower tonight or in the morning?"

"I'll go in the morning if that's okay with you." Then I realized I had left my duffel bag in the back room of the café. "Oh no, I just remembered."

"What's wrong?"

"I don't have any shampoo or a toothbrush with me. You know, the basic essentials."

She smiled. "No worries. You'll find an extra toothbrush in the cabinet and shampoo in the shower. Help yourself."

"I owe you."

Vivian waved her hand at me dismissively. "You can buy me a drink at The Lava Pot some night after work so I can lust after the hot bartender."

"You've got a deal."

I unpacked my nightshirt, went into Vivian's bathroom to brush my teeth and wash my face, and then settled on the couch with the blanket and pillow she had provided. Benny cuddled on my chest, purring up a storm again. I stroked his soft head while I thought about how my life had changed in a few short days. Despite Hale's murder, I was feeling a little more positive now. Maybe things were finally looking up.

*　*　*

"Carrie!" Poncho shouted from the kitchen. "Table two's order has been sitting here for five minutes. My food's not the same quality when it gets cold."

Egads. Poncho had done nothing but scream since Vivian and I had arrived at noon for the lunch service. Lola was acting sullen and ignored both of us. Maybe she felt territorial and didn't like that I had spent the night at Vivian's.

"Lola and Alana were upstairs arguing earlier when you were waiting on that table outside," Vivian whispered suddenly. "I thought I heard Carmen's name mentioned. Maybe Alana thinks both of them slept with Hale. Personally, I'm not sure why anyone would want to, but hey, what do I know?"

"I thought Alana was taking Tuesdays off."

Vivian snorted. "She's keeping an eye on us. She left, but I bet you anything she'll be back later. Alana has no life, so why not make ours miserable while she has the chance?"

I liked Vivian and thought Lola was okay, but the underhanded gossip was getting to be a bit too much. Sure, everyone was on edge about Hale's murder and this was an extra-tense environment, but it was all starting to wear on me.

"Aloha, gang!" Tad pushed his way through the kitchen doors and out into the café. He pointed at the large plastic bag in his hands. "Lots of pretty napkins for pretty servers! I've already put the clean aprons in the cubbies as well."

"You're a prince, Tad." Vivian took the bag from him and placed it under the front counter. She looked at me. "When it quiets down between the lunch and the dinner crowds, you and I will make up some more table settings. We're getting low, but we should have enough to last until then." She looked at Tad. "Did you get all the dirty ones?"

Tad's face twisted into a pout. "Really, Viv, do you think this is my first day on the job?"

She rolled her eyes. "I think I saw one of Poncho's dirty chef jackets in the kitchen this morning. I'll go grab it for you."

"Viv needs a man," Tad commented as she pushed through the swinging doors. "So where's that delicious Keanu boy toy this morning?"

I couldn't help but smile. Tad was the dose of fresh ocean air this place sorely needed. "He was out here earlier to help Lola with the breakfast rush, but he went back upstairs."

Tad leaned over the counter. "Guess who I ran into on the path outside?"

"I give up. Who?"

"Carmen."

"Do you think she was on her way over here?"

He shrugged. "No idea. She's working at Sir Spamalot's now." It was an outdoor eatery Vivian had mentioned that was located near the resort and specialized in different ways to serve spam. "I didn't know Hale had fired her. She practically spat his name out when she told me."

My pulse quickened. "Maybe you and I could go grab a quick bite to eat later and talk to her." I couldn't believe I'd actually said that. I hated spam.

"Detective Carrie," Tad teased. "Are you a super sleuth now?"

"Look," I said. "I don't like working in this kind of environment. Everyone is on edge about the murder. I just want to see if she'll talk to me."

He sighed. "I'd give anything to come along, love, but I'm swamped today. Text me later, and tell me what you find out. God knows I adore a good gossip session."

Yeah, and so did everyone else around here, apparently.

Vivian appeared with the dirty chef's jacket and handed it to Tad. "That's it for today."

"No problem." Tad examined my face. "Have you heard back about the audition yet?"

I shook my head. "Nothing. Guess that means I didn't get it."

He stuck his nose proudly out in the air. "Jeff called me personally last night. He wants me to be assistant stage manager. I told him no problemo."

My heart felt like someone had wrenched it out of my body. I was thrilled for Tad, but since I hadn't heard anything myself, it seemed I was out of luck. "That's awesome. Are you happy?"

"Totally, girl. Jeff is a top-notch director. Sometimes you have to pay your dues in the theater business. That might mean I'll get an actual part next time."

"Congratulations. That's great."

My voice must have sounded a bit wistful, because Tad reached over to tweak my nose. "Cheer up, hon. It might be taking them a few days to go through everyone, so you never know. You might still hear some good news. Each director does it differently."

I sighed. "Hope you're right."

"Keep the faith, love." He blew kisses to both of us and left by the lobby entrance.

Keanu pushed through the kitchen double doors, holding a tissue to his hand. He moved aside some of the items underneath the counter, and I heard him curse under his breath. Cripes, everyone was in a bad mood today.

"What's wrong?" I asked.

He held up his hand and frowned. "Paper cut. Hazards of being an accountant, I guess. It's actually pretty deep, and as usual, the Band-Aids in the first-aid kit are nonexistent."

Vivian grimaced at the sight of blood on the tissue. "We always forget to fill that thing."

I held up a hand. "Hang on. I think I have one in my duffel bag." When I'd left for the showers at the resort yesterday, I'd thrown a Band-Aid into the duffel along with my razor case and shampoo. I was notorious for cutting my legs while shaving.

I went into the employees' back room and opened my duffel bag. My dirty clothes from the other day were on top. I reached underneath them, and something with a sharp edge brushed against my fingers.

"Ouch!" I yelled. How could I be so stupid and not put my razor back inside its case? Unfortunately, this wasn't the first time I'd done this. Peeved at myself, I turned the bag upside down and angrily dumped all the contents out of it.

A white pearl-handled knife clattered to the floor. The blade was covered with dried blood. I let out a small gasp of terror as realization set in.

This was the knife I'd seen Poncho using the first day I started here. The same knife that had been sticking out of Hale's chest when I found him—aka, the murder weapon.

Boy, was I in trouble now.

CHAPTER FIFTEEN

The room started to spin, and the blood roared in my ears. No, this couldn't be happening. Not only was I concerned that there was a killer among the Loco Moco workers, someone was now trying to frame me for my boss's murder. *Me.*

I opened my mouth to scream, but no sound came out. I stood transfixed, staring at the knife that lay on the floor. All of a sudden, I was standing in front of Hale's dead body again. It was as if I had been transported back in time. My legs grew heavy and went numb. I covered my mouth with both hands and tried to force the piece of pizza I'd eaten earlier at Vivian's back down my throat.

"You know, I could bleed to death at the rate it's taking you to find me a Band-Aid." Keanu's voice teased from behind me.

I turned around to look at him but still couldn't speak. His eyes shifted from me to the knife on the floor, with an alarmed expression.

"Holy—is that what I think it is?"

My throat was parched, and I forced the words out in a feeble whisper. "It's the one th-that was sticking out of him…Hale…when I f-found him."

Keanu's pale face undoubtedly mirrored my own. For a moment we both stood there, too shocked to say anything. Then Keanu pulled his phone out of his pocket.

"What are you doing?" I asked.

"I've got to call Detective Ray," he said.

I whined like a baby. "They'll think it was me. It was in my duffel bag."

Keanu clutched me by the arm. "Someone planted it there. Did you touch it?"

"Only the blade," I confessed. "I felt something sharp in the bag and thought it was my razor. I got annoyed so I dumped everything out." I pointed at the floor. "As you can see." Thankfully, my bikini panties were hidden from sight. I started to put the clothes back into the bag, and Keanu stopped me.

"I don't know if you should touch anything," he said.

"What's going on? I—Oh my God!" Lola screamed. She looked from the knife to me and then at Keanu, horrified.

Keanu put a finger to his lips. "We don't want to alarm the customers. I'll go upstairs and call Detective Ray." He disappeared from the room.

Lola grabbed my arm. "Where was it?"

"My bag." I trembled with anxiety. "What am I going to do?"

She put an arm around me. "Look, they won't think you did it. I mean, you just started here. You'd never met Hale before, had you?"

I inched away from her. "Are you suggesting I killed him?"

Lola's eyes widened in surprise. "No, of course not. I— oh God, I don't know what to think. One of us might be a murderer."

I shivered and turned away from the knife. "I can't stand to look at this anymore."

"What's all the commotion about?" Poncho came charging from the kitchen, spatula in hand, with Vivian right behind him. He looked down at the knife that was covered in blood, and his face turned a sickening gray. "Sweet Lord. That's the knife that killed Hale? *My* knife?"

Keanu ran back down the stairs. "Detective Ray is on his way out here. He recommended that we shut the place down. I called Alana, and she's on her way too."

"Great," Vivian said through clenched teeth. "Is he going to want to question everyone again?"

Keanu gave me a sympathetic look. "Probably just Carrie."

That was all. I was jinxed. I was sure of it.

Poncho swore. "We lost a day's pay on Friday. What does this Detective Ray think, that we are millionaires? I say we stay open."

Keanu looked at him in disbelief. "Do you think people are going to want to continue eating here if they think a killer is serving or fixing their food?"

Poncho's eyes were as dark as storm clouds. "And what exactly are you implying, Mr. Hot Shot Assistant Manager?"

"Nothing," Keanu assured him. "I've heard the rumors. Most of the customers think it was a robbery gone wrong. If they find out about the knife, we might as well shut down the place for good."

Poncho swore again and then stormed back into the kitchen, brandishing his spatula in front of him like a weapon.

"Cripes," Vivian said. "Alana's going to freak when she gets here. Can I leave, Keanu? I don't want to be a witness to the show she's going to put on."

He shook his head. "Go out front, and put up the *Closed* sign. Traffic's light, and there are only a couple of people inside finishing up. If anyone asks, just say that we uh—"

"Had a small fire? The chef is ill?"

"Negative," Keanu said. "Tell them the refrigerator's on the blink. We hope to reopen later but no guarantees. Hurry up before someone else comes in."

Vivian turned and practically ran through the kitchen, with Lola following close behind. It was just Keanu and me now. He took a step closer to me. "Are you okay?"

"Not really," I whispered, fighting back tears.

"Hey." He stepped forward and placed his arms around me. I leaned into the hug, letting him support me, hoping some of his strength might seep into my bones. The air around us suddenly became charged like an electric current. I wrapped my arms around his waist and placed my head on his hard rock chest. The heat threatened to suffocate me. He lifted my chin with his fingertips and peered into my eyes.

Then in a brief second, he released his hold on me. I went from terrified to content to confusion in a span of about thirty seconds. *What gives?* Had I done something wrong?

He cleared his throat. "Alana could be here any minute. I—uh—don't think this would please her. Hale didn't like the staff acting too friendly toward each other, and I'm guessing she'd feel the same way."

Then I understood. If she caught us in an innocent embrace—or would it have ended up innocent?—that might mean both of our jobs. Could Alana have another reason for not wanting her employees to get along with each other? Maybe she was secretly carrying a torch for Keanu. He was young, handsome, and unlike her husband, not a low-down, dirty womanizer. Of course, he was also about 15 years younger than her. Wait a second. Did Keanu like her that way too? No, that was ridiculous. Or was it?

"I can't stand this." Frustrated, I sat down on the bench heavily and put my head in my hands. "I don't want to work here anymore, Keanu. I'm terrified."

"Carrie, you need to think. How long was that bag in the locker?"

"Since yesterday morning. Maybe—" Then I gasped. "If Alana finds out I slept here—"

Keanu shook his head. "Alana was aware you were coming in to clean yesterday. She didn't know what time, so you'll be okay. Who's been in here since then?"

I gave a collective shiver. "You, me, Poncho, and Vivian, Lola. Wait, and Leo and Anna." Whom I had only seen in passing. "Alana was here this morning too. Who else?"

"That's what I'd like to know too."

We whirled around to see Detective Ray standing there with another policeman. He nodded to both of us and then reached into his pocket for a pair of disposable gloves. The other policeman took some photos, and then Detective Ray slipped the knife into a plastic bag.

"So it seems we have found our weapon," Detective Ray said to us. "Is this the knife that killed Hale, Carrie? Do you remember now?"

"Yes," I said in a feeble voice. "I'm pretty sure it's the one."

Poncho was standing in the doorway, watching the scene play out. "Carrie, why would someone put the knife in your bag?"

Detective Ray scowled at him and then handed the bag to the other policeman. He reached into the breast pocket of yet another Hawaiian shirt to remove a tiny pad of paper and pen. This shirt was beige with large red and blue flowers emblazoned on it. Did the man own anything else?

"Excuse us, Poncho and Keanu," he said. "I'd like to talk to Carrie alone."

I pointed at Keanu. "Can't he stay?"

"It's all right," Detective Ray said smoothly. "You're not under arrest. Not yet anyway."

Well, that was reassuring. Poncho gave me a somber look and departed. Keanu seemed more hesitant to leave, and his blue eyes were anxious as they bore into mine. Detective Ray shooed him away with his hand. "It's all right. We won't be long."

Detective Ray sat down on the bench and motioned me to sit as well. "Carrie, the knife was found in your gym bag?"

Nothing got past this guy. "Yes, sir."

"When was the last time you looked inside it?"

"Yesterday morning."

He raised an eyebrow. "Isn't the restaurant closed on Mondays?"

"Uh, yes." Oh man, I wished Keanu would have been allowed to stay. How was I going to explain this one? "I came in at Keanu's request to do some extra cleaning for a few hours."

"What time did you arrive?" Detective Ray asked.

Great. If Alana found out about this, I was doomed. "About ten o'clock or so."

I hated to lie. I mean, I *really* hated it and wasn't any good at it either. But what else could I do? If the detective knew that I'd slept here two nights ago, he'd start thinking all kinds of crazy things.

He made some more notes on his pad and nodded to the policeman who was standing there patiently. "Go ask Keanu to come in here—the young guy. Then take the bag with the knife and wait for me in the car. We'll get it run through the system for fingerprints immediately."

My mouth went dry. I had only touched the tip of the knife. Would my prints be found on the weapon too?

Detective Ray broke into my thoughts. "So how do you think the knife wound up in your bag, Carrie?"

Gee, that's a tough one. "Well, I would guess that someone's trying to frame me for Hale's murder."

"Any idea who?" he asked.

I gave him an incredulous look. "I have no idea whatsoever, Detective Ray. I just started here and had never met Hale before. I'm telling you the truth."

"Carrie didn't do it." Keanu was standing in the doorway. "I'd stake my life on it."

Detective Ray glanced from me to Keanu. "Would you now?" His mouth twitched into a faint smile. "What I need from both of you is to tell me who exactly would have had access to this room in the past two days. The restrooms are on the other side of the café, so I'm guessing you don't get customers in here."

"They'd have to come through the kitchen, unless they snuck in through the back door somehow," Keanu said.

I counted on my fingers. "Me, Keanu, Poncho, Vivian, Lola, Leo, Anna, Alana—"

"Tad Emerson," Keanu said in a low voice. "He works for Lovely Linens. He was in here this morning dropping off fresh aprons and napkins."

I realized that Keanu had to name everyone who had access to the room, but I hated to see Tad implicated. Then again, I liked Tad, but what did I really know about him, besides the fact that he was a regular hoot to be around? Plus, he hated Hale. Enough said.

Detective Ray was busy scribbling away on his pad. "I'm familiar with the place. I'll see if I can track him down. There's no one else that you can think of who might have been in here?"

"No, sir," I replied.

He rose to his feet. "I may want to question you both again later. I spoke with Mrs. Akamu right after you called her, Keanu. She's out of town shopping but assured me she would be back within the hour. There's no reason not to reopen the place if she wants."

Keanu nodded. "The servers are hard pressed to get breaks around here, so I'll let them take off for a few minutes before she gets back."

Detective Ray nodded. "Of course. If I were you, Keanu, I would refrain from telling customers about this, unless you want to be out of business. I believe most people at the resort think Hale's death was the result of a robbery. Mrs. Akamu—er—Alana—assured me that she would have more security cameras installed by tomorrow. There have been a few concerned patrons at the resort who left early and demanded a refund, but for the most part, curiosity seems to be the bigger factor."

"We already know about that." Keanu pursed his lips together.

Detective Ray nodded. "I'll be seeing you both soon."

"Wonderful." I watched as he departed through the swinging doors. "What am I going to do if he comes back with a warrant for my arrest?"

Keanu placed his hands on my shoulders and turned me around to face him. "They can't arrest you solely based on the knife in your bag. At least, I don't think so. But it's pretty obvious that someone here committed the crime. So if it's not you or me, that leaves Viv, Poncho, Lola, Leo, Tad, or Alana."

A lightbulb clicked on in my head. "Holy cow. We forgot one person."

"Who?" Keanu asked.

"Carmen. Tad said he saw her on the path before he came into the café."

Keanu raised his eyebrows. "What would she be doing here?"

"Tad said she's working at Sir Spamalot's." I picked the clothes up off the floor and threw them back into my locker. Detective Ray had taken the gym bag for evidence as well. "I'm going to talk to her."

Keanu shook his head. "You don't even know Carmen. She won't tell you anything."

I untied my apron. "I don't care. I have to try. I'm not going to jail—" My hands started to shake. What *would* I say to this woman? *Excuse me, did you plant a knife in my bag? Did you kill Hale?*

Keanu laid a hand on my arm. "We have a little while before Alana gets back. Come on. I'll go with you."

"Really?" I was stunned but thankful at the same time.

He nodded. "Carmen won't talk to you, but she might tell me something. I want to get to the bottom of this too."

We crossed to the patio door. Keanu held it open and then followed me out. We started down the boardwalk in silence. It was another beautiful day, and there were several people outside on the beach area, soaking up the sun. All of the tables were filled at The Lava Pot. Casey was outside chatting with a customer and waved at us when we walked by. We smiled and waved in return but didn't stop.

"It's starting to look like one of our fellow employees might have done this." I wished Keanu had divulged to me his reason for wanting Hale dead. I really didn't think that he could have killed him, but the only person I knew for certain was innocent was me.

Keanu looked straight ahead, his face expressionless. "Do you think Carmen could have done it? What would be her motive? I know he fired her but that doesn't seem like enough of a reason to me."

"I'm not sure, but someone told me that Carmen was taking antidepressants."

Keanu cleared his throat. "There is another suspect you keep forgetting to mention. Your theater buddy."

I winced at the thought. "I adore Tad, but would he have killed Hale based only on the fact that he insulted and embarrassed him that one time?"

Keanu shook his head. "It was more than one time, Carrie. I think Tad tried not to make a big deal about it because he didn't want his uncle to lose business. But Hale always had something demeaning or insulting to say whenever he saw Tad. He bullied the guy constantly when there were other people around too. Okay, next suspect please."

"I hate to say this, but Poncho has to be considered as well, especially since he—"

I covered my mouth with my hand.

Keanu stopped walking and turned to look at me. "Especially since Poncho is what?"

I couldn't tell him I'd been snooping, but I didn't see any other way around it now. "He told me that he once killed a man."

Keanu ran a hand through his dark silky-looking hair. "But that wasn't his fault."

"Yes I understand but—" Oh, I'd really worked my way into a fine jam this time. "I have a confession to make."

He folded his arms across his muscular chest and studied me with apprehension. "Go on."

I bit into my lower lip. "It would be nice if you had something to confess too. You know, to even the score."

Keanu gave me a shrewd look, but his mouth twitched into a genuine smile. "Let's go visit Carmen first. Then we'll go down to the pier and have a long talk. We're due."

CHAPTER SIXTEEN

———

Like the Loco Moco Café, Sir Spamalot's was situated near the beach, but we took Keanu's moped to save time. The place was a casual, open-air eatery with a grass hut feel to it. The counter ran in a square with high stools perched around the perimeter of it. There were two people behind the counter, and one of them was Carmen.

As I had thought earlier, she seemed to be in her mid to late thirties, with some premature gray peppered into her light brown hair. Her opaque gray irises regarded me suspiciously as we sat down. She was attractive, but there were already fine lines forming around Carmen's eyes, a telltale sign that her life may not have been an easy one so far.

There was only one other customer in the place—a pretty redhead reading a magazine. She had an expensive camera perched on the counter in front of her.

"So." Carmen directed her question at Keanu. "Why are you here when you can dine at the King's Lair for free? Oh, pardon me. The *Dead* King's Lair."

Keanu ignored her sarcastic remark and gestured at me. "Carmen Stacey, this is Carrie Jorgenson. She's a new server at the Loco Moco."

I extended my hand across the counter, but it was left dangling in the air as Carmen merely grunted at me. "My replacement, no doubt. What'll you have?"

Keanu waited for me to go first. I didn't want to make it obvious, but I was not a spam fan in any shape or form. My mother used to serve the canned meat to me as a child on a regular basis, and I'd had more than my fill to last an entire lifetime. "Just coffee, please."

She looked at me like I had pineapples growing out of my ears. "Try again, honey. We don't have coffee here. We have spam and more spam. Spam kabobs. Spam musubi. And we've got soda or iced tea to drink."

"Soda," I said quickly. "Any kind is fine."

She produced a can of Sprite for me and looked at Keanu. He studied the menu. "Make that two."

Carmen slammed his can down on the counter. She started to walk away, but he leaned over to touch her arm. "Can we talk to you for a minute?"

"Carmen." The young woman waved a bill in the air. Carmen ignored us and hustled to her side.

"Thanks for the meal. Keep the change."

"No problem, Autumn. Good luck on that gig of yours today."

"It's a perfect day to photograph a wedding, isn't it?" Autumn nodded at my coworker. "Hi, Keanu. Sorry to hear about your boss."

We'd been hearing the same utterings of sympathy for a couple of days now. I had to wonder if anyone really was sorry that Hale had died. In my mind, I pictured Tad doing a hula dance to the news and forced a giggle back down in my throat.

"Thanks, Autumn." Keanu smiled at her, and for some odd reason I was instantly jealous.

She leaned closer to him. "I heard that it was a random robbery. Do they have any leads?"

It was good to know that Detective Ray's earlier assumption was spot-on. If people thought there was a murderer working at the Loco Moco, would they be coming in to sample Poncho's famous pineapple salsa or Hale's Hamburger Platter? My guess was no.

Keanu took a sip of soda. "I really don't know much, Autumn."

She sighed wistfully. "I bet they got some cool photos of the crime scene." She gave a wave to all of us, including Carmen, and left the hut.

The place was now deserted. The other woman who'd been behind the counter said good-bye to Carmen and left, obviously having finished her shift for the day. Carmen sauntered back over to us. She focused on Keanu, deliberately ignoring me. "So, what'd you want?"

Keanu didn't mince any words. "Someone murdered Hale, and we'd like your thoughts on the topic."

She snorted. "Look, I'll admit I'm not sorry he's dead, that's for sure. But I didn't kill him."

I remembered the argument they had when he fired her and the check register entry for the money he had paid her. Carmen was involved in some detail of his life, and I wanted to know exactly how. "The day Hale fired you, he said it was because of the way you reacted to a customer's tip, but you told him that was just an excuse. I think there was something else going on between the two of you."

Carmen scanned me up and down. "You're quite the nosy little thing, aren't you?"

Keanu cut in. "Do you want to tell us what's going on, or would you rather speak directly to the police? I'm getting to know Detective Ray pretty well. I'm sure he'd be interested in what you have to say. He hasn't questioned you yet, right?" He pulled out his cell phone.

Carmen's eyes registered with sudden alarm. "They don't know I'm working here—yet. *Please* don't call him. I can't deal with that right now."

Okay, so we were making progress.

"Come on," Keanu urged. "Level with me. You can trust us."

She sighed heavily. "I guess it doesn't matter anymore. Yeah, I did sleep with Hale. It was only once, but I assure you, that was more than enough."

Good grief. "Is that why he fired you? Because he was afraid you'd tell Alana?"

Carmen shook her head. "It's a little more complicated than that."

Keanu and I exchanged glances. I thought again about the check register in the desk. The pieces were starting to fit together like those jigsaw puzzles my mother always enjoyed doing. I had a sudden hunch, based in part on Carmen's earlier comment, but couldn't be positive my assumption was correct. If I was wrong, Carmen might grab me by the hair and throw me across the beach. She looked strong enough. "Were you pregnant?"

Her face registered shock and alarm, while Keanu watched me, clearly impressed.

Hey, Nancy Drew's got nothing on me.

Carmen's eyes filled with tears. "How did you know?"

Bingo. "Call it a woman's intuition. Once is all it takes." The same words my mother had probably told my father years ago when she discovered she was pregnant with Penny. "What did Hale do when you told him?"

Carmen wiped at her eyes with the back of her head. "He asked me to get rid of it. He said he'd pay me enough money to make it worth my while." She paused. "I didn't want to, but I also didn't know how I was going to raise a baby all by myself, without any help. He gave me five thousand dollars up front and promised me more." Her face became pinched with pain. "The next day I suffered a miscarriage. The doctor said it might have been brought on by all the stress I was suffering from, but there wasn't a way to know for sure."

My heart went out to her. "I'm so sorry."

She straightened up and glared at me. "I don't want your sympathy. Anyhow, I'd already cashed the check, and Hale thought I'd made the whole thing up. He was totally pissed. I even offered to put him in touch with my doctor, but he was still convinced I was lying. A few days after I came back to work, the incident with the customer happened. I guess he saw it as his chance to be rid of me. I even called him later that evening to tell him he'd better give me my job back or I'd tell Alana. Hale just laughed and said 'go ahead.'" She twisted a napkin between her slender fingers. "I didn't kill him, but I'd like to thank the person who did."

Yikes. "But why would you—" I stopped myself, afraid to sound judgmental if I asked her why she would even consider sleeping with him. Sure, Hale had been attractive and rich, but the thought of being with him in an intimate manner was enough to make me want to retch.

Carmen blew out a long, ragged breath. "I get it. You want to know why I'd sleep with such a pig. The truth is, I don't know. We went out for drinks one night after work. We got to talking, and he actually seemed like a nice guy—even human. I guess I had a little too much to drink. I remember getting into the car with him, but things went fuzzy after that." Her face turned a shade of crimson. "Sometimes I drink a bit more than is good for me."

Vivian had said that Carmen was a regular at The Lava Pot, but I wisely kept that piece of knowledge to myself.

"The next morning I woke up in one of the Aloha Lagoon resort rooms, alone." Carmen's voice was low. "No note from him, zero acknowledgement of any kind. When I saw him at work the next day, he acted like nothing had happened."

Keanu broke in. "I knew about the extra money, Carmen. I thought maybe you were blackmailing him for some reason."

Head smack. Why had I not surmised that Keanu, who handled the finances, had also seen the checkbook? Was he on to my snooping as well?

Carmen's lower lip began to tremble. "I should have gotten more from the louse while I had the chance. I should have told Alana. She thinks we slept together anyway. Lola stopped by yesterday and told me what she's been saying about me." She placed a protective hand over her stomach. "I wish the outcome could have been different for someone else."

I wanted to believe her, but Carmen had suddenly jumped to the top of my suspect list.

"I don't sleep around," Carmen said defensively. "He and Alana were separated, and it's not the first time he'd been unfaithful to her. I've heard the rumors. Those two have always been off and on like a faucet. She had spies too, or so I've been told."

What a great foundation for a marriage. I exchanged a doubtful glance with Keanu. If her account was true, I was genuinely sorry for Carmen. Still, I was not convinced that she could be trusted or that her story held water.

Realization dawned in her eyes, and she jutted her chin out in defiance. "Look, I had nothing to do with his murder. That's why you're both here, right? You think I did it. No, wait. The police think one of *you* did it, so you're trying to pin it on someone else."

Keanu shook his head at her. "You're wrong on both accounts. We only want to find out who did this before someone else gets hurt."

Carmen glared at him. "I earned that money from Hale fair and square. My doctor would verify the pregnancy if I asked him to. I couldn't care less about Alana's feelings when she finds out I was carrying her husband's child. Now, I think you two have overstayed your welcome." With that, she abruptly turned and walked over to a couple who had just sat down on the other end of the counter.

I opened my mouth to say something, but Keanu laid a firm hand on my arm. "Let's go, Carrie."

He threw a ten-dollar bill down on the counter but made no further comment to Carmen, who stood there watching us, hands on hips, as we walked away. When I turned my back to her, I could almost feel those scorching eyes burning a hole through my skin.

Even though there had been rumors about Carmen and Hale, her confession had rocked me, and if the story was true, I was appalled at how Hale had treated her. Alana whining to me how Hale had been a "kind and gentle soul" was ludicrous. I walked swiftly, the anger growing inside and threatening to consume me.

I'd almost forgotten about Keanu until he touched my arm. "Hey, wait up, will you?"

I turned to face him. "Sorry. This whole thing disgusts me. I'm sorry he had to die, because I wouldn't wish that on anybody, but I can't believe how vile the man was. If Carmen's story is true, he took advantage of her when she was drunk and then asked her to have an abortion. Personally, I'd rather stab myself in the eye with a fork instead of have sex with that man."

Keanu choked back a laugh.

"It's not funny," I spat out, and started walking again. We were back at his moped.

Keanu laid a hand on my arm and whirled me around to face him. "Hey. I wasn't making fun of you. I'm sorry."

He was standing very close to me. I looked up at his striking features—the high forehead, the silky-looking dark hair, strong, well-defined jaw, and the thin lips drawn together in concern. I again wondered what it would feel like to be kissed by them. Keanu's eyes were even bluer in the sunlight as he smiled down at me, the dimple alone enough to make me swoon.

He reached down onto the bike and handed me a helmet. "Let's go back to the Aloha Lagoon. We'll sit on the pier and have a long talk."

CHAPTER SEVENTEEN

I removed the phone from my back pocket and placed it on the beam next to me. When I sat down next to Keanu, I tried not to think about the fact that our legs were touching as they dangled over the water. My mind drifted back to the conversation with Carmen. I was still shocked about her confession—if it was true, that was.

"So do you think she's lying?" Keanu asked, as if reading my thoughts.

I paused for a moment to consider. "I'm not sure." If the story was true, and she had killed Hale, what would it have solved? She'd already lost her baby and would have no way of getting further money out of him. "If Carmen was drinking heavily and mixed prescription pills along with the alcohol, her behavior could have been erratic. Maybe she came to confront Hale that night at the café after he had fired her. He might have insulted her, they fought, and then she killed him in a sudden rage."

"I've heard of that type of scenario before," Keanu remarked. "I didn't know she was taking pills, but one night after work I stopped off for a beer at The Lava Pot. Casey told me he'd had to call a cab for Carmen. She was so drunk that she could barely stand."

I thought back to the night Hale was murdered. "Alana told me that she thought Carmen was the last person to call Hale the night he died. And I'm pretty sure I know how the conversation played out too."

Keanu's expression was puzzled. "What do you mean?"

"Do you remember when you told me that Hale wanted to see me? I was certain he was going to fire me. When I got to the top of the stairs, I heard him talking to someone on the phone. He was laughing and saying something about cutting them off without another dime. They had threatened him, and he said it wasn't the first time he'd heard that line."

"Carmen did say she called him," Keanu said. "So that definitely would fit."

"I wish I knew for sure." Deep down, I wanted the killer to be Carmen. I hated to think it was someone I was working with at the moment—or Tad. With the exception of Alana, I liked everyone else at Loco Moco Café.

I looked out at the water and instinctively moved backward so that my legs were no longer hanging over the side. The ocean was peaceful and serene, but I didn't want to tempt fate.

Keanu watched me intently. "You're all tensed up. You don't like the water, do you?"

I had to hand it to Keanu—he was pretty perceptive. "I almost drowned as a child. My mother brought me to the beach and then let me wander into the water alone. I went out too far and—" I hated reliving the memory, which sometimes woke me up in the middle of a deep sleep at night. "Thankfully, someone saw and rescued me in time."

His jaw tightened in anger. "Wow. Was that a common thing for your mother to do? Let you wander off on your own?"

When I didn't answer, Keanu blew out a breath. "I'm sorry. That was uncalled for."

"I don't like talking about my childhood," I said honestly. "It wasn't a very happy time for me."

Sympathy and kindness filled his eyes. There was also a question I assumed was on the tip of his tongue, so I quickly reassured him. "I wasn't abused. Not physically anyway. My mother never wanted me, and neither did my father." It was tough to say the words out loud.

He reached out and took my hand between both of his. They were strong but gentle as his fingers stroked mine. "I can't imagine someone not wanting you in their life."

The waterworks threatened to make an appearance. "It's all in the past. I don't want to feel sorry for myself."

"It's all right. You're allowed."

He was so easy to talk to, but I still didn't want to get into this. What was there to tell him—stories of a mother who'd wished I'd never been born? Or maybe I could regale him with tales of the older sister who'd told lies about me and thrived on being the perfect daughter, never once coming to her little sister's defense about anything. "I'd rather hear about your family."

Keanu leaned back and stared up at the sky. "I'm an only child. My parents are terrific. They own a chain of supermarkets in the Pacific Southwest."

Wow. I wondered if they were as wealthy as the Akamus. "So why aren't you working for them? Or maybe you don't even need to work at all?" I wanted to bite my tongue off as soon as the words came out. "I'm sorry. That was rude."

Keanu's eyes locked on mine, and he smiled. "It's all right. To tell you the truth, I don't know what I'm doing here either. Didn't we say we were going to play confession earlier? You know, before we went to talk to Carmen? You go first."

Great. I sighed. Keanu was going to hate me when he found out I'd been snooping. He'd probably walk away and leave me at the pier, but I wanted to be honest with him. "The other night, when I slept in the office? I kind of did some snooping."

Keanu waited. "Go on."

I shifted uneasily. "I um—looked around in Hale's desk. I thought maybe I could find something to tell me who the murderer was."

He nodded. "I appreciate you being honest with me."

I gaped at him. "You knew already!"

He grinned. "Guilty. I could tell someone had been in the files."

I hung my head in shame and wished I could disappear. "I don't know what to say. This is so embarrassing. Are you going to tell Alana?"

He was silent. Panicked, I raised my head to look at him.

"No. I might have done the same thing if I didn't already have access to them," Keanu admitted.

Relief washed over me. "I also found an agreement between Poncho and Hale."

Keanu's expression was grim. "Yeah. I asked Hale about that once and was pointedly told to mind my own business, so I never asked again. I can't be positive, but I always figured it had something to do with Poncho's past. Why would Poncho agree to something like that? What if he killed Hale in an attempt to get out of it?"

"You really think he was the one—" I couldn't go on. I didn't want to. I remembered when Poncho had spoken fondly of his children and wife, saying how his marriage had been given a second chance. He'd also made me breakfast and been so kind when he'd found me sleeping on the couch—well, after he'd almost scared me to death. "No. I don't believe Poncho did it."

He reached for my hand again. "But *someone* did it, Carrie. Only an employee would have been able to put that knife in your bag. Or someone else who had easy access to the room."

"Could a customer have snuck in?" I asked.

He frowned. "It's doubtful, unless, like Carmen or Tad, they knew the layout well and where the employees kept their stuff. I hate the thought that there might be a killer among us, but we need to face facts here."

We sat in silence for a couple of minutes and watched the white foam skimming the surface of the gentle waves of the ocean. It was mesmerizing and threatened to lull me to sleep. I was tired. My brain resembled a jumble of mixed-up conclusions as to who might have committed the crime. I had come to Hawaii in hopes of starting over—with my boyfriend by my side—finding a career, developing my singing, and someday maybe even having a family, complete with the dog and little white picket fence. Instead I was currently homeless, had a cheating ex, and my voice had been compared to that of a wailing cat. It was also safe to say I'd become one of the lead suspects in the murder of my boss. The only way out was to discover who had killed Hale.

I glanced sideways at Keanu. "So, I told you my secret. How about you?"

Amusement brimmed in his eyes. "What do you want to know? I'm an open book."

Yeah, right. "Well for starters, you told me the night of the murder that you had a reason for wanting Hale dead."

Keanu turned his head and stared out at the water. "Sure, I hated Hale like everyone else. Do you know what it did to me to watch him treat his servers like dirt? Do you think I enjoyed watching him coming on to you? No. The guy was pure vermin. But the real reason I couldn't stand him was because of what he did to my sister."

Dread as heavy as a mountain settled in my chest. I fervently hoped that this was not something revolting, like the situation between Hale and Carmen. "You said you were an only child."

He looked at me sadly. "Let me finish, okay? Twenty years ago when the café was up for sale, my parents tried to buy it. They've always wanted to be in the restaurant business. Hale's parents were extremely wealthy, while mine were just starting out. They had one small supermarket at the time and were easily outbid by the Akamus. Hale's family was one of the most prominent to settle in Hawaii, and his grandfather made a fortune in the real estate market. His parents started buying up businesses left and right. Hale's sold most of them, with the exception of a shopping center in Oahu."

"I've heard about that place," I volunteered.

Keanu's jaw clenched. "Yeah, it's one of the biggest in the state. I've been there. The place is the size of a small town. It actually figures prominently in the story I'm about to tell you."

I had no idea what he meant. "Go on."

"My parents were disappointed when they couldn't buy the Loco Moco," Keanu continued. "They loved the place—still do."

"So, did you come to work here because you were angry at Hale about that?" After all these years, it seemed like an odd thing to do.

Keanu stared down at the water and blew out a long, ragged breath. "No, that's not the reason. I had a sister, Kara. She was ten years older than me. That's how my parents knew about the restaurant going up for sale. She worked at the Loco Moco as a waitress back then and told my parents the original owner was selling. After Hale's parents died, she continued to work here for a few more years." He gripped the pier, his knuckles turning white suddenly.

My stomach convulsed. "Oh no. Hale—he didn't…"

"No," Keanu said. "He didn't have a relationship with her. He'd just gotten married to Alana. Not that it would have made any difference to him, but Kara had a boyfriend and no interest in dating her boss. Anyhow, after a few years she scraped together some money and moved to Oahu with her boyfriend. My parents didn't like him, but in all fairness to the guy, he did help her get her business started. Kara was always so fiercely independent, and my parents were overprotective. She had enough money to rent a spot in Hale's shopping mall. It was a small clothing boutique. The place didn't make a ton of money, but she loved it anyway. It was her lifelong dream."

He paused and closed his eyes for a moment. "I remember going there a few times. I was just a punk of a kid and couldn't care less about that kind of stuff, but she was so damn proud of it. And I was of her."

This sounded like way too much interaction with the entire Akamu clan for my taste. "Go on," I said softly.

He rubbed a hand wearily across his eyes "Kara got sick—cancer. She didn't have health insurance. My parents weren't as well off as they are now—they were just starting out in business themselves back then but did what they could to help her. She didn't tell them how bad things were financially at first and refused to move back home. Kara got behind on her rent at the store. She asked Hale if she could have a few extra weeks to come up with the money, and he refused. One day she got to the shop and found she'd been evicted."

"What a horrible thing for him to do," I murmured.

His nostrils flared. "Hale knew about her condition and didn't care. Hell, everyone knew. She'd lost all her hair and a ton of weight, but she never once complained. Hale didn't need her money that bad—he had more than God. You'd think after he lost his parents it would have made him a better person. Nope. So you know what he told her when she begged for more time? 'Business is business.' He had the place rented again a few days later. Probably at a higher rate too."

My insides went hollow. "Wh-what happened after that?"

Keanu's face was stony as he watched a ski boat cross the water in the distance. "It broke her heart. She came home to my parents and then died a few weeks later."

His voice shook, and tears started to gather in my eyes as I covered his hand with mine. "I'm so sorry. How awful for you and your parents."

When Keanu turned his head to look at me, I saw the face of someone whose world had once been shattered. "I've watched the progress of the café and Hale's shopping mall over the last few years. When Hale had an opening for an assistant manager months ago, I applied. The last name didn't even register with him."

Uneasiness washed over me. "Keanu—"

He cut me off. "Since I also had an accounting degree, Hale was thrilled and hired me on the spot. It was his typical speed—getting two jobs out of a person while actually only paying for one. Hale also asked if I could help out with some paperwork at the shopping mall from time to time. I knew he had to take on some investors a few years back when the place was briefly in the red. So when he asked for help, I jumped at the chance. This was what I'd been hoping for."

Oh no, he didn't. "What exactly are you saying?"

"I wanted to get even with him," Keanu explained. "I was going to fudge the books so that it showed Hale was performing illegal activity, like embezzling from his own investors. Hell, I don't know what I was thinking. I wanted some type of payback for Kara. I thought it would make me feel better."

Incredulous, I rose to my feet. What was going on here? The one person I thought I could trust was also deceitful?

"I don't believe this." Perplexed, I started to walk away from him.

"Carrie!"

Keanu gripped me by the shoulders and whirled me around to face him. I was startled by the authority in his voice. "I didn't do anything. I swear. I chickened out. I realized it wouldn't bring my sister back. And when my parents found out I was working here, they were furious. I promised them that I wouldn't do anything wrong, and they believed me." He paused. "I hope you will too."

My lower lip trembled. "I do believe you. But why would you stay here—if you didn't plan to harm Hale?"

He sighed. "I'm not sure. I've thought about leaving, but I really do love the place and the customers. I'm not so sure that I want to be an accountant anymore. This is the type of establishment I'd like to own myself someday. I guess restauranteering is in my blood. Plus, I think the coworkers are pretty terrific too." His eyes locked on mine.

We stood there, looking at one another as a golden ray of sunlight streaked across the bright blue sky, and I felt my resolve weaken. There was something about Keanu that spoke to me and said he was different from other men I'd known in my life—especially the likes of Brad. Sure, he'd had a moment of weakness and wanted to make Hale pay, but he hadn't followed through. Heck, Keanu was human. Who was I to judge? No one was perfect, least of all me.

"You're lucky to have such wonderful parents," I said hoarsely.

We were standing very close to each other. When I stared into his eyes, I found myself wondering how the ocean had settled there.

"I am lucky," Keanu agreed. "My parents are good people. They've worked hard for everything they have. I don't like people to know my family is wealthy, because then they treat you differently. Sure, I've had opportunities that most people haven't been afforded, but my parents wanted me to learn to depend on myself and not them. That's how they raised Kara and me. I don't know any other way. Does that make sense?"

More than he knew. "Totally."

He stared at me thoughtfully. "Something tells me that's why you left Vermont. Because your family was less than wonderful."

"Keanu, please don't." I tried to turn away again, but he placed his hands on my shoulders and forced me to look at him.

"Talk to me, Carrie." His voice was gentle and soothing, like the tropical breeze.

"I told you—I don't want anyone's pity." But even as I said it, the tears began to gather behind my eyes. "Here's the deal, and then let it go, okay? My father got my mother pregnant when she was very young. She was crazy about him, and I suspect she might have even trapped him into it. After my sister was born, they agreed on no more kids. He had never wanted any in the first place. Then three years later, I was born. The accident waiting to happen."

He smiled. "I'm sure your father must have been crazy about you when he first saw you."

"I don't have any memories of him," I confessed. "From what my sister told me, he was hardly ever home, and even when he was, all they did was fight. When I was four years old, he left home for good. We haven't heard from him since, except when he used to send money. Over the years, whenever my mother would get angry at me for a bad report card or making a mess, she'd throw it in my face that I was the reason he left. She once told me she wished I'd never been born."

The silence that followed my confession was deafening, and it was as if I had been stripped naked for the entire world to see. I had never revealed that last part to anyone, not even my best friend. I figured Penny probably knew, but since we'd never been close, it hadn't been a topic of discussion between us.

A tear leaked out of my left eye. "Jeez, what a cry baby I am."

Keanu reached over with the pad of his thumb and gently wiped at my lashes. "It's all right. I'm here for you."

He was so close that I was positive he must have heard my heart thundering against the wall of my chest. It echoed inside my head.

When our gazes met, I knew what he was about to do next. His eyes brimmed over with desire as he regarded me in silence. I didn't dare breathe for fear it might break the spell.

Keanu brushed my hair gently back from my face, his fingers lingering for a few moments on the strands. Then he ran a finger down the side of my cheek, and my entire body tingled with anticipation.

"Is Carrie short for another name?" His tone was soft, his mouth near mine.

"Carolyn." Unconsciously I licked at my lips as if about to taste something delicious—which of course, I was.

"You're very beautiful, Carolyn." Keanu's voice was barely above a whisper as we continued to stare at one another. His deep-set eyes were so easy for me to lose myself in. I could forget everything now—my parents, Brad, the murder. Everything except Keanu.

He placed a hand on my waist and drew me closer. When he lifted my chin with his finger, my lips automatically parted, like a reflex action, ready and eager to taste him.

"Keanu!" A voice yelled.

We both turned around, startled. Lola was running down the pier toward us, a terrified look upon her face. Instantly, we both moved apart.

"Lola, what's wrong?" Keanu asked.

She paused to catch her breath. "Detective Ray is here. He has a warrant for Poncho's arrest."

CHAPTER EIGHTEEN

———

By the time we returned to the café, we were just in time to catch the police car departing. The lights on top flashed merrily away, and a slumped-over, rounded figure was in the backseat. *Poncho.*

My heart constricted inside my chest. "He didn't do this," I said to Keanu, Vivian, and Lola. "Someone is setting him up for the fall."

Alana greeted us at the patio door. "And where have you two been? Busy getting a room by the hour?"

My lips curled back in distaste. "That's it? Your chef has just been arrested, and all you care about is where we've been?"

Keanu narrowed his eyes. "Easy, Carrie."

"I don't care anymore."

Alana turned on her heel, and I followed her inside the café. A small crowd of people had gathered on the boardwalk to watch as the police car with Poncho drove away. They'd been pointing and whispering. Yeah, definitely not good for business.

I walked at a brisk pace to keep up with the Ice Queen. Maybe she'd killed Hale and wanted Poncho to take the rap for it. She didn't need this place for income—she had her blasted shopping mall, after all. "You told Detective Ray to arrest Poncho, didn't you? Maybe you helped by making up a few lies about him?"

She gave me a brittle smile. "My, you're quite the cheerleader in Poncho's camp. Sleeping with him too?"

That was it. I was going to kill her. Maybe they'd give me a cell right next to Poncho's. I lunged forward, and Lola caught me by the arm. "Don't, Carrie. She's not worth it."

"We will be reopening the place in twenty minutes, so I suggest you all get busy." Alana crooked a finger at me. "I want to talk to you alone upstairs. *Now.*"

Maybe I should have been grateful that I was being fired. Maybe I could manage to put this mess behind me, although somehow I doubted that would be possible. This would continue to follow me like a dark shadow until whoever responsible was caught. My gut told me Poncho hadn't done this, and I was sticking to that theory.

Keanu put a hand on my arm. "I'm coming with Carrie."

Alana whirled around, furious. "No. I want to talk to her alone."

"It's all right," I said to Keanu. Having no choice, I followed the queen of mean upstairs. I wasn't afraid of her any longer and suspected she knew this. She sat down behind the desk while I stood there, arms folded across my chest. "Well?"

"Look," she said. "I'm sorry about Poncho. But I had to tell Detective Ray the truth."

"Which was?" I prompted.

A flicker of annoyance crossed her face. "I'm still your boss for now. Treat me with respect."

"You have to earn respect with me to gain respect," I said. "So far, you're not doing a great job."

Her nostrils flared. "Poncho didn't want to be here. He and Hale had some type of agreement worked out that he had to stay for five years. I didn't know all the details. Detective Ray said that Poncho's fingerprints were found all over the knife."

"Gee, maybe because it *was* his knife?" How could they arrest him based solely on that?

It was as if Alana had guessed my thoughts, and she stared down at the floor. "I heard Poncho threaten Hale the other day, and I had to tell the detective about it. I don't want to believe that he'd kill my husband, but I have no proof otherwise."

"How can we reopen if Poncho isn't here?" I asked.

"Leo is on his way in," Alana explained. "Lola can cover in the kitchen until he gets here. I'm about to place an ad in the paper and online for another chef. Perhaps Poncho will be let out on bail, but I can't have him working here under these circumstances. Everyone's aware of what happened. What would the customers think?"

I clenched my fists at my side. "You're destroying a man's life without any concrete proof. He didn't do this. Someone planted that knife in my bag, and it wasn't Poncho. For all I know, it could have been you."

She rose to her feet, trembling with rage. For a moment, I was afraid she might strike me. "How dare you. You know nothing about me or my husband. You might have seen him as a ruthless powerhead and womanizer, but there was more to him. Once upon a time he was just a normal kid trying to live up to his parents' expectations. He adored them. Then there was a horrible car accident, and everything changed."

We were back to the accident again. "I heard about that. How did it happen?"

She shrugged. "Hale never liked to talk about it, but it seems he and his parents might have been having an argument. He lost control of the wheel, and the car veered into the opposite lane. A young woman was driving the other car. Hale's parents and the woman died as a result. Hale didn't suffer any real serious injuries, but after that night he was never the same."

Okay, I understood that Hale had suffered a terrible loss. But something told me car accident or no car accident, he still would have turned into a horrible person. I wished I knew more about the woman in the other car and thought of the article I'd found. Could this woman be connected to Hale's death somehow? Was that even possible, after all these years? "The woman who died in the other car. Did you or Hale know her?"

She shook her head. "Her name was Elizabeth something. I guess she had recently moved here from the mainland. Look, I'm sorry about what's happened, but the fact remains someone killed my husband. And unfortunately, all the evidence points at Poncho. There's nothing I can do."

"He's being framed," I said angrily. "We both are, for some reason. And you can bet I'm going to find out why." Without another word, I stomped down the stairs and was just in time to see Keanu opening the door to the lobby. We had a few stragglers come inside, but word had apparently gotten out. It seemed that no one wanted to eat in a restaurant where a killer had been preparing the meals.

The rest of the day passed slowly and uneventfully. The dinner crowd was light, even for a Tuesday. At eight o'clock, the place had emptied out, and Alana surprised us by putting up the *Closed* sign and locking the door.

"What are you doing?" Lola asked.

"Go home," Alana said as she walked back toward the kitchen. "I can't deal with this anymore today. The phone calls from the resort, the press. We'll start over tomorrow."

Vivian and I were silent as we wiped down the tables and counters. Leo grunted a good-bye to us and left. Unlike Poncho, he wasn't fastidious about the kitchen, so we went in to finish the cleanup. Keanu joined us soon afterward to help.

"Hey," Vivian said to me. "I hate to do this to you, but I have a date tonight. And I might want to bring him back to my place." She winked. "Can you find another place to crash tonight?"

Her speech took me by surprise, and I tried not to show my disappointment. Where was I going to find another place on such short notice? "Sure, no problem."

Lola interrupted us. "I'm out of here, guys." She glanced at Vivian. "I'll stop by later for the rest of my stuff. Thanks for letting me hang out."

Vivian scowled at Lola's retreating figure. "She stays at my place for a week and never even offered money. Not that I would have accepted it, but you know what I mean. She brought takeout home only once. I tell you I'm too nice for my own good."

She went into the back to grab her purse out of a locker, and Keanu folded his arms across his chest, watching me. "But it *is* a problem. You *don't* have another place, do you?"

When I said nothing, he placed a hand on my arm. "Come on, Carrie. 'Fess up."

"I'll think of something. Don't worry."

"Hey," Keanu said. "I think I might have a solution. How much longer until you're finished here?"

I had cleaned the stove and countertops while Vivian mopped the floor. "I just need to rinse the coffeepots out. I don't know. Maybe five minutes?"

His phone beeped, and he glanced down to read the screen. "Okay. I'm going out on the patio to return a call. I'll meet you back here in a few."

Alana thundered down the stairs and let herself out the patio entrance without a single word to anyone.

I needed some answers *now*.

A distant memory from the night of the murder stirred in my brain. Someone had made a comment that struck me as strange at the time. What was it? I wished I could remember. Would talking to the police help? Maybe, but was there any chance that Detective Ray might be willing to talk to me about the investigation? Probably not.

Vivian walked past me with her purse. "Are you sure you're going to be okay for the night? I feel really bad about this."

"Sure. Keanu said he has an idea. Listen, thanks for letting me crash at your apartment last night. I do need to go back and get my stuff though."

"My," Vivian said coyly. "What kind of an idea? I thought he might be interested. I've seen the way he looks at you."

I rolled my eyes. "I don't think that's what he means."

She winked. "He must be lonely since he and Tammy broke up. Such a shame to think of that hottie sleeping all by himself."

"Oh stop," I growled, and she laughed. "Seriously, thanks for letting me stay last night."

No problem," Vivian said. "There's a key under my front mat. Just leave it inside when you're done. I'm meeting my date at The Lava Pot for a drink first, so there's plenty of time for you to get your bags before we return to my place for what I hope will be one *wild* night."

Yeah, okay, way too much information for me. "I'll see you in the morning."

She winked. "Wish me luck." With that, she was gone.

A minute later, Keanu reappeared. "Are we all battened down for the night?"

"Looks that way." I watched as he set the alarm, and then we exited through the back door of the kitchen. I still had no idea where he was taking me.

"I didn't want to say anything around Alana," Keanu said, "but that call was from Poncho. He told me that he was out on bail."

My mouth went dry. "What's going to happen to him now?"

Keanu shrugged. "I guess he'll have to wait until they schedule a trial."

"We have to find some way to help him." I told Keanu what Alana had said to me earlier in her office. "I don't trust her."

We were standing next to Keanu's moped, which he had parked at the rear of the café. "I think I'll ask my parents to call some of their friends who are in the life insurance business," he said. "They might be able to find out if Hale had any policies floating around. If we can learn who the beneficiary is— especially if it's someone besides Alana—that might give us a potential lead to go on."

"Isn't that illegal?" I asked.

He smiled. "You can find out anything if you know the right people. Come on—hop on. Do you need to get your stuff at Vivian's?"

"Yes, but—"

Keanu put his helmet on and handed me one. "I'll take you to her place and then bring you back to the resort. I got you a room there for the night. For as long as you need, in fact."

I stared at him in amazement. "What kind of girl do you think I am?"

To my surprise, he laughed out loud. "Carrie, it's not like it sounds. You're not going to be a kept woman, so to speak. My parents have a standing suite at the resort. It's a beautiful place. Sometimes they like to use the hotel's conference room for meetings, or they'll call staff to come in from out of town. If the employees choose to stay overnight, my parents want them to be comfortable. I'm simply offering it to you in the meantime."

It was a generous gift but one that I didn't feel comfortable accepting. "I can't do that. It wouldn't be right to have your parents pay for my stay."

His baby blues shone with amusement as they watched me. I looked up at the sky and could have sworn that the moon winked at us, as if wanting to share in the moment.

"They get charged for it either way, so it makes no difference," Keanu said. "Would you please let me do this? I happen to care about you and don't want you sleeping on the beach tonight."

"All right. Thank you," I said gratefully.

He moved the bike forward, frowned, and then looked down at the wheel. He got off the seat and bent down next to it. "What the—"

I was clueless as to what was going on. "What's wrong?"

Keanu swore under his breath and then sighed in frustration. "Flat tire. Let's walk back over to the resort's main lobby. We'll at least get you situated in the room first. Then I'll get the bike fixed and run you into town."

"You've already done more than enough," I objected. "I can walk to Vivian's. It's really no big deal."

"I insist," Keanu said, and we started down the path to the resort together.

The wind had picked up, and the air was breezy and somewhat cooler. I'd heard rumors all day about an impending tropical storm, and it appeared as if they might be true.

The loud roar of an engine behind us jerked me out of my thoughts. A white sedan with high-density LED lights was moving down the path at a furious pace toward us. I put a hand to my eyes to try to shield the brightness, but it was of no use.

"That car is going way too fast," Keanu remarked. "The speed limit is only 15 miles per hour over here. He needs to slow down before someone gets hurt. Probably some crazy tourist who had one too many mai tais." He waved his hands at the car in a futile effort. "Slow down!"

Call it intuition, but something alerted me to the fact that this was no crazy drunk. The car's speed intensified, and the engine roared again. This was no random act. The driver had his sights set on one thing only—us. The vehicle zoomed toward us at a frightening pace.

"Look out!" I screamed.

CHAPTER NINETEEN

Before I could even attempt to get out of the way, Keanu gave a hard push to my back that sent me flying. I sailed through the air and landed face down in the white sand next to a giant banyan tree. I sat up, spitting the grains out of my mouth as the car screamed past us.

I made a low moaning sound. "Keanu?" Slowly I rose to my feet and took stock. Nothing was broken, thank goodness. There were a few scrapes on my hands, but other than that I seemed to be fine.

"Keanu!" I screamed his name this time, panic setting in.

"I'm okay." His faint voice was coming from behind a palm tree only a few feet away from me. He was lying on his back, his face white and drawn.

Alarmed, I knelt by his side. "Are you all right?"

He reached for my hand and raised himself into a sitting position. "I think I sprained my ankle. No big deal."

"Lean on me." I placed an arm around him.

"I always wanted to be a hero," he joked, but it was clear to see that he was in pain.

"It could be a fracture," I said. "You shouldn't put any weight on it."

He waved my comment off with a look of annoyance. A couple of men dressed in the hotel uniform of polo shirts and khaki shorts came running toward us from the resort's main entrance.

"Are you two all right?" The taller man's name tag read *Jimmy*. He was definitely a native Hawaiian, and I couldn't help notice how good looking too, with dark curly hair and large brown eyes. He towered over Keanu, who I surmised was about six feet tall, and made me feel about as big as a bug.

"He might need medical attention," I said, gesturing at Keanu.

Keanu shook his head, clearly irritated by the attention. "No. I'll be fine." He stared at both men. "Do you guys have cameras out here? Someone deliberately tried to mow us down."

Jimmy nodded. "We'll check the footage on the computer right away. Hopefully we can get the license plate number and report it to the authorities. Are you two guests of the resort?"

"I'm Keanu Church. My parents have a suite here."

"Oh of course," Jimmy said. "I should have recognized you from the Loco Moco. Are you and your girlfriend on your way to the room now?" He looked at me expectantly.

Good grief. Another one of life's embarrassing moments, and I'd had a lot of those lately.

"As a matter of fact, we are," Keanu said, ignoring the girlfriend reference. With my assistance, he managed to stand but seemed a bit disoriented.

"We can get a wheelchair for you, sir," the other security man offered.

Keanu frowned. "Not necessary. I need to walk it off. I'm all right."

But I could tell from the way he clenched his teeth together that Keanu wasn't all right. He was in more pain then he was letting on. Fortunately we were close to the main entrance, so he didn't have to walk far.

The small crowd that had gathered near the beach dispersed as we hobbled inside. Jimmy rang for the elevator and gave us his card. I glanced toward the reception desk. "What, no check-in needed?"

Keanu shook his head and grinned, producing a passkey from his pocket. "Already taken care of."

We slowly made our way down a plush carpeted hallway, and Keanu slid the card into the door of suite 505. When the door opened, I tried not to gape at the surroundings. There was a king-size bed with a luxurious-looking silk duvet on top. A private balcony ran between the two adjoining rooms, which offered gorgeous views of the ocean and the resort's swimming pool. The brilliant moon was fading fast in the night sky, another sign that a storm was looming on the horizon.

The adjoining room next to the master suite held a large comfortable couch, a table with plush chairs, and a wet bar in one corner. There were 70-inch flat screen televisions mounted to the wall of each separate room, and a spacious bathroom with a full Jacuzzi. Keanu's parents kept this year round? Mr. and Mrs. Church were doing quite well for themselves.

Keanu hobbled over to the bed and collapsed on it, his face contorted with pain.

"There must be a doctor at the resort," I said. "At least let me call the front desk and ask."

"I'll be fine." He reached for the phone on the nightstand. "I'm going to call and ask them to send a cab so you can get to Vivian's house for your things. I think I'll just hang out here until you get back, if that's all right with you."

"Of course." Heck, it was his room, so who was I to say? He could stay as long as he wanted—even the night—with no objection from me. "I hope I get there before Vivian does. I don't want to interfere with her date."

Keanu was already on the phone. "Hi, this is Keanu Church. Please send a cab for Miss Jorgenson. She's staying in our suite tonight." He listened. "Five minutes. Perfect, she'll be downstairs waiting. Thank you."

"I'm paying you for the cab fare." I dug into my purse, which was the only thing I had with me. Everything else was still at Vivian's.

Again, he waved me off. "Forget it. If you try to pay me, I'll make you clean out the walk-in-freezer tomorrow."

I grinned. "Okay, you win."

"You'd better get downstairs." He lay back down. "When do you think you'll be back? Maybe I'll take a quick shower while you're gone."

My pulse quickened at his words. *Okay, get your mind out of the gutter, Care.* "Well, the cab ride will be about five minutes each way, another ten to get my stuff—I'd say in about a half hour or so."

"Perfect." He removed his sneakers and tossed them on the floor. "I'll order us some food from the Starlight on the Lagoon restaurant when you get back."

I'd seen their menu. That place made Loco Moco Café look like McDonalds by price comparison. "They're way too expensive. You don't have to—"

Keanu narrowed his eyes. "Carrie, please let me do this."

I sighed in resignation. "Okay, sounds good. And thank you." My voice quivered with emotion. "For everything."

He flashed me a gleaming white smile. "My pleasure."

I arrived downstairs just in time to see a cab pull up at the curb. The driver was a heavyset Polynesian man who nodded politely at me. "Miss Jorgenson?"

Fortunately I knew Vivian's address, or this might have been embarrassing. With no car, it was difficult for me to offer someone driving directions. Her address had been easy for me to remember though—77 Kilo Drive.

When we pulled up in front of the building, I tried to pay the driver, but he assured me that the fare and tip had already been taken care of. My heart warmed to Keanu and how generous he was.

"Will you wait for me?" I asked the driver. "I won't be long."

He smiled and nodded. "Take your time, Miss."

I didn't want to take my time though. This was costing Keanu money. It didn't matter how much cash he or his parents might have—I didn't like taking advantage of anyone. I lifted the mat outside of Vivian's apartment and grabbed the key, turned it in the lock, opened the door, and hesitated.

"Viv?" I called.

There was no answer, and I breathed a sigh of relief. How embarrassing would it be to come in and find Vivian and her date kissing or, worse, in bed together? I grabbed my cosmetic bag and suitcase then looked around to see if I'd missed anything.

Benny meowed in greeting. It looked like I'd just interrupted his nap. He was perched on the top of Lola's cardboard boxes in the corner of the room. He must have jumped from the back of the couch to get up there. He stood and stretched his legs, making a squeaking sound in the process. He boldly jumped off the stack and sent the top box tumbling to the floor. A large book, papers, and photos scattered everywhere, and he meowed again, as if pleased with himself.

I groaned. "Come on, Ben. I'm in a hurry here." I sank to my knees and began to pick up the mess. Cripes. Why hadn't Lola taped these boxes tighter? Benny proceeded to rub his body against mine, purring with the intensity of a vacuum cleaner.

I laughed and stopped for a minute to pet him. "Okay. Be a good boy and let me clean this up."

The book was actually an album. *Memory Lane* was printed across the front of the leather-bound cover in gold block letters. I quickly shoved the photos back inside, barely glancing at them. I knew they were out of order, but what could I do? I'd have to apologize to Lola later.

"Jeez, Ben," I muttered. "You really made a mess."

There were a few newspaper articles mixed in with the papers, and some had yellowed with age. I carefully inserted them back into the bursting plastic pages, hoping they would not tear. My eyes caught the headline of the last one.

Three locals were killed in a horrific car accident last evening...

Bile rose in the back of my throat. Why did Lola have a copy of this article? It was the same one I'd found in Hale's desk. What did the accident have to do with her? Did she know Hale and his parents from years ago?

There was something Lola had said the night of Hale's murder that had seemed odd at the time, but for the life of me, I couldn't remember. A detail that I had managed to overlook. I tried to concentrate. All of a sudden, the light switch clicked on in my brain, and I sucked in some air. There was only one person who would have the answer to my question. I needed to call Detective Ray immediately. He might not talk to me, but I had to try.

My cell wasn't in my purse. What had I done with it? I racked my brain trying to remember. I'd last seen it on the pier that afternoon when I'd been there with Keanu. We were about to kiss, and I'd laid it on the beams. Then Lola had startled us, and we'd run back to the Loco Moco Café. Ugh. *I left my phone on the pier. Please let it still be there.*

There was a tear on the side of the box, and I couldn't remember if it had been there before. I stood on a chair and managed to lift the box back on top of the others. I gave Benny another pat on the head, left the key on the coffee table as Vivian instructed me to do, and turned the lock on the door before closing it. The driver was quick to get out of the car and help me load my suitcase into the back.

He watched me with genuine concern. "Are you all right, Miss? You don't look well."

That was an understatement. "Is there any way I could use your cell for a minute? I lost mine this afternoon. It's very important."

He reached into his pants pocket and handed it to me. "Not a problem. Help yourself."

Shoot. I couldn't remember Detective Ray's number. I could dial for police help and track him that way, but I did remember Keanu's, so I went that route. I prayed he'd pick up even though I knew he wouldn't recognize the number.

"Hello." His tired voice was low and sounded sexy.

"It's me," I whispered.

Keanu came to life on the other end. "Where are you? Is something wrong?"

"I'm on the cabbie's cell. I think I left mine at the pier this afternoon. Do you have Detective Ray's number?"

"Carrie, what's wrong?"

I noticed the driver watching me in the rear view mirror. "I'll tell you everything when I get back."

Keanu recited the number. "He's not going to give you any information."

"I'm aware of that. But he may be willing to answer another question I have. Listen, let me phone him before I forget the number. I'll call you back."

"Carrie—"

I disconnected and quickly dialed Detective Ray's number. "Please pick up. Please pick up."

"Ray Kahoalani."

Relief flooded through me. "Detective Ray, this is Carrie Jorgenson from Loco Moco Café."

"What can I do for you, Carrie?"

I clutched the phone tightly in my sweaty hand. "I'm hoping that you might give me some particulars about Hale's death. There are details that have escaped my memory."

The silence on the other end was deafening. "I'm not sure what you're suggesting."

I wasn't sure what I was suggesting either. "Detective Ray, I'm positive that Poncho didn't do this. Why would someone be trying to frame both him and me? It doesn't make sense."

"Carrie, I don't share details of my investigation with anyone except my coworkers. No offense, but I especially would never share them with someone who's under suspicion for committing the crime, either."

How nice. "But people already know details," I protested. "They were asking me the other day about how I'd found Hale."

"I'm not sure what you're getting at," Detective Ray said. "This is why suspects are questioned separately. No one would know anything about you finding Hale—unless you told them yourself. I don't divulge that information, *ever*." I heard him talking to someone in the background. "Carrie, I'm afraid I have to let you go. I'm in the middle of another investigation. Why don't you give me a call back later?"

"Okay," I whispered into the phone but was already talking to dead air. I looked up and saw that the cabbie was turned around in his seat, watching me. We were in front of the resort.

I handed the phone back to him. "Thank you so much." When I tried to give him a ten-dollar bill, he refused again. "Already taken care of, Miss."

"Please take it," I urged. "It's my way of thanking you for the use of your phone." Then I remembered about mine. "Could you possibly get a bellboy to take my luggage up to suite 505? I need to walk over to the pier first."

"I can drive you," he offered.

"Not necessary," I said. "Thanks again."

The truth was that I wanted to walk, for my brain was a mass of jumbled confusion. As I hurried toward the pier, I went over the night of the murder in my head again, trying to see what I was missing.

Keanu had helped me back to the patio after I got sick. I had talked to Detective Ray, Keanu drove me back to my apartment, the confrontation with Brad—no wait. Someone had called before that. Detective Ray had left a message for me about coming in the next day, but there had been another call.

The tiki torches shone in the darkened sky as the palm trees whipped in the wind, and I felt a spatter of rain from above. Maybe I should have taken the cabbie up on his offer. I hated the dark, especially when paired with deep water and my lack of swimming skills. This wasn't exactly my favorite choice of places to be right now. No one was around because of the weather. The tide had turned, and the usual gentle waves rocked against the wooden beams with great force. I couldn't wait to get back to my cozy room for the night—and of course, Keanu.

Lola had called me after I found Hale's body. What had she said to me? I sucked in some air as her words slowly registered, hitting me like a blunt slap to the face.

That had to be horrible for you to find him like that.

An ice-cold chill ran down my back. Yes, that was it. How had Lola known I'd found Hale's body when I hadn't told her yet? At the time I'd assumed Detective Ray mentioned it to her when he called. Sure, he wasn't the sharpest crayon in the box, but even he wouldn't have divulged that. So how had Lola known?

Because she'd been there—inside the café—watching me.

I spotted my phone lying on the pier and sank down next to it with my hands against the beams, trying to steady myself. The pieces were finally starting to fit together. As I scrolled through my contacts for Detective Ray's number, hands shaking, the nearest tiki light went out, and I was submerged into semidarkness.

"Hello?" I yelled. Could the wind have blown it out?

I heard the sound of someone running toward me and could see the outline of a shadow. Before I could even attempt to react, something flat and hard connected with my forehead. The phone shot out of my hands, and my face smacked against the hard surface. *That was going to leave a mark.*

I moaned and struggled into a sitting position. My head was reeling, and my stomach was tied in knots. The surrounding blackness did nothing to help as I fought to remain conscious. Even in the dark, my world did somersaults. A sharp object, perhaps the heel of shoe, pierced me in the side. I cried out in pain and collapsed on my stomach, hugging the side of the pier in desperate panic.

"You should have stayed out of this, Carrie."

The voice was soft and demure in the darkness, and I slowly turned my head in the direction it came from. I couldn't see who the voice belonged to, but that didn't matter. I already knew who it was.

Lola.

CHAPTER TWENTY

"You were in Vivian's apartment—looking at my album," Lola said. "Something or someone tipped you off, so you went to investigate."

I groaned and managed to sit up, but Lola pushed me down again. She was holding something in her hand—my phone. In the dim light I saw her face as she stared menacingly down at me. She was wearing a sweatshirt with the hood pulled up over her head. Her eyes paralyzed me with fear. While sweet and Bambi-like before, they brimmed with hatred now. Her intention was apparent. She planned to kill me.

Lola giggled. "I figured you might be up to something, so I've been following you around all evening. I got back to Vivian's right after you drove away in the cab. I saw the box had a slight tear in it when I removed it from the pile, so it was obvious that you'd gone through it."

I said nothing as I tried to grope my way around in the dark. The sky suddenly burst open, and the rain descended from it like a cleansing shower, as if whispering for me to confess the truth. "The woman in the other car—she was your mother. Hale killed his parents and your mother in that car accident back in 1997."

There was silence for a moment, with the exception of Lola's heavy breathing. Then she put her hands together in a mock clap. "Little Miss Detective. You're better than I thought. How did you make the connection?"

I wanted to rise to my feet and charge her but suspected she must have a weapon. She'd hit me with something—what it was I couldn't be sure. Plus I was dizzy and couldn't see well. Not to mention that I was terrified. If I took a step in the wrong direction, I might plunge into the water below. I continued to sit there, helpless, praying someone might come along.

She kicked me, and my face hit the concrete again. "I asked you a question."

"Don't," I groaned feebly. "Hale had the same article in his desk. It was an accident. He didn't mean to kill her. He lost his parents too."

Her response was to kick me viciously in the back of the leg, and I cried out. "It doesn't matter. I had to grow up without a mother because of him. Do you know what that's like?"

Actually, I did. "Yes."

"Don't make jokes!" she screamed. "He should have rotted away in jail for what he did. Instead, he went on to inherit his parents' business, while my father had to borrow money to pay for funeral expenses." She hiccupped back a sob. "He ruined my life."

"So is that why you took the job here—to kill him? Did you grow up in Aloha Lagoon?" It hurt to talk. Tiny men were running around inside my head with hammers, merrily pounding away at the surface.

Lola wiped her eyes. "I actually grew up in Lihue. My mother was in Oahu for the weekend at some banking conference for her job. She was on her way home to me and my father when the accident happened. Later, when I was old enough to understand what Hale had done, I vowed to myself that someday I'd find Hale and let him know exactly what I thought of him."

She paused for breath. "About six months ago, I moved here and came into the Loco Moco with a friend for lunch. I had to see him for myself, you know? Thought I'd spit on him and then leave. But there was a sign in the window for a server. I had experience, so I applied for the job and got it. At first I just wanted to learn more about the accident. I bided my time for a while, and then about a month later, hit pay dirt. He was standing at the register, talking to some old guy who'd known his parents. The guy mentioned the accident, and you know what Hale said?" Her voice rose to a high accolade. "He told him it was the girl in the other car's fault. He blamed the entire accident on my own mother!"

She started to wail, the sound resembling a wounded animal. The noise intermixed with the screaming wind around us. "Hale Akamu killed my mother and deserved to die. He was a hideous pig."

"But you tried to frame an innocent man," I argued. "You used Poncho's knife for the murder. This was right after Alana said he had threatened to kill Hale. You knew he'd be implicated." I slowly crawled forward in her direction. I couldn't judge the distance to the other side very well but knew it wasn't far to the edge.

Lola snorted. "Not my problem. He's already got a rap sheet, so what's the big deal about adding another murder to it?"

She laughed then, a cold, hollow one that formed icicles between my shoulder blades. "I decided to throw suspicion on everyone, including myself, to confuse that detective. If you remember, I planted a sheet from Keanu's order pad on Hale's body. I found Vivian's bracelet earlier when it fell off her wrist and placed it inside Hale's pocket for good measure. The piece of pineapple was for my benefit, since I'd been talking about it earlier to you and Vivian. If I was going to incriminate everyone, I couldn't forget about myself, right? That would have made me look even more obvious. I told Detective Ray, and he ate it up, so to speak."

"Nice moves," I muttered.

"And of course, I couldn't forget you. Sweet and innocent Carrie, the newbie. That's why I planted the knife in your bag. Poncho's *favorite* knife. It was easy to confuse the cops, and kind of fun too. You should be proud of yourself. You figured it out before they did. Very impressive since you didn't have much to go on."

I sat back on my haunches. There was a faint glimmer of light coming from the nearby hotel in the distance. My only hope was that Keanu might be worried that I hadn't returned yet. Did I tell him I was coming to the pier? I couldn't remember. "You forgot one thing. The night of the murder."

"Oh?" She sounded puzzled. "What was that?"

"No one ever told you I was the one who found Hale," I reminded her. "Detective Ray said he never gives away details like that in a case. When you called that night and said you couldn't believe I'd found him, I figured it was because Detective Ray had already told you."

She gave an exaggerated gasp as if putting on a performance, then laughed. "Oops. My bad."

"You tried to kill me and Keanu earlier tonight," I said. "Why?"

Her voice was icier than a rural road during a Vermont blizzard. "You were getting too nosy, hon—you and Mr. Stud there. What, do you think you're the dynamic duo or something? It's pretty obvious something's going on between you two. Such a shame that nothing will ever come of it though."

"They'll find your car." I tried to use stalling tactics, but it was difficult when your body was filled with paralyzing fear.

"The car belongs to a neighbor of mine. He's an old guy who always leaves the key inside. He doesn't even know where *he* is half the time, let alone the car. I've already gotten rid of it."

I was chilled to the bone, but it wasn't a result of the downpour. I realized that tonight might be my last night on earth and that I was at the mercy of this crazed woman—someone I'd worked with, who I had actually started to think of as a friend. Poor Vivian. She had no idea that for the last few days she'd been sharing her apartment with a psychopathic killer.

I had to keep Lola talking. "Wha—what are you talking about?"

Lola took a step toward me. "Sorry to tell you this, but your life ends tonight, Carrie. Right now, as a matter of fact."

Panic set in. "Wait. Tell me about that night. Why did you do it then? Because I had just started working there and Carmen had been fired the day before?"

She laughed. "Yeah, the timing was perfect. Hale had an argument with Poncho, and he told Hale he'd love to kill him. Bingo. A perfect day or what? Then Hale got a phone call from someone who had been threatening him."

"Carmen." The fog inside my head was starting to clear.

"Anyhow, I was across the boardwalk, behind a group of trees, and saw you and Keanu leave together. I figured he was taking you home. What I didn't realize is that you were coming back to the café. I had just taken the pineapple from the fridge when I heard you at the door. There wasn't any time to remove the knife or even get out of the building. I hid in the back room with the cubbies and hoped you wouldn't come back there." She paused. "I had another knife—just in case."

I shivered at her words, understanding their full meaning.

"I heard you run out the door and knew you were going for help," Lola continued. "I panicked and grabbed the knife out of Hale's body, then ran out the patio door while you were down at the water puking your guts out. I didn't know till I came outside that Keanu was there too." She whistled softly in the night. "Close call for me."

"Then you decided to hang on to the knife and plant it on somebody else, like me. You figured you would confuse things even more by trying to implicate both me and Poncho."

"Pretty much," she confessed. "Poncho's plastic gloves came in handy that night—let me tell you. Then today, when you and Keanu went off together, I thought you two might have figured it out. You guys looked pretty tight. So I had no choice but to scare you. With any luck I might have injured one of you or put you permanently out of commission. Hey, a girl's gotta do what she's gotta do, right?"

"That's sick," I muttered.

"You are a first-class snoop," Lola snickered. "I had you pegged right from the beginning. Too bad Keanu pushed you out of the way. It would have been easier for you to go like that. Now you have to confront your worst nightmare."

As the waves continued to crash against the pier, I understood what she meant. Ever since I was a child and the incident at the beach occurred, I'd had the same recurring dream about drowning, except that I always woke up afterwards. This nightmare didn't come with those perks.

"How did you know about that?" I asked.

"Remember those two guys who were outside the café the other day flirting with you?" she asked. "They invited you to go out on their boat, and you said you couldn't swim." Lola made a *tsk-tsk* sound. "You shouldn't give away secrets like that, Carrie. They could be used against you."

She reached down and pulled my head back by the hair. When I raised up my hands to fight her off, she smacked me across the face. A ring on her finger cut my lip, and I tasted blood. Lola must have had cat's eyes, or else she knew the pier like the back of her hand. She started dragging me toward what I assumed was the edge.

"Let go of me!" I managed to kick her, and she lost her grip for a second. In panic, I rose to my feet and tried to run, but she landed another blow to the side of my face.

"Somebody help me!" I screamed into the night. Damn this storm. All the guests were probably snug in their rooms. There was no one around to save me. I stifled a sob. If I had to die, I didn't want it to be like this. The thought of the deep, dark water below was too frightening a prospect.

She gave me a hard shove, but my fingers grabbed one of the beams, and I held on as tightly as I could. Then I lifted my legs and connected with Lola's stomach.

Lola emitted a groan and hit the base of the pier. "Don't you dare ruin this for me!"

The tiki torches lit the sky once again, and we both squinted as our eyes adjusted to the sudden light. I spotted Keanu standing on the other side of the pier, slowly limping toward us.

He pinned his eyes on Lola. "Let her go."

Lola squeezed my neck tightly between her hands. "Turn around and go back, Keanu," she ordered. "Walk away, and pretend that you didn't see anything."

We were at the edge of the pier, too close to the water below for my comfort. I was struggling for air but managed to insert my elbow backward into Lola's chest. Lola let go of me, and I started to rise. Keanu rushed toward us, but Lola struck me across the forehead with her hand. She reached for me, and I managed a sharp kick to her face with my shoe. Her eyes rolled back in her head as she landed on top of me, then we both fell off the pier and into the darkened water below.

Panicked, I screamed and flapped my arms like a crazy person, but the current was strong and dragged me under immediately. I knew nothing but the dark water and a deep-rooted fear inside that threatened to suffocate and consume me. The waves started to draw me further out into the ocean. I kicked with all my might and managed to lift my face above the water for a split second to gulp some air. Bits of my life flashed before my eyes, and suddenly I was six years old again, bobbing up and down in the water, looking for my mother…

"Help me!" I shrieked.

Two strong arms went around my waist. A wave rushed over us, and I was momentarily blinded from the water. My face was then above the surface, and I started to choke and sputter. I continued to kick and scream, in full-blown panic mode now.

Keanu's face was next to mine. He held me around the waist with one arm and fought the waves with the other.

"Carrie, stop fighting me!" he yelled. "I've got you. Relax. I won't let go. I promise."

I clung to him and those words as the picture of me as a child fighting the water started to fade from my brain. I was dead weight to Keanu as he dragged me along in the water. Emotions overwhelmed me, and I started to sob.

"It's all right." Keanu was breathing heavily, but he spoke soothingly to me as we reached the shore. He released me, and we both fell on our backs in the sand. I rolled onto my stomach, coughing and gagging. Keanu slapped me on the back a few times and then turned me over. His face was directly above mine. The tiki lights reflected off his blue eyes, perhaps the most beautiful thing I had ever seen.

He reached down to brush the damp hair out of my eyes. "Are you okay?"

I was crying again, and he wrapped his arms around me. "Thank you," I whispered.

"I'm going after Lola," Keanu said.

Before I could even respond, he released me and turned to go. I clutched at his soaked shirt, but he shook me off and dove back into the water.

"No!" I screamed into the night as the rain continued to cascade around me. I was terrified that he might not make it back this time. He'd probably further aggravated his ankle by saving me. I staggered to my feet but had to stop for breath. I was still dizzy from the blow to my head, and the beach turned upside down a few times. I staggered back into the sand and sunk to my knees, breathing hard.

"Please God," I whispered. "Please bring him back safely."

I started to crawl back towards the pier. When I heard Keanu's voice, he sounded panicked.

"Carrie!" he shouted. "Where are you?"

"Here." I started to rise to my feet unsteadily.

Keanu came into view, and when he reached me, he sank onto the sand, pulling me down with him. "I was scared half to death when I didn't see you at first." He pushed the wet hair off his face and stared down at me, his expression somber. "The waves are too high. I had to turn back."

I reached for his hand, and he covered mine with both of his. "It's not your fault," I said. "You did everything you could."

He raised himself on one elbow and reached down to examine my forehead where Lola had struck me. I winced, and Keanu clenched his jaw. "You've got an awful lump from where she hit you and bruises across your cheeks. Maybe even a concussion. We've got to get you some medical attention."

My teeth were chattering, I was soaked from the rain and the ocean water, and every bone in my body ached. I moved closer, and he wrapped his arms around me.

"You saved my life. I don't know how to thank you."

He observed me thoughtfully in silence. "I'm just glad I was here. Thank God the cabbie told me you were down at the pier. After a couple of minutes I started to get nervous and figured I'd walk down to check on you. Of course it took me forever with this bum ankle." He stroked my hair gently. "That had to be terrifying for you."

Tears started to well in my eyes. Ashamed, I looked away.

"Hey." Keanu slowly turned my face back toward him. "Don't cry, Carrie. The nightmare is over. You're safe now. I always want you to feel safe—with me."

The rain had stopped, and our eyes locked on each other. He continued to stroke my hair as we lay there in the wet sand. Finally, I couldn't take it anymore.

"Oh, hell." I put my arms around his neck. "Please kiss me, okay?"

Not waiting for an answer, I pressed my lips against his and felt his mouth open for me. He was gentle at first, his mouth warm and wet and tasting of salt water. Then the kiss turned more urgent. He gently pushed me back into the sand, his body on top of mine. His arms went around me as our bodies blended together in the sand.

"I do love a forceful woman." Keanu grinned when we finally came up for air. "Just so you know—I was planning to get around to that part eventually. I was worried about your head."

"Stop worrying." I ran a hand through his wet hair, and he leaned down to kiss my cheek. "I told you I'm fine."

"You don't look fine," he admitted. "Where's your phone? I lost mine in the water. We've got to get some help for you."

I pointed in the direction of the pier. "It's on the pier somewhere, I think. And yeah, I must look like a train wreck."

"No, you're still beautiful," he assured me. "Nothing will ever change that."

Lights streaked across the sky, and we spotted a police car making its way in our direction, followed by an EMT vehicle.

Keanu lifted his head and watched them approach. "Someone must have spotted us down here."

I started to move away, but Keanu tightened his grip around me. I raised an eyebrow at him as he ran a finger down the side of my face, and I trembled—now with desire.

"What are you doing?" I asked. "They'll see us."

He grinned. "Who cares? I've been thinking about kissing you ever since we first met. Give me those lips again, Miss Jorgenson."

CHAPTER TWENTY-ONE

I was standing on stage, in front of a packed crowd at Lincoln Center in New York. It was our two hundredth consecutive sellout. I bowed modestly in front of the audience that roared with approval. Everyone in the house was standing on their feet and shouting my name. I bowed again and then ran backstage, but the applause rang louder. The audience started stomping their feet on the floor, threatening to bring the house down.

My costar, Neil Patrick Harris, gave me a gentle push. "Carrie, honey. Go give the crowd what they want."

I made my way back to the stage, amid thunderous applause. The stomping grew louder and louder as I covered my ears. It was all too much.

"Okay, everyone, clapping is good enough. Thank you!" I shouted.

The knocking thundered in my head, and I opened my eyes. Disoriented, I realized after a few seconds I was in Keanu's suite at the Aloha Lagoon Resort. Dang, what a dream. It didn't get much better than that.

The knocking continued, and a male voice called through the door. "Miss Carrie, are you in there?"

Poncho. "One minute." I stared down at the outfit I'd gone to bed in, a T-shirt and panties. Yeah, definitely not enough. I searched around the room frantically. My suitcase stood in one corner, but I didn't have time to sift through it right now. I ran into the bathroom. A complimentary robe and slippers were on the counter. I tore open the package and threw the robe on, tying the sash while I opened the door.

Poncho was standing there with a tray between his hands. A smile quivered underneath his moustache.

"What are you doing here?" I asked.

"I thought you might be hungry, *ho'aloha*." He walked past me into the adjoining room of the suite. He set the tray down on the table then looked at me. "Here or on the balcony?"

"Oh wow. It's fine right here, thank you." I glanced at the clock on the wall. It was eleven in the morning. After spending a couple of hours at the hospital the night before—where I was informed that I had a mild concussion—I'd returned to the hotel with Keanu. Because he had aggravated his ankle with his rescue antics, he'd been given a walking boot and told to stay put for the night. Ever the gentleman, he'd given me the bed and taken the couch in the separate sitting room. I glanced around. There was no sign that he'd even been there. Emptiness settled in the bottom of my stomach.

"Come." Poncho held out a chair for me. "How are you feeling? Keanu said you had a concussion."

I sat down. "Where did he—is he at the café?"

Poncho shook his head. "He was there earlier but said he had to leave. Things to take care of." He poured a cup of coffee for me from a plastic carafe. "You are both very lucky that woman did not get you killed."

I glanced out the window in the direction of the ocean. While we had been at the hospital last night with Detective Ray questioning us, he had received a call that Lola's lifeless body had washed up on the shore. Guilt riddled my body. Even though I had been forced to defend myself, I assumed the sharp kick I'd given her must have knocked Lola unconscious, thereby resulting in her death. "She wasted her whole life with hate. It's such a tragedy."

Poncho watched me in silence. "Do not blame yourself, Miss Carrie. Hale was a lot of things, yes. God knows I had my reasons for hating him too. But he did not deliberately kill Lola's mother in that accident. He did not deserve her revenge or to die like that. No one does." He stared down at his hands for a minute. "That incident at the bar that night—I will regret it to my dying day."

My heart swelled inside my chest as I reached out to pat his hand. "You didn't mean for that to happen. With Lola it was a little different."

Poncho looked up and smiled at me. "Enough. I came to feed you, not make you feel bad." He lifted the silver lid off the plate, and I stared down at the food before me. It was a mixture of white rice with a hamburger patty and a poached egg on top, smothered in gravy. My mouth immediately began to water.

"Do you know what this dish is called?" Poncho asked.

I shook my head. "I've never seen it at the café."

Poncho put a small dish of hash brown potatoes next to my coffee cup. "It is called the Loco Moco."

I laughed. "Seriously? How come we don't serve it then?"

Poncho scowled. "It is a common islander breakfast food. Hale never cared for the dish himself and refused to put it on the menu. I think it is safe to say that it will be making a comeback though."

I was intrigued. "Then why is the café named that?"

"Hale and his parents did not name the café. The original owner did. The Akamus thought it might be bad for business if they changed the name. Now, no more questions. Eat," he commanded.

I took a bite, and my taste buds practically sang out loud. A fabulous comfort food that for me ranked right up there with the likes of macaroni and cheese, ice cream, and chocolate cake. "This is amazing."

He beamed. "I am so glad you like it, Miss Carrie."

Curiosity was already getting the best of me again. "Was Alana at the café this morning?"

Poncho nodded. "For a little while. I think that there may be some changes coming our way since she knows who killed her husband."

Uneasiness stirred from within. Was she still planning to fire me?

Poncho wore a pleased expression on his face. "Do not look so worried, Miss Carrie. Everything will be fine. Keanu seemed to be in very high spirits. I wonder what could have brought that on."

Heat burned my cheeks, and I looked away in embarrassment. The kisses that we'd shared last night seemed almost like a dream today. After the police and medical help arrived, we'd been taken to the hospital and been examined. Detective Ray had driven us back to the resort himself in the wee hours of the morning. I'd insisted Keanu stay as well—heck, it was his room—but nothing further had happened between us. I'd remembered him waking me up a couple of times during the night to check on me, his fingers gently stroking the side of my face. However, he'd made no attempt to crawl into bed beside me. What a bummer.

Poncho interrupted my thoughts. "Leo is holding down the fort for now with Sybil and Vivian. Keanu will be interviewing for new help this afternoon. Anna and Sybil have agreed to more hours until we get new staff trained." He moved my empty plate on top of the tray and straightened up. "I came in early to make your breakfast."

"You didn't have to do that."

He brushed my comment aside. "I heard what you did for me. You told the detective that I did not do this. You were determined to prove my innocence, and I happen to think that is worth at least a little food for a hungry young lady." His voice turned gruff. "*Maholo*."

My inquisitive nature had to know. "Will you leave the café, or can Alana make you stay?" I hoped he wouldn't leave, but with his culinary skills, why should he remain there when he could make more money elsewhere?

He looked at me, thunderstruck. "You know about the agreement? But how?"

Me and my big mouth. There didn't seem to be a way out of this one. "Ah, I might have happened to see it."

Poncho gave me a doubtful look. "Well, it does not matter anymore. When I was out of prison I could not find a job anywhere. I was desperate to help my family. I came to see Hale and put on a cooking exhibition for him. He was quite impressed until he ran a background check on me. Hale decided to hire me anyway—provided that I promised to sign an agreement that I would stay for at least five years. If I did not measure up, he could let me go at any time and would not provide a reference."

I still didn't understand. "But you still could have left, right? What would Hale have possibly done to you if you quit?"

Poncho was silent for a moment. "Sure, *ho'aloha*, I could have left. But Hale and his family carry a lot of clout in this town. He would have told lies about me, and then when he mentioned that I had been in prison—" He sighed. "I do not know if anyone would have hired me and did not want to take a chance. I have a family that must come first. They are happy here, and I did not want to uproot them."

I was suddenly envious of Poncho's children. How I wished I'd had a parental figure like him in my life. What a wonderful husband and father, putting his family first above his own needs. "But why did you agree to it in the first place?"

He shrugged. "Simple. My wife and I had no money. She lived with relatives while I was in prison. When I was released, they did not want a killer in their house, so we had to find another place to live. No one else would hire me, so I had no choice. Hale promised to at least give me cost-of-living raises every year, and it was all a lie. It made my blood boil to look at him each day, but what else could I do? Well, besides kill him, that is. Sorry, bad joke there."

I grimaced at the words. "Ouch. So now what?"

Poncho was quiet as he lifted the tray in his hands, so I posed a new question. "Are you going to leave us?"

He shook his head. "That is being addressed today. I am pretty certain that I will be staying. With more money of course."

Something was up. Poncho acted like a little boy who was dying to tell a secret. "What's going on? Do I still have a job?"

He chuckled. "I believe so, but you will have to find out for yourself."

"Wait!" I clutched his arm. "You know something. Spill it."

"Spill it?" Poncho feigned mock horror. "You *never* say that expression to a chef, Miss Carrie."

I sighed in resignation and opened the door for him.

Poncho gave me a perfunctory bow. "I thank you for everything—for being my friend and your faith in my innocence.

The Loco Moco Café and I are both lucky to have you. If I ever had a daughter, I would want her to be just like you."

His words touched me deeply, and I was forced to turn away and blink rapidly for a moment. "Thank you for breakfast. I mean, *maholo*."

Poncho smiled. "I will see you tomorrow. Come in a half hour early, and I will teach you how to make the Loco Moco."

"Sounds good."

I closed the door noiselessly behind him and stared around at my luxurious accommodations. It would have been easy to sink back into that amazing soft bed for a little while longer, but I didn't want to waste my day off. I planned to sit on the balcony for a while with my coffee, soak up the sun, and do some soul searching. I had so many things to be thankful for today—my life, for one. Plus I was young, in paradise, and had a new man—or did I?

First things first. I needed to find a new place to live. I didn't plan to sponge off Keanu and his parents any longer, no matter what he said. I grabbed the coffee mug and picked up my cell and started toward the balcony with it. The police had found it on the pier the night before, where Lola dropped it. Despite some scratches, the phone still worked—another miracle in itself. I noticed that Vivian had texted me while I had been talking to Poncho.

So glad you're okay! I'm at the restaurant and probably will be all day since we have no other help now. Smiley face emoticon. *I'll stop by and see you on my way home. I want to hear all about your night with Keanu.* Another smiley face emoticon.

Good grief. I could only imagine what she must have said to Keanu when she saw him at the restaurant earlier.

She had sent a separate message below it. *Lola's landlord called me this morning. Guess he found out from Detective Ray that she was staying here. I gave him your number. Later.*

No sooner had I read the text, than my phone buzzed in my hands. Startled, I glanced down at the number, a local one but unknown to me. Why would Lola's landlord want to talk to me? "Hello?"

"I'm looking for Carrie Jorgenson," a scratchy male voice said.

"This is Carrie."

The man cleared his throat. "Hi, my name is Arnie McCabe. I'm the landlord for an apartment building on Hani Drive. A Vivian Banks gave me your number."

Speak of the devil. "How can I help you?"

"My tenant, Lola Simmons, died last night."

No matter how many times I heard this, the words still made me shudder. "Yes, I worked with Lola. Did you know her well?"

"Apparently not well enough, from what I heard," he admitted.

Yeah, join the club.

"Detective Ray Kahoalani called me this morning with some questions," Arnie went on. "He told me that Lola had been staying with Miss Banks while the repairs were going on in her apartment. I called Miss Banks to see if she would be cleaning the place out. She put me in touch with Lola's boyfriend, who referred me to her father. Anyhow, Miss Banks said you might be interested in the apartment yourself."

The thought that I'd actually slept near a murderer was enough to creep me out. While I appreciated Vivian putting in a good word for me, I couldn't see myself staying in Lola's apartment after everything that had happened. I debated about what to tell Arnie. "Ah, it's probably a bit out of my league. Too bad because I really do need to find a place."

"That's all right. I shouldn't have any trouble renting it." Arnie coughed into the phone, a phlegmy sounding one that made me think he was a heavy smoker. "I do have an efficiency apartment one floor up from Miss Simmons' if you're interested. The tenant just moved out last week."

My pulse quickened. "How soon will it be available, and what's the price?"

He told me the amount, and it seemed manageable. "Tomorrow," Arnie replied. "I have someone in there cleaning today. The previous tenant was pretty meticulous, so for once I don't have to make any repairs. I don't allow dogs, but you can have a cat for a fifty-dollar pet deposit."

"I don't have a pet." Benny crossed my mind, and I was heartbroken when I realized that he was now homeless. As much as I adored Vivian, she had made no bones about her dislike of the cat. "Did Lola's father say if he was taking her cat?"

Arnie snorted. "I mentioned the animal, and he asked me to take it to the pound. Poor little guy. I'd keep him myself, but my wife's allergic. Can you let Miss Banks know? She didn't mention the cat when I talked to her."

"I'll take him if that's all right." It was obvious that Vivian wouldn't. "I can swing the deposit okay."

"Sure thing," Arnie replied. "Mighty nice of you to do that."

"He's really a sweet cat, and I don't want him to end up at the pound." I was excited about having my own place and becoming a pet owner, all in one day. It was wonderful to finally be independent.

I made arrangements to stop by later, fill out an application, and bring some references. True, I hadn't seen the place yet but was fairly certain I'd want it. I only had enough money for the security and pet deposit and half a month's rent, but since we were in the middle of the month, Arnie said I could pay the next month at the beginning of February. I couldn't afford any furniture yet, but hey, one thing at a time, right?

I went out onto the balcony with my coffee. Despite a slight headache, I was happy and content. Poncho's words from the other day rang out in my head—*I treat every day like it's my last one on earth because we are never promised tomorrow.* That was what I fully intended to do from now on.

My thoughts returned to Keanu. Where had he gone after leaving the café? My phone buzzed again. I recognized the number and groaned inwardly. "Hello, Brad."

"Hey, babe." His sensual voice greeted me. "I heard about what happened last night. You okay?"

I was surprised that he had reached out to me. "I'm fine, thanks."

He paused for a moment. "Listen, I guess I did act like kind of a jerk. It wasn't until you left that I realized how much I liked having you around."

Brad always had such a way with words. "Look, we tried. I'm not blaming you entirely. I made mistakes too. You didn't want me to tag along to Hawaii because you were afraid I'd want some type of serious commitment."

"Kind of," he confessed. "I'm not the marrying type, babe."

"Yeah, I get that. I don't wish you any ill, Brad, but I don't want to be a couple anymore. We're not in love with each other, and I honestly don't think we ever were."

"What's love got to do with it?" he asked, sounding genuinely confused and not like Tina Turner at all. "You're beautiful and fun to be around—well, most of the time. Plus we had some good times in between the sheets. Who says we have to be married? Can't we just party for now? I'll try hard not to stray again. Promise."

He just didn't get it. If there was one thing I regretted in my life, it had been rushing into a physical relationship with Brad. Next time would be different, I promised myself. "You cheated on me, Brad. I really doubt I could ever trust you again. Take care of yourself."

Maybe he'll grow up someday. I disconnected and leaned over the balcony, watching the sun as it shimmered on the surface of the resort's swimming pool below. To my left was a picture-perfect view of the ocean. It looked calm and serene compared to last night. I winced, allowing myself to relive those awful few moments again for a split second.

Brad's philosophy about life and love was certainly original. His mind had never run deep, so to speak. It was sad that he didn't understand the message I was trying to convey.

"Men." I sighed out loud.

A soft laugh sounded from behind me. "You say that word with such enthusiasm."

I whirled around to find Keanu standing in the doorway, his eyes locked on mine.

CHAPTER TWENTY-TWO

———

"How long have you been standing there?" I asked.

"Long enough." Keanu remained in the doorway, his eyes unwavering. "I assume that you must have been talking to your ex."

I placed the phone down on the glass-topped table and looked back up at him. "Yes. He wanted me to move back in."

Keanu's jaw clenched ever so slightly. "What did you tell him?"

"Well no, of course," I said. "I'm not in love with him. Sure, it made me angry when he cheated on me, because I thought we were exclusive. But I don't think I ever planned to marry him. I wanted to run away from my life, and he was the excuse I needed to do it."

He watched me in silence for a few seconds. "I know you're short on funds, so you're welcome to stay here for as long as you want."

I shook my head. "There's a vacancy in Lola's building, but not her apartment. It's available tomorrow. I think I can swing the rent okay. I'm taking her cat too."

A huge smile broke across that adorable face of his. "You're a big softie, Carrie."

At a sudden loss for words, I stared down at the floor. My mind was instantly flooded with insecurities. Could he have regretted what happened last night? Did I want to get involved with someone else again so soon?

Keanu walked over and stood directly in front of me. He placed his hand underneath my chin and tipped it upward with his finger. "I think you have some questions for me."

I nodded. "I wanted to know if—"

"It can wait." Keanu pulled me toward him and captured my mouth with his. My arms went around him, and I forgot what I wanted to say as I felt his kiss everywhere, from my pulsating heart to the tips of my toes. He moved his lips to the side of my neck and trailed a path down it.

"In case you had any doubts," he whispered in my ear, sending delicious shivers down my spine, "I don't regret kissing you last night. Since the first day you came into the café, I haven't been able to get you out of my head." He placed my hand over his chest. "You're in here now too."

Keanu kissed me again. My knees started to buckle from the want and desire, but he tightened his hold around my waist, supporting my body. The heat flooded through me until I thought I might erupt like a volcano. When we broke apart, I was breathless and buried my face in his shoulder. To say I didn't want to be with him in an intimate way would have been one whopper of a lie. At that moment, an image of Brad flashed through my mind. I'd done the same exact thing with him. I wanted this to be different.

"There's something I should say before we go any further," I murmured as he kissed my hair.

He gently lifted my face until our eyes were level. "Okay. What is it?"

I reached for his hand. "I think you're terrific but—"

"Uh-oh." He smiled, but his eyes regarded me with caution. "This isn't another rejection, is it?"

I was confused. "Another one? What are you talking about?"

He leaned back against the rail of the balcony and ran a hand through his hair. "This is exactly how things started out with my ex a few weeks ago."

"Tammy?" I asked.

He looked at me and grinned. "Asking around about me at the café, eh?"

The heat rose through my face. "You know you don't have to ask anything over there. Everyone is more than happy to volunteer information."

He roared with laughter. "What were you going to say?"

"It's not a rejection," I said, suddenly talking very fast. "I want to be with you. I'm attracted to you and think you're terrific. But I need to take things slow this time. That was my mistake with Brad. I jumped right in without looking first." I shivered. "Jeez, I hate that expression. It makes me think of the water. Am I making any sense?"

Keanu reached forward and put his arms around my waist, pulling me toward him. "Yes, you are. The last thing I ever want to do is hurt you. I was attracted to you since the minute you walked into the Loco Moco. I wanted to ask you out when you said you'd broken up with Brad, but was afraid to rush you. I figured you were upset."

Relief spread through me. "Thank you for that. So why did you break up with Tammy?"

"She broke up with me," Keanu explained. "We were growing apart. It was really for the best. She also wanted to focus more on her career, which can be pretty demanding at times."

"What does she do?" I asked curiously.

He pushed a piece of hair back behind my ear. "Tammy's a hula dancer. She performs at the Aloha Lagoon, but other places as well. As you can imagine, her services are very much in demand around this state."

I was suddenly jealous of a woman I'd never even met. "She must be beautiful."

"Yes," he admitted. "But so are you. Inside and out."

"I can live with that." I reached up and kissed him lightly on the mouth. "What about the address for Poipu? Do you live with your parents?" That might make things a little awkward if we were going to be spending time together in the future.

Keanu grinned. "So you looked at my folder too?"

I lowered my head in embarrassment. "Guilty as charged."

"I have my own apartment. That address on file is from when I first started here. I moved out shortly afterwards. Tammy was living with me briefly, but she left about a month ago when we broke up. Anything else you'd like to know?" A smug smile hung at the corners of his mouth.

"That should do for now," I said, feeling slightly reassured that he didn't live with his mother and father. I wasn't positive that I was up for meeting them—yet.

Keanu kissed the tip of my nose. "I've got a great idea. How about I take you out to dinner for a real date tonight? I promise I won't rush you into anything you're not ready for. We'll take things as slow as you want. Let's just have a fun evening getting to know each other better."

"As long as it's not the Loco Moco," I teased. "I'm not a cheap date."

"How about Starlight on the Lagoon?" Keanu asked. "You never did get to sample their cuisine last night."

"Sounds wonderful."

He looked like he wanted to kiss me again, but we were interrupted by the ringing of my phone. I wondered if it was Detective Ray. He'd hinted last night that he might have more questions for us. "Hello?"

A deep, ethereal male voice answered. "Carrie Jorgenson, please."

"This is Carrie."

"Carrie, it's Jeff Temple from the Hana Hou Theater."

My heart stuttered inside my chest, and I didn't dare breathe. I stared at Keanu, pointed to the phone, and then mouthed *Oh my God.*

"Who is it?" Keanu whispered.

"Hello?" Jeff called.

I gulped in a couple of mouthfuls of air. "Hi, Jeff, how are you?"

"Carrie, we enjoyed your audition the other night."

My lips formed another *Oh my God* at Keanu. "Did you really?"

He paused on the other end. "Well, let me be honest. We enjoyed your *acting* audition. Your singing leaves a little to be desired."

"Oh." I was crestfallen. This was a *thanks, but no thanks* call. I was surprised he had even bothered to phone me. Calls were usually reserved for those who'd been chosen for actual parts. Still, I tried to take the positive away. "Well, if I continue to work on it, maybe you'll consider me for the next show?"

He laughed. "I'd like to offer you the part of Beth in *Little Women*."

I pumped my fist in the air. "That's the one who dies!"

"Who died?" Keanu asked, confused.

I put a finger to my lips. "Yes! I'll take it!"

Jeff chuckled on the other end. "Beth doesn't have much of a singing part in the show. I think we can work around your—ah—lack of experience there. My assistant and I agree that you have a special stage presence. You practically glided across it. I think you're exactly what we're looking for."

His words amazed me. In my twenty-four years on this earth, I didn't think I had ever glided at anything. My mother had been excellent at making me feel clumsy and awkward. The only time I'd ever been truly happy was when performing. For years I'd been more focused on singing instead of my acting ability. *Did I really have a talent for theater*? Maybe I was able to perform well because I'd spent most of my life pretending to be someone else, like the waitress game when I was a child. Maybe I… "Thank you, Jeff. You don't know how much those words mean to me."

"I have no doubt you'll be an asset to our show," Jeff said. "We're having a read-through tomorrow night at seven o'clock sharp. I'll see you then."

I couldn't stop smiling as I put the phone down and turned to face Keanu. "You won't believe this."

"Let me guess." He folded his arms across his broad chest and surveyed me with amusement. "You got a part in the musical."

"*Little Women*."

"That's it. Tad was at the café this morning, talking about it."

I laughed as his face came to mind. "Yeah, he's going to be assistant stage manager. He'll be at most of the rehearsals, so I can bum rides with him. This is going to be a blast."

Keanu edged closer to me. "I can't wait to see it."

I raised an eyebrow. "You'll come to the show?"

"Of course I'll come. I'll be front row center. You'll have your own personal cheering section."

"I like the sound of that. Everything does seem to be falling into place for me," I admitted. "Maybe it's a sign I do belong here."

His blue eyes sparkled as if they held their own secret. "Hm. Want my take on it?"

My breath caught in my throat. "Sure."

Keanu nuzzled my hair with his lips then brought his face level with mine. For a moment we stood there, lost in time, our eyes locked upon one another. The tension in the air was thick enough to cut through one of Poncho's prized pineapples.

"Do you believe in fate?" he asked.

"Sometimes," I confessed.

"I think it was fate that brought you here. Brad didn't have anything to do with it. You were meant to come to Aloha Lagoon, work at Loco Moco Café, and hook up with a great guy like me." Keanu winked.

"All in that order?" I teased, relieved that Keanu was willing to move slowly. This proved that not only did he care about me, but he also respected me. I had never before had a man in my life that I could count on. Maybe that was about to change.

Keanu traced his finger over my lips. "You're special, Carrie. I knew it the moment you gave me first-degree burns."

I laughed, but at the same time, there were also tears forming in my eyes. I placed my arms around his neck. "It does feel right to be here with you. I already owe you so much. You saved my job and my life."

"Like I told you last night, I always want you to feel safe with me." He lifted my chin and kissed me again. His lips were warm and moist, and I had to fight the urge to moan inside his mouth. It was a gentle kiss, as if to echo his previous sentiments. "I'm only going to date you on one condition though."

"Oh? What condition is that?"

"You let me teach you how to swim," Keanu said. "Everyone who lives in Hawaii should at least be able to dog paddle."

"Okay, it's a deal."

We stood together for a long time, holding hands and looking out at the ocean. Things had never been so perfect for me before. It was almost surreal, and I found myself wondering if the other shoe was about to drop somehow.

"So," Keanu breathed into my hair, "do you think you'll feel well enough to come back to work tomorrow?"

I smiled at him. "I could come in this afternoon if you need me."

He shook his finger disapprovingly. "No work today. Doctor's orders."

"Is there any way I can shift my hours around? The rehearsals will be at nights—mostly Monday thru Fridays, I believe. I'll work all day on Saturday and Sunday if I have to."

His mouth formed a slow, sexy smile. "I think that can be arranged."

"Really?" I asked. "You don't think Alana will mind my changing shifts? I was afraid she might fire me."

He laughed softly. "That reminds me of something else I have to tell you."

Uh-oh. I braced myself for the worst. "Is it good news or bad news?"

"It's pretty good," Keanu admitted. "Alana sold the café today."

My mouth fell open in surprise. "Get out. What brought this on? And to whom?"

Keanu's face was stern as he leaned back against the rail and watched me thoughtfully. "Alana wasn't happy there. She confided to me right after Hale died that she was thinking about selling the place but didn't want to act on it until the killer was found. Alana doesn't care to run the place and never did. She said she needs to go away and find herself again."

Although I hadn't liked the woman, I felt nothing but pity for her now. She had loved Hale, after all. "I know something about that—the finding yourself part, that is." A worrisome thought occurred to me. "Do you think the new owners will clean house? Does this mean I might have to look for another job?"

Keanu shook his head. "Nothing will change, except maybe the hours. We'll probably stay open seven days a week, and more staff will be brought on in order to make this happen. The restaurant does rely on tourism, after all. It never did make sense to me that Hale wanted the place closed on Mondays, but he was the owner, so who was I to argue with him?"

Curious, I searched his face. "Did Alana tell you all this?"

"Not exactly."

"Okay." I took a step away from him, but Keanu laughed and drew me back into his arms again. "Do you happen to know the owners?"

He waggled his hand back and forth. "Pretty well, in fact. My parents are buying the café from Alana, and I'll be managing it. When I told them it was available, Mom and Dad jumped at the chance. They didn't even argue over Alana's asking price."

A knot formed in the pit of my stomach. It may have been indigestion from Poncho's delicious rich breakfast, or maybe it was plain fear. "Y-your parents? They'll be my boss?"

Keanu grinned wickedly. "Well, technically *I* will be your boss. They'll stop by a few times a week. But it's nothing for you to worry about. They're going to love you."

Oh boy.

Poncho's Pineapple Salsa

1 cup finely chopped fresh pineapple
½ cup diced red bell pepper
½ cup diced green bell pepper
1 cup frozen corn kernels, thawed
¼ cup chopped onions
2 green chili peppers, chopped
¼ cup orange juice
¼ cup chopped fresh cilantro
½ teaspoon ground cumin
Dash of salt and pepper

In a large bowl, mix together pineapple, red and green peppers, corn, onions, green chili peppers, orange juice, and cilantro. Season with cumin, salt, and pepper. Cover and chill in fridge until serving. Serve as a side dish or with tortilla chips.

Pumpkin Roll

3 eggs
1 cup sugar
1 tsp baking soda
½ tsp salt
½ tsp cinnamon
2/3 cup solid pumpkin
¾ cup flour

Filling:
1 package (8 ounce) soft cream cheese
2 tbsp butter
½ cup sugar
1 tsp vanilla
Dash of lemon juice

Preheat oven to 350 degrees Fahrenheit. Beat eggs and sugar together. Add soda, salt, cinnamon, and flour. Add pumpkin and mix well. Line cookie sheet with parchment paper and spread mixture over paper. Be sure to reach into the corners.
Bake for 15 minutes, and then cool for 20 minutes. Lift off the cookie sheet; put waxed paper on top, and then roll up. Put in fridge for 1 hour.
Filling: Whip all ingredients with mixer until creamy. After refrigerating, open pumpkin roll and remove paper from both sides. Spread filling on roll. Roll again, and wrap in wax paper, then Saran Wrap. Roll must then be refrigerated. Serves 8-10 people.

Pulled Pork

3 lbs of pork butt (without bone)
1 cup water
1 tsp flour
1 tsp Worcestershire sauce
¼ cup brown sugar (dark or light)
½ cup apple cider vinegar
½ cup ketchup
1 cup barbeque sauce
½ of a medium onion, finely chopped (optional)
Hamburger or sub rolls

Use a Reynolds slow cooker liner for the Crock-pot so there will be less of a mess to clean up afterward. Add flour, water, and pork butt. After cooking on high for an hour, add the rest of the ingredients. Stir every ten minutes or so. After an additional three hours, remove pork mixture from the Crock-pot and shred apart with a fork. Spoon pork onto buttered rolls. Makes 6-8 servings.

Mai Tais

1 ounce spiced rum
1 ounce light rum
1½ ounce Triple sec
½ ounce orange juice
1 ounce pineapple juice
¼ ounce cranberry juice
Ice cubes (as required)

Fill shaker with ice cubes. On top of the cubes add dark rum, light rum, orange and pineapple juices, cranberry juice, and triple sec. Give combined liquids a shake. Pour drink into glass and enjoy.

ABOUT THE AUTHOR

USA Today bestselling author Catherine Bruns lives in Upstate New York with a male dominated household that consists of her very patient husband, three sons, and assorted cats and dogs. She has wanted to be a writer since the age of eight when she wrote her own version of Cinderella (fortunately Disney never sued). Catherine holds a B.A. in English and is a member of Mystery Writers of America and Sisters in Crime.

To learn more about Catherine Bruns, visit her online at:
http://www.catherinebruns.net

Visit the official

website!

Trouble in paradise...
Welcome to Aloha Lagoon, one of Hawaii's hidden treasures. A
little bit of tropical paradise nestled along the coast of Kauai, this
resort town boasts luxurious accommodation, friendly island
atmosphere...and only a slightly higher than normal murder rate.
While mysterious circumstances may be the norm on our corner
of the island, we're certain that our staff and Lagoon natives will
make your stay in Aloha Lagoon one you will never forget!

www.alohalagoonmysteries.com

If you enjoyed *Death of the Big Kahuna,* be sure to pick up these other Aloha Lagoon Mysteries!

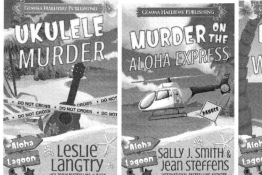

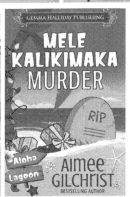

www.GemmaHallidayPublishing.com

Made in the USA
Middletown, DE
19 January 2018